THE GHOULS
OF
CALLE GOYA

When Malice Results From Good Intentions!

by

Owen Jones

Copyright

Dedication

This edition is dedicated to my wife, Pranom Jones, for making my life as easy as she can - she does a great job of it. Our daughter, Chalita, has been incredibly kind to us during the creation of this book, which is based on elements of truth on more than one level.
Karma will repay everyone in just kind.

Inspirational Quotes

Believe not in anything simply because you have heard it,

Believe not in anything simply because it was spoken and rumoured by many,

Believe not in anything simply because it was found written in your religious texts,

Believe not in anything merely on the authority of teachers and elders,

Believe not in traditions because they have been handed down for generations,

But after observation and analysis, if anything agrees with reason and is conducive to the good and benefit of one and all, accept it and live up to it.
Gautama Buddha

Great Spirit, whose voice is on the wind, hear me. Let me grow in strength and knowledge.

Make me ever behold the red and purple sunset. May my hands respect the things you have given me.

Teach me the secrets hidden under every leaf and stone, as you have taught people for ages past.

Let me use my strength, not to be greater than my brother, but to fight my greatest enemy – myself.

Let me always come before you with clean hands and an open heart, that as my Earthly span fades like the sunset, my Spirit shall return to you without shame.

(Based on a traditional Sioux prayer)

"I do not seek to walk in the footsteps of the Wise People of old; I seek what they sought".
Matsuo Basho

"Have I not commanded you? Be strong and courageous. Do not be afraid; do not be discouraged, for the LORD your God will be with you wherever you go".
Joshua 1:9

"Whatever misfortune befalls you [people], it is because of what your own hands have done- God forgives much-"
Quran 42:30

Myself when young did eagerly frequent
Doctor and Saint, and heard great Argument
About it and about; but oft-times
Came out, by the same Door as in I went.
Omar Khayyam
The Rubaiyat XXIX.

Contents

1. LAKE MJØSA, NORWAY

The old Baron was seated at the large, highly polished, teak and leather desk in his study looking out over the lake before him. He was short for a Norwegian, about five feet eight inches, had distinguished curly grey hair, a rather round face with brown, bespectacled eyes and was dressed casually in a dark green cashmere cardigan, open-necked shirt, and grey flannel trousers, since he was not expecting any visitors until possibly after lunch. The perfect silence was only occasionally broken by the sound of ice cracking on the lake outside or birds foraging for small fish in the shallows. The old castle had stood secluded in its large grounds for five centuries and the current baron had spent all of his time there after finishing his education. Quietness was ingrained in him.

When the long-awaited tap on the door eventually came, he answered it in a surprisingly loud voice.

"Enter! Ah, Maximillian, I hope that you have good news for me". There was more than a hint of impatience in his voice.

"Yes, Herr Baron, I am certain that I have. The telephone line and the satellite dish have been restored to fully functioning order after the storm last night and the post has been delivered". Maximillian proffered the silver tray he was carrying to the Baron, who picked up the dozen or so envelopes on it.

"So, that means that telephone, broadband and satellite communications have been completely restored?"

"My tests suggest that that is indeed so, Herr Baron".

"Very good. Thank you, Maximillian. You may proceed with the preparations. Is everything progressing as planned in that matter?"

"Yes, sir, there are no problems".

The Baron fanned the letters and the butler left in complete silence, although, before he pulled the door to behind him, he did allow himself one glance at his employer's face. He thought it an extremely courageous and cheeky thing to do, but he liked to be aware of the Baron's mood at all times.

Maximillian had been the Baron's manservant at university in Heidelberg, when they had both been young men. He was German, and was the only person allowed to call him Herr Baron. He was completely trusted by the whole household. They had been together for more than fifty years and they knew each other better than they did their own wives.

The Ghouls of Calle Goya

The Baron was looking for the heavy, dark-green envelopes that signified that they came from the closest members of his family and the community within which he worked. These he opened with an obvious sense of trepidation, putting the others aside until later. He was smiling as he withdrew the RSVP cards one after the other. There were eight of them. He held them up before him and spoke to an old family portrait.

"The clan is gathering, grandfather Peter. We will be one again and continue the ancient family tradition!"

The walls of the panelled study were lined with family portraits, but there were two in particular that the Baron wanted to view at that moment. However, they were not on display to everyone, not that many people ever made it into the intimacy of his private study anyway. Only a handful of business managers, solicitors, accountants and the like had ever been through its door.

However, the Baron had another room, a secret room, off his office. It had always been there, since the castle was constructed, but along with millions of dollars of other restoration work, it had been brought into the Twenty-first Century with state-of-the-art security, life-support and communication systems. He activated the remote-control device in his pocket and a perfectly hidden panel slid open - silently.

The room was large by any standards. In the centre, stood a perfect, round, table with thirteen matching chairs; a seemingly unnecessary antique chandelier hung over its centre, but its candles could be lit with piezo lighters and doused with puffs of air from canisters of compressed air that were operated by the same remote control. However, it was only ever used on very special occasions because the room was already perfectly illuminated by concealed lighting, which could be adjusted to suit the circumstances. As he entered what he referred to as The Sanctuary, he pressed another button on the remote and half of the opposite wall came to life with a scene from outside the castle. It was a special one-way window, which could be made to give a view or not by passing an electrical charge through the glass.

However, the Baron paid scant attention to the swans foraging on the lake outside. He pushed more buttons, and two other panes of glass were activated revealing his most prized possessions. One oil painting and a sketch in controlled environments became visible. The Baron held up the RSVP cards to the man in the painting and spoke.

"The four-hundredth annual gathering of our clan is about to take place, O Most Revered Ancestor. They have long-tried to deny your connection to our family, but we have never been cowed. We have never denied you and nor will we ever! We know that we are of the same blood and we will keep the faith! Just three more days and we will all be reunited again - I trust that you will be able to honour us with your presence on that auspicious day, even if only for a short while?"

The Baron smiled as he felt that he had been answered in the affirmative silently in his head. He smiled at the wiry-haired, middle-aged gentleman in the picture and again felt an answer. He moved to the woman in the second picture. It was not a portrait, but depicted only one person in the scene. He bowed slightly and clicked his heels in the best way of showing the deepest respect that he knew.

"Revered Ancestors, your will will be done according to our ancient family tradition". Having said that, he bowed again to each painting, turned on his heels, left The Sanctuary and pressed the button necessary to put the room into lock-down once more with only a barely audible swoosh from the door. He returned to his desk, switched his computer on and called his butler again.

"Maximillian", he said, "it appears that communications have indeed been restored to normal again. The letters I received this morning indicate that the traditional family gathering will proceed as planned. Be so good as to implement the ancient procedures for the combined four-hundredth gathering and one hundredth special initiation. You have prepared for a dozen initiations before, have you not, Maximillian?"

"That is correct, Herr Baron, this will be the thirteenth time".

"Your service is much appreciated, Maximillian, not only by myself but by the whole family. Have the new members of staff been appraised of their duties during the gathering and been instructed where they may and may not go during the two days of the celebrations?"

"Yes, sir, everything is as it should be".

"Accommodation, for our staying guests, food, drink, special needs, etc?"

"Yes, Herr Baron, I have taken care of all those details personally".

"Is there anything you want me to deal with?"

"No, sir, only those things, about which I know nothing".

"Very well, you may continue with your duties, Maximillian".

"Yes, Herr Baron".

With that, the Baron turned his attention to his everyday business activities and paid the butler no further heed.

∞

The thirty-one staying guests arrived almost at the same time the following afternoon. They arrived in their own vehicles, mostly by car, although two flew in using their own helicopters. There were eleven members of the Inner Circle, four candidates, ten spouses and six teenagers. Spouses were allowed, as were children over thirteen, but they were not classified as Inner Circle, which comprised the Baron, the Baroness and eleven other close friends and family members. The non-Inner Circle guests were kept at a distance from the main purpose of the event. Partners, girlfriends and boyfriends were strictly forbidden.

The eleven other Inner Circle members were all blood relatives, however distant, and they had ten spouses and ten children between them. Four of those children had been selected for 'special attention'.

At the First-Degree Ceremony, the candidates are willing, but trepidatious, excited, but wary, and those who knew more about what would be happening to them were saying nothing, although their sponsors were hoping that their own apprentice candidates would pass the test and prove that their judgement had not been impaired by the ties of parenthood. If they passed the test, they would become acolytes - aspirants to join the Inner Circle and learn the secrets of its members, when one of them passed on to meet the Great Ancestors.

The Inner Circle members were old but not ancient, and, being rich, they had access to the best medical care anywhere in the world. The Baron, at seventy, was the second youngest on the Board, as the Inner Circle was sometimes called, after his wife, Ingrid, and was its president. His wife was a decade younger and its chairperson. They had not been blessed with children, so they could not populate the Board with their offspring, but they held virtually full control of the group in any case. It was the way that the organisation had been set up four hundred years before.

In actual fact, in many ways its constitution, such as it was, was quite progressive, in that men and women had equal opportunity, but once a leader had been chosen, he or she could be autocratic, if they so wished. The Baron was so well respected because he always listened to dissent and sometimes accepted the opinions of others as superior to his own, but he didn't have to.

Presidency and chairpersonship of the Board was for life, or as they put it 'for the duration of the elected person's life on Earth'. The Baron and Baroness were expected to fulfil their rôles for another ten to twenty years, but no-one felt any resentment about it. He was, after all, the world's closest living relative to the 'Revered Ancestor', as far as they were concerned. Certainly, others claimed ancestry and some could even prove it, but the Norwegian branch considered that they were the only true family, the only ones who truly understood him and the only true holders of the Faith, even though they were not recognised by mainstream historians or anyone else for that matter.

However, that didn't concern them one jot. They revelled in it. As far as they were concerned, they knew their ancestry and had no regard for the opinions of outsiders. Sometimes, over the centuries, rumours concerning the secret society had slipped out, but they had always been quashed. In the earliest days that would have been achieved by the use of merciless violence, but in the more merciful spirit of modern times, law suites had been just as effective. The Sedolfsen family had access to the most conniving lawyers in the world and were prepared to unleash them at the slightest whiff of scandal.

It didn't happen very often because newspaper editors knew of the risk they ran if they attacked the Sedolfsens, but a few brave seekers of truth had been bankrupted in the past for trying to expose more than they could prove and the next round of potential exposure was about to begin.

Disgruntled failed potential candidates were the greatest risk. Being young, they often got drunk and revealed details to friends that they should not have. Sometimes, these 'friends' then sold their stories about the powerful, though secretive Sedolfsens on to the press. It would be during the next month or two that they would be at their most vulnerable. The full celebrations were to last two days. The first day was to include local dignitaries and those from farther afield who could make it, but these guests would not be invited to spend the night. When asked the reason for the annual bash, the answer was always the same.

"Oh, we don't know why any longer! One of our relatives, er, great times twenty uncle Peter, we think, started the tradition of a party on this date four hundred years ago, and no-one has ever thought up a good enough reason to cancel them. We have been holding them every year ever since!"

That had always produced a laugh and an end to the matter. However, the real reason for the first night of the celebrations was to charge the castle with energy that the Inner Circle could harness for use in its own private rituals on the second day.

Not many people understood that and even fewer people noticed that the largest parties occurred every four years, when potential new apprentices were selected.

And this, the one hundredth selection, was to be a spectacular event.

2. THE SEDOLFSENS' ANNUAL BALL

The Baron wanted the four hundredth annual ball and the one hundredth apprentice selection to be the best ever. To that end, first, he had done some thinking, then he and his wife had put their heads together and finally he had asked The Board for its recommendations. It was the way he usually did things, and one of the reasons that he was so popular.

The result was that three hundred and ninety guests were invited and fifty extra staff were taken on. The Baroness was well aware that nothing was allowed to go wrong this year even though the ballroom would be filled to almost double the capacity it was designed for. Therefore, she had called in the assistance of the best party organisers in Norway and Sweden to check her figures and supply extra staff.

Von Knutson were the best in the business and it was rumoured that the royal houses of both countries had availed themselves of the company's services in times of need.

"What is the weather report, Francisco?" asked the Baroness of her husband. "Do you think that the gods will look upon us favourably this year?" She was only an inch taller than her husband, but she was naturally thin and elegant, whereas he was prone to putting on weight. However, that, her hair and her heels made her appear a lot taller, not that the Baron minded. In fact, he was rather proud of having a taller wife, as many shortish men are.

"I think that they will, Joie", he replied using his pet name for her. "The ice has gone from the lake; the birds and foxes are coming back... it's not so cold and the weatherman says that we are in for an exceptional spring. So, yes, I think we've hit it lucky".

"It was also a stroke of genius to invite so many people that whatever the weather is like outside, people will find it too warm inside just because of their own body heat".

"It's very kind of you to say so, my dear. I am rather proud of that little touch myself. I really liked your suggestion to have concealed entertainers dotted about between the ballroom and the marquee too. That'll make them jump about a bit! By golly, I should say so".

"Thank you, darling. Catering for two hundred in the dining room and two hundred in the marquee should ensure some circulation and there's the smoking room, the verandah and the gardens. I think we can safely say that our guests will have ample opportunity to regulate their body temperature themselves".

"I agree, Joie, a well-deserved pat on the back for all concerned. Ah well, let's get on with it then. The first batch of guests is due at eight, aren't they?"

"Yes, Frank, we had better start getting dressed. It's time to let the staff and caterers sink or swim on their own. There's nothing more we can do until we are ready ourselves".

"Very well, Joie, I'll call by your dressing room at eight to pick you up".

They embraced lightly, pecked each other on the cheek and parted company.

∞

The Baron and Baroness were standing by a table of drinks about twenty feet in from the entrance to the ballroom. The Master of Ceremonies announced each of the guests as they arrived, but the hosts only remained there for thirty minutes while the most important guests entered, those who had been given the earlier arrival time of eight pm. Others who had been told eight thirty would have a harder time of making it to shake the Baron's hand and express their gratitude for being invited.

Dress was formal, but this wasn't a problem for most of even the local tradesmen who already possessed dinner jackets to wear to their Masonic or Round Table Lodges, both of which the Baron was a member, although he rarely attended the meetings any more. He had joined because it was traditional, a gesture of goodwill, a publicity exercise, more than because he was looking for a good night out with decent local people.

The majority of the local population understood this and respected him for making the effort to support the neighbourhood charity fundraisers. The aristocratic Sedolfsens enjoyed a good reputation with the overwhelming majority of people living around about the castle and in the province as a whole.

They both put on their best smiles to match their aristocratic-cum-military dinner attire. The Baron sported medals, a cummerbund and a sash, while the Baroness wore a full-length dark green silk ball gown, a tiara and a sash. They extended a white-gloved hand, one after the other, to each of the early guests. Occasionally, the Baron would bow slightly and click his heels and his wife would courtesy, when someone of royal blood stood before them. As the ballroom began to fill up, the members of the Inner Circle mingled seamlessly from the French doors, the dining room or the main entrance according to their preference.

The event was spectacular; everyone said so. The party was reported in the local paper by the editor of the newspaper personally since he was there, as was his boss from Oslo, the owner of the paper.

There was a small orchestra providing appropriate music in the ballroom for those who knew how to dance in the older styles and there were quite a few. There was a harpist in the dining room for those who wanted a break and there was a small theatre troupe performing sketches in the marquee. The crowd modulated itself very well by moving between the venues, and the weather could best be described as fresh, but it was certainly not cold.

People wandered between the three main hotspots and stood on the patio or walked in the gardens, which were lit by a multitude of lights regulated by a number of computer-controlled, pre-programmed sequences. The surprises went down well though. Scantily clad men and women in tights and body stockings, who must have felt the cold, sprang out from alcoves and small arboreta in a flood of coloured light, and fire-eaters spat flames from concealed spots at random. Hoots of laughter and screams of surprise could be heard in the grounds all evening.

With so many guests present, and so much going on, it was a simple task for the thirteen of the Inner Circle to slip away whenever they wanted to. Rarely was it a concerted effort to leave and meet up all together, but nevertheless, it was not unusual for two-thirds of the Board to find themselves in The Sanctuary at the same moment.

The Baron had opened the one-way window onto the ballroom as the two rooms adjoined. There was also CCTV of the grounds and the marquee fed from the castle's main security cameras.

"What an atmosphere, Francisco!" said one of the Inner Circle seated around the table. "You really have excelled yourself this year".

"Pardon, Claus?" asked the Baron, who was slightly hard of hearing, if the voice was not completely familiar. Claus waved at the screens and held up a thumb. "Oh, yes, I see what you mean. Thank you so very much. Joie put a lot of work into the event".

"I particularly like that ingenious touch of having thirty guests to each member of the Board. It gives the atmosphere that extra frisson, don't you think?" commented another member.

"Yes", added Claus, "it should provide a real boost for tomorrow. Well done, both of you. I think I'll wander over to the marquee and have a smoke on the way. It looks pretty lively over there. Anyone fancy a wander?"

"Yes, I'll go with you", replied another and they exited into the study.

The whole castle was filled with the sounds of people enjoying themselves, but the events outside in the garden and the marquee seemed to be marginally the most popular, partly because the weather was so mild and partly because the ballroom soon became stuffy when it neared its intended capacity.

The most active revellers of them all though were the thirteen members of the Inner Circle who appeared to thrive on the excitement of those around them. Baron Sedolfsen and his wife seemed to be everywhere. Everyone wanted to talk with them and they were willing to cooperate - nay, more than willing, they were enthusiastic about it. They literally dined on the joyous mood of their guests.

When the party was officially over at midnight, the hosts posted themselves near the exit from the ballroom so that they could personally thank all those who wanted to bid them goodnight and that was all of those who hadn't had to leave early.

When the last few guests had left shortly before one, and the servants were securing the castle for the night, the Inner Circle came together in the middle of the ballroom floor as if from out of the woodwork. Each was smiling broadly.

"Well, my hat's off to you, Franky, and you, my dear Joie, you really have done us proud this year". There followed a round of cheering.

"Thank you, uncle Hakon, thank you all, on behalf of Joie and myself. Now, if you will excuse me, I have a few things to do before I retire, but you can carry on until you drop if you like. I'm sure there must be some food and drink lying around that you can scavenge, otherwise just ask the staff who are still cleaning the place up. Goodnight".

The Baron remotely locked down the Sanctuary and went to his room feeling exhilarated, but also wanting to preserve the energy for later on that evening.

3. THE 100th APPRENTICES' NIGHT

Most of the Inner Circle spent the following morning in bed, and the afternoon lounging around the castle, walking in the grounds or fishing in the lake, which was well stocked and famous for its trout. The Sedolfsens had a few items to check on, but left most of the organising to Maximillian, since the caterers were no longer needed.

Breakfast and lunch were served, but they didn't lay on any food after that because it was traditional for everyone to dine together after the meeting had closed at around ten o'clock.

The rooms of all of the Inner Circle had been granted access to the footage of the party the previous evening and all of the members spent an hour or two running through the highlights as they were getting ready in order to relive the party and psyche themselves up for the evening before them.

The ceremony began at seven. All the lights in the public area of the castle were put out at the main fuse box, only the kitchen was left using electric light so that the staff could prepare supper. Torches of greased twigs were placed in their holders along the passageways and candles and open fires were used in all the rooms. The flickering lights made it look from outside as if the castle were ablaze. When Maximillian struck the gong at seven, thirteen figures in full-length black cloaks with hoods left their rooms and proceeded to the study bearing a burning fifteen-inch candle before it. When they had all arrived at the study door, the lead figure produced a large black key and ceremoniously opened the door. They filed into the office, which no longer looked quite as it used to and waited while another key was produced and The Sanctuary was made accessible to them. As each figure stood at the threshold to the inner sanctorum, a challenge was given: "Who was the last and yet still the first great Master?"

A muffled reply from each of the twelve, inaudible to any other than the Guard of the Sanctuary, and if correct, earned admittance. Each of the twelve passed the test and stood behind his or her seat.

"I say to all standing here, what is the first requirement for opening this meeting?" asked the bearer of the keys.

"To prove to you, O Inner Guard, that we are just members of the Inner Circle loyal and true, and that we have earned the right to a seat at this table", the twelve chanted as one.

"And how will you achieve that, pray?"

"We will achieve that, Inner Guard, by revealing our true identities in the time-honoured fashion", came the reply.

"And what is that time-honoured fashion of which you speak?"

"We will step out of the Darkness and into the Light, so that we may be recognised as true and loyal members".

"Very well, let it be so, starting from number thirteen".

A figure took one step nearer the seat before him, placed his candle in the holder on the table and began to disrobe. He hung his cloak over the back of his chair and stood in front of it. He was wearing a white smock, which bore several daubs, streaks and patches of colour on it.

"My name is Erik," he said placing two fingers of his right hand over his heart, "and I am the Master Artist of the Odense Atelier of Artists. I bring you greetings from all the Artists, Painters and Apprentices from the loyal and true Odense Atelier".

"Thank you brother Artist. Your qualifications being the artist's smudges over your heart have been recognised and your greetings noted. Welcome to the Inner Circle. Number twelve..."

A similar routine was carried out with numbers twelve to two, which was the Baroness, who represented the Mjøsa Lake Atelier. When the twelve Master Artists had revealed themselves, the Inner Guard spoke again.

"And I, as the Inner Guard of your Sanctuary, will now reveal my true identity in honour of your candour and trust".

He removed his hood revealing a Basque beret, and then his cloak to show his artist's smock.

"Greetings, Brother and Sister Artists, from the Inner Circle Atelier here at Lille Mjøsa Castle. Please convey my deepest regards to the artists and apprentices of your respective Ateliers and now let us be seated.

"Fellow Artists, before we are seated, let us take the time to open the Atelier properly. What is the one item that the world needs more of?"

"Enlightenment!" came the universal reply.

"Yes, my Brothers and Sisters, but universal enlightenment, not that of a few for the few, so let us take a leap of faith into the Darkness and trust in Higher Forces. Extinguish the personal lights that have guided you here this evening and trust in the common good now".

On the word 'now' each candle was put out and The Sanctuary was left in total darkness.

"Great Artist of the Universe", wailed Joie, "please help us in our moment of blindness, we beseech you!"

There was a spark in the blackness above them and a candle flickered into life, then two more, followed by four and then eight more. Fifteen, a magic number to them, the length of a tool of enlightenment, an artist's paintbrush.

"As you are all aware, this is the 100th. Apprentices' Night, so it is very special to us. Not only does Apprentices' Night come but once in four years, this is the one hundredth such occasion and we have four would-be apprentices. I am sure that you are all aware that we had 390 guests last night, which equates to thirty guests for each member of this Inner Circle Atelier and that our Atelier meetings are held but once a year on the 30th. of March. All the significant numbers are in force this year, so let's make it a good one. Erik of Odense, would you once again don your cloak and hood and prepare the apprentices in the outer chamber, while we who are left prepare for your return". He tapped a block of cedar with the rear end of a fifteen-inch paintbrush to signify that that subject had been dealt with and the Master Artist from Odense left the room incognito.

While he was admitting the apprentices to the study, and advising them how to present themselves to the Board, the other twelve members were preparing The Sanctuary. They removed various artefacts from the walls and placed them around the room and donned masks and singlets that they had made themselves and brought with them. Then they put their cloaks and hoods back on, and secreted themselves at various locations around the room. Finally, the window to the outside was activated, the candles were relit and taken by their owners to wherever they were stationed, and the lights in the chandelier were extinguished. Francisco pushed a button and a tiny red light flashed high up in the far corner of the study. Eric was watching for it and was the only one who saw it. Everyone heard the howling of wolves and evil cackling.

"The time has come apprentices for you to show your worthiness to join our esteemed organisation". The howling and cackling continued and as each apprentice showed signs of rising tension, Eric said, "Turn to your right so that I may blindfold you... All right, about turn left and await my signal to enter the Chamber of Trials, where ghouls, demons and other terrors may be lurking. Your sponsor will guide you, so trust in your sponsor and nothing evil can befall you. Via con Dios, trust only in Him, yourselves and your sponsor. I will see those who survive in the Otherworld very soon".

A single crash of a gong somewhere in or outside the castle rang out and the door to The Sanctuary opened with a loud, eerie creak.

"Take fifteen paces forward on my mark, apprentices, but pay heed, fifteen, no more and no less. There you will find your sponsors. Good luck! Forward into Darkness, brave fellows!"

They took off gingerly in single file, each one counting carefully and stopped at the fifteenth step.

"Go no further!" shouted one sponsor over the din as he grabbed his ward's left arm above and below the elbow.

"Stop for pity's sake, before it is too late!" pleaded the second and grabbed his charge. The third and fourth apprentices were treated likewise and they were led off to the four corners of the room sometimes having to avoid obstacles that lay in their path or to bear the howling and cries of Board members as they passed them by. This was all frightening enough for the young apprentices, but their blindfolds had been made so as not to cover the eyes completely, so that the wearer could catch glimpses from time to time.

When the terrified apprentices had made it to the apparently safe refuge of their corners still in the grip of their sponsors, the picture wall came to life revealing a scenario of a pack of timber wolves feeding on a carcass in a thunder and lightning storm. Shadowy ghoulish figures clad all in black but flashing occasional glimpses of pale-green skin darted about among the wolves. It was so lifelike that many would have believed that they were outside in the woods at the terrible scene.

"Apprentice Artists, you have been blindfolded to shield your sensibilities from the wickedness that goes on all around you in this world. However, some of you, the bravest, the humblest and the truest, will catch glimpses of the horrors that can befall mankind even through the blindfolds that they are wearing. If you are one of those, I salute you and bid you to take courage from the knowledge that your Brothers and Sisters are here to ensure that you come to no harm. Sponsors, I call upon you to lead your apprentices around our hallowed grounds but to guide them carefully, and protect them from Evil".

The couples meandered around the room, roughly following the walls, but trying to disguise that that was what was happening. As they passed the round table or any of the posts where members were stationed surprise interactions would take place all to the backdrop of the terrible sounds of wolves feeding and ghouls enjoying themselves in the way that men assume that they do.

One candidate stumbled and nearly fainted, but for the encouraging words of his sponsor.

"Courage, Robert, you are almost through this ghastly night. Let me be your comfort, guide and shield".

Robert walked on, but certain that he had failed the test and disappointed his Sponsor.

"I see approaching Brethren," called a voice in the Darkness. "Brethren, be ye of good heart?"

"Aye, Brethren, and you?"

"Yes, we are looking for shelter from this madness!"

"Would you join us?"

"Gladly", came the reply. Three more such greetings were given and the band of eight returned to the table where the other nine members were already seated. The first sponsor rapped the tabletop with his knuckles.

"Who is without?" called Francisco.

"We are eight brothers and sisters, loyal and true, seeking shelter and sustenance. It has been a most foul night".

"Eight, you say? But we only have room for four more. Whom would you leave behind?"

"No-one, Brother, if you cannot accommodate all of us them we must move on for we are loyal and true to one another too".

"In the face of such loyalty, I will call up four more chairs that you may all dine with us. Enter Brothers and Sisters loyal and true".

With that, the members removed their ghoulish masks and singlets and placed them in the drawers in the table before them.

"Step up Brothers and Sisters that you may be recognised"

The first sponsor removed the cloak from his apprentice. "May I present Millicent, a sister apprentice from Oslo, and I am her Master, Willem of Oslo". So, saying, he removed his own cloak. The other three couples followed suit.

"Master Artists, before I can allow your apprentices to join our illustrious gathering, I have two questions: one for you and one for them. Why are they blindfolded?"

"So, that their eyes might be spared the horrors of the night".

"So, if Darkness brings horrors, what would you like most right now apprentices?"

"Light!" said three in unison, but the fourth said, "Lights!" before realising he was out of sync and said "Light!"

It produced a barely-audible chuckle from some members.

"Well, if our guests desire Light, or even more than more than one, let there be Light and as the chandelier dropped a few feet and the candles were lit, the sponsors whipped away their apprentices' blindfolds.

"Before you join us at this table, in honour of your candid nature, we will also reveal our true identities. Number thirteen?" and the disrobing began again. When Francisco had taken his cloak off, the sponsor Master Artists and their apprentices were directed to their places.

"Well done, Apprentices", said Francisco, "let me be the first to shake your hands and welcome you to this the Mother Atelier. We will dine tonight and tomorrow you will return to your Mother Ateliers in the knowledge that one day you may be called back to this table to take a permanent seat as do we thirteen here now".

The Apprentices looked around them but only the table was clearly illuminated the walls some distance away were in shadows and the picture wall had been turned off.

"Brothers and Sisters, please sit back from the table a few inches".

Francisco pushed a button in his pocket and the table sank slowly out of sight. Moments later, it was replaced with an identical table bearing seventeen servings of soup in bowls of gold, and bread rolls on golden side plates. The Apprentices were awestruck at the extravagance.

"No silver service tonight, Brothers and Sisters, tonight all the metal on the table will be of twenty-two carat gold. We don't use it often, but as tonight is the one hundredth Apprentices' Ball, Joie, my wife, and I thought it appropriate. Joie, would you say Grace? Bon appétit everyone!"

The tables revolved thirteen times for thirteen courses, and the banter around it was jovial and lively. The four Apprentices were particularly pleased to hear that they had been awarded two weeks' holiday in Spain. This was not a complete surprise to them, because there were rumours about the holiday apartments that the organisation owned around the world, but it was twice the normal length of time given to an Apprentice.

"And don't worry", Francisco reassured them, "we have already squared it with your bosses, parents or whomever.

"One word of advice about your vacation: you will all be expected to behave in a manner that will bring honour to our illustrious organisation. We have owned most of our overseas properties for many years and so, we, naturally, have contacts in the vicinity, who will be able to report back on your conduct. Make sure that it is exemplary. Having said that, we all hope that you enjoy yourselves at your destination. You have earned it. Well done, one and all!" Francisco started the round of applause and the members of the Inner Circle followed his example with great enthusiasm.

When the ceremony and the meal were over, everyone had had his or her fill of food, drink and speeches, and they were all happy to go to bed.

4. FRANK AND JOY

Frank was a tall, handsome, fifty-something-year-old banker, who worked in the City of London, but as a specialist in commercial loans; he often had to travel to other branches than his own to meet clients nearer to their premises. Every lunchtime, and sometimes after work too, he would visit one of the pubs or restaurants in the area where he found himself for something to eat. He was a bachelor, and, living alone, found cooking for just himself a chore. If he fancied a drink to relax himself in the evening, he could take a taxi home since he never took his car to work anyway.

He was well off, or at least well paid and had saved quite a lot in nest eggs provided by the bank at preferential rates. However, he was lonely. He was beginning to regret never having made the time to look for that special someone. These days, he found that he was finding himself more and more often on his own. He was bored with drinking and eating too much just to be able to convince himself and his colleagues that he was having a good time being single at his age. Pick-ups were becoming rarer, but he hadn't given up hope just yet.

One Friday lunchtime, he noticed a party of Thais from the Embassy nearby celebrating across the bar room. There were about twenty of them and they were roughly evenly split between the ages and sexes. However, one of the women, whom he judged to be about thirty years of age and just about the most beautiful woman he had ever seen, seemed to be responding to his stares. At first, there was brief eye contact, and then a smile quickly covered by a hand, and then, as time passed by, more open responses.

He checked his watch. His lunch hour had flown past and it was time to leave, but how could he go now, after being presented with a rare opportunity like this?

Frank reconsidered his thoughts. 'Rare?' 'Rare?' Rare did not even come close. This was more than rare, it was unique. He made a snap executive decision and phoned in sick.

"I'm at that new wine bar down the road. Look, I'm terribly sorry, but I feel a little queasy. Perhaps one of the moules in the marinère was off... No, there's no need, really... Honestly... I'll sit here a while longer, go to the toilet a few more times and then get a taxi home. When I feel that I can trust myself... if you know what I mean... Yeah, sure, thanks. Yes, it is a bummer, but there you go. Maybe it's better not to eat seafood on a Friday after all. It can spoil your weekend.

"Oops, something's bubbling down below, I'd better go back to the bog and sit down. See you on Monday... Thank you, bye".

When he was certain that the Thai party would not be breaking up any time soon, he ordered a decent bottle of red Rioja, and sat back to stare at the Thai woman, who had caused him to lie to his boss for the first time that he could remember in thirty-odd years.

He was in a cavalier mood after lying to Mike, his manager, so he decided to take a big risk. He held up his glass to the Thai lady and mouthed the word 'Cheers!' His heart was in his mouth, but he came over light-headed when she reciprocated with her glass of white liquid.

He cursed himself for ordering a full bottle of red, when she was drinking either white wine or water. It was impossible to tell from the distance, but he could not see any wine bottles on the table. For a few seconds, he toyed with the idea of sending the wine back as corked and ordering a glass of Chablis, but he had already told one lie and didn't like the feeling.

When he saw her and three other women stand up to go to the Ladies, he decided to make his move. As they passed by his table, he gave her his best smile. He thought he would die when she smiled back, but she did not stop. He wondered how long it would take four women to go to the toilet. Three to five minutes, he reckoned, but he knew that he could not be too generous, so he began counting down four minutes. Halfway through, he remembered that he had a stopwatch on his Omega, but it was too late and he nearly lost count.

At what he hoped was the four-minute mark, he got up to stand at the bar close to his table. They would have to pass by in single file, and if she were last, he would ambush her.

Sure enough, after three hundred and twelve seconds had passed, the women started to walk past him, but they all smiled.

Two almost giggled.

He guessed that he had been a topic of conversation in the loo, but his prayers were answered and 'his girl' brought up the rear of the line. He stepped out in front of her.

"Oh, I'm dreadfully sorry. I do apologise! Are you all right? I don't know what I must have been thinking!"

"Don't worry, no harm done", she said stopping and smiling at him broadly for his clumsy approach. After a few seconds, she started to look embarrassed.

"Oh, look, silly me, I'm blocking your way. I couldn't help noticing you... and your friends... are you having some kind of a party?"

"Yes", she replied, giggling at his awkwardness and obvious intentions. "It is our king's birthday, so we have the afternoon off. We are celebrating his happy birthday... December 5th. is a very big holiday in Thailand".

"Oh, you're Thai, are you? How interesting", he said feigning ignorance. "My name is Frank by the way" and he held out his hand.

"Nice to meet you, Frank. My name is Joy", she replied, still seeming to be laughing at a joke that he was not aware of.

"When you are finished with your party, Joy, might I be permitted to buy you a drink to celebrate your king's birthday as well?"

She hesitated for just the right amount of time for propriety and then accepted.

"My friends are leaving at three. I was going to go back with them, but... I suppose I could join you for one drink... in honour of our king, of course".

"Yes, of course, in honour of your king's birthday. I will wait for you right here".

Frank had never been much of one for royalty, but at that moment, he was thanking God that there was a king of Thailand.

They had a wonderful afternoon and evening, but like Cinderella, Joy wanted to be back in the Embassy by midnight and so Frank duly walked her home. He felt as if he were on a cushion of air. He already knew that he was deeply in love with the Eastern Beauty, and she knew that he was too. For her part, Joy liked the Englishman as well, but like most women who find themselves in this situation, she was much more guarded than he was.

However, when he asked to meet her the next day, she threw caution to the wind and accepted. On Saturday, she agreed to meet him on Sunday too, and by the end of that day, there was no doubt in either of their minds that they were in love.

They spent every lunch break they could, and every evening together, but Joy refused to move into Frank's apartment, insisting that she wanted everything done in the 'old English style'.

They spent Christmas and the New Year planning their wedding with the help of Frank's parents, but they also talked for hours to Joy's mother in Uttaradit by video-phone. Her mother did not speak English, but Joy translated for them. The old English style wedding was set for March 30th, after which they would have a honeymoon in Spain, somewhere that Joy had always wanted to visit, before flying on to Thailand for civil and Buddhist weddings there with her family and friends, since they could not make it to the UK.

Frank was Church of England and came from Walton Downs in Surrey and Joy was a Buddhist from a small village in northern Thailand, although she had lived in Bangkok for quite a while before being posted abroad. Her parents had been rice farmers, but her mother had had to lease the land out when her husband had died a decade before. Ninety-odd percent of her family still lived in the area. However, none of this presented a problem to their marriages. They decided to hold the civil wedding in Bangkok, where she had many friends and the Buddhist ceremony in her village, so that her family and old school friends could attend.

Joy was fond of saying that three weddings in four weeks was more than any woman could hope for, especially when they were all to the man she loved. Frank was a little less enthusiastic. He had the money, and could get the time off, that was not a problem, but he didn't like the idea of being the centre of attention so often in such a short space of time.

In fact, it made him feel queasy, but for real this time.

"Don't worry about it, my darling", she used to reassure him, "Thai weddings are very laid back. I think that they are much more fun than the old style English ones I have seen in films".

All of Frank's friends and colleagues took to Joy immediately and his boss even offered them the use of his apartment in Fuengirola for a fortnight. When they looked up Fuengirola on Google Earth, Joy was ecstatic.

"That is just where I have always wanted to go! I want to see Torremolinos, Benalmadena, Los Boliches, Marbella and Gibraltar. The Costa del Sol just sounds so romantic, doesn't it? It will be just perfect".

So, Frank had accepted the offer gratefully. He also allowed his future bride and his mother to attend to all the details of the Surrey wedding. Joy gleefully immersed herself in the tradition of the British wedding ceremony. She read up on it and insisted that every detail be correct, because, although no-one knew it, she, like most Thais was deeply superstitious. She particularly insisted on wearing 'something old, something borrowed and something new', but she also followed other traditions such as getting engaged, wearing a veil, having Mike for Frank's best man and a woman from the embassy as her chief bridesmaid, and handing out wedding favours of hand-carved Welsh love spoons.

The wedding ceremony duly took place at a small, but beautiful village church nearby that they had managed to find at relatively short notice.

Only sixty guests were invited to attend the ceremony and small reception in a local hotel, and that included ten of Joy's friends from the Embassy. Frank would always wonder thereafter whether his mother had restricted the numbers because either his wife was not British, she was not European, she was not Church of England, or because she was Buddhist, was brown and was Thai. He would never ask, but he would never stop wondering about it either until the day he died. Joy, for her part, didn't seem to notice his doubts, or never mentioned them if she did. She was the most beautiful and happiest bride he had ever seen, and that made him overflow with pride and joy.

Joy was not her real name, of course, it was Pranom, but all Thais adopt a nickname that they like to use amongst friends. Some choose Western names, but most do not.

Frank thought that Joy suited his wife perfectly, because she brought happiness wherever she went and everyone was always glad to meet her. He counted himself the luckiest man on Earth, but then so do most bridegrooms.

Joy thought that she would die from happiness when Frank took her by the arm and led her back down the aisle in her fluffy white wedding dress with all the people looking on. It was easily the most important moment in her life and she had ten friends and a professional photographer there to ensure that the day would be captured forever. A copy of the professional video was to be placed on line immediately, so that her friends and family could download it at will.

After the reception, Frank and Joy took a taxi down to a small village hotel not far from Gatwick. It was too late in the day to make it worthwhile flying out that night, so they had booked onto the midday flight to Malaga for the next day.

They travelled first class and were given a champagne lunch on the very comfortable three-hour flight. Joy's Schengen visa had been pre-arranged, so it was just a question of walking off the plane, through customs and into a pre-booked taxi.

"Malaga, isn't it, sir?" asked the taxi driver in an almost perfect English accent.

"Er, no. Fuengirola... Calle Goya. I forget the number of the apartment block, but here is a photo".

"My apologies, sir, but no worries, we'll have you there in twenty minutes. Honeymooners, eh? Lovely! The province of Malaga is a great place to be. You'll have an unforgettable time here. I can promise you that for sure. Take my word for it".

With that, the driver pulled away from the curb, put his foot down and said no more. The motorway hugged the coast for the forty-kilometre journey - the Mediterranean Sea glittered blue and silver in the afternoon sun. Villages and towns sped by on either side of the road, seemingly deserted for the afternoon siesta, for which Andalusia is famous. The province virtually shuts shop between two and five every day. Joy hugged her husband's arm in love and excitement... it was everything that she had always dreamed of, and she was everything that he had always wanted.

It seemed far too soon that the Mercedes-Benz left the motorway and entered the ghost town of Fuengirola south.

"I can see the look on your faces the both of you, but don't be fooled. It's only four thirty. In half an hour, this place will be a hive of activity and if you walk down this road, the Comina de Coin, for twenty minutes, you'll be on the beach. There's no siesta there! Now, let me see", continued the cabbie adjusting the SatNav. "Calle Goya, you say? Yes, here it is just off the Camino de Coin, the very street we're on. It's a nice area... no riff-raff, if you know what I mean... and your apartment block is... this one. Would you like a hand upstairs with your luggage, sir?"

"No, we'll be fine thanks, drive. I'm told there's a lift in the building".

"Very well, sir, that'll be forty-one Euros eighty... call it forty for cash. Thank you, and welcome to our province and country, I hope you enjoy your stay".

"Yes, I'm sure that we will. Thank you. Goodbye".

Joy and Frank took one look up the facade, before opening the street entrance and calling the lift to the first floor where they would be staying.

"I just simply adore it", gasped Joy as Frank fumbled with the key in the lock.

5. LA RESIDENCIA 'HOME FROM HOME'

"Come on in then..."

"No, you have to do it again".

"What? Oh, that, but I did it last night".

"Yes, I know you did, but that wasn't our home. It was only practising".

"OK, but nor is this our home".

"I know, but it is for a while and it will give you some more practice. I just love your quaint British traditions; they are nothing like our Thai ones".

Frank put the cases inside the doorway, picked up his giggling wife and carried her over the threshold. They kissed before he put her down.

"Is that any better, Thaiger?"

"Oh, yes, but I can't get enough of being in your strong arms... Oooh, it makes me go weak all over".

"I know the feeling, darling. Having you in my arms, even just looking at you makes me go weak all over... except in one place".

"Yes, I know. I can feel it sticking in my bum. If it hurts, Mummy will massage it for Daddy".

"Yes, please Mummy. Daddy wants that very..." but he broke off when he heard stifled laughter on the stairs above them. He put Joy down quickly and closed the door quietly.

"Oh, my God, I think someone was listening".

"It doesn't matter, Daddy. We're both adults, we are allowed to have fantasies. Besides, we're married and this is our love nest for the next two weeks, so who cares if someone heard us or what they heard?"

"What if it was someone from the bank?" He couldn't fathom her expression. "What if it gets back to the bank? I'll be a laughing stock!"

"I don't know... some people might be jealous that you are having your thing massaged by a beautiful Thai woman who is half your age".

"That's true", he said more to keep the peace than because he wasn't afraid of being talked about at work. "Let's see what you can do, it is getting awfully big and sore now, Mummy".

"Well, you just leave that to Mummy, Daddy. She'll sort it all out for you. Come to Mummy" and she pulled him down onto the hallway floor just inside their closed door.

When they had finished, and got dressed again, Frank carried the cases into the bedroom and they began their exploratory tour of the apartment there.

The first impression was that every room was of a decent size. It wasn't a huge flat, but both had lived in much smaller ones, especially when they were students. It was sparsely decorated with off-white matt emulsioned walls wherever there were no tiles. As non-Spaniards, both of them thought that it looked very typically Spanish - even Andalusian, although neither of them would have been able to explain exactly what that meant. The apartment ran the length of the building, so there were large patio windows in the bedroom at the back and in the lounge at the front, which opened out onto small verandahs, and also provided a pleasant crosswind. Besides that, there were fans in each room and air conditioning throughout. The bathroom and the kitchen, the latter being part of the lounge, were modern and stylish. There was a huge flat screen TV set on the wall, which was fed by fibre optic cables and distributed around the flat by Wi-Fi.

The fridge contained two bottles of wine: one of red and one of sparkling cava. There was a note too, which read: 'The boss, Mr. Michael, he say to put these here for you. Welcome and happy honeymoon'.

"That was nice of him, wasn't it?" asked Joy.

"Yes, it could have been champagne, but…"

"Oh, please, Frank. He has loaned us this beautiful apartment and put wine in the fridge. Let's just be grateful, no? Perhaps, he did ask for champagne, but the manager bought cava. Who knows? Let's just be grateful, or give him the benefit of the doubt, if you like. Just be happy, my love".

"Yes, you're right, Joy. What have I been like all my life without you to show me the way to see things clearly? I must have been a real tosser".

"What is a tosser?"

"Oh, it's a man who massages himself like you just did to me. Well, that's the literal translation anyway. It means a fool".

"You are not a fool, Frank, but I think that all men are literally tossers".

He laughed and hugged her to him.

"You make me feel twenty years younger, my darling, I love you so much. What shall we do next?"

"I want to unpack my clothes before they become too creased. Anyway, they say that if you live out of a suitcase for too long, you may live out of one all of your life, and I do not want that for us. I want us to live in a nice home and be happy together".

"Yes, so do I, but surely one night, or even two, is not too long?"

"The proverb does not specify, but I think the length of time is different for everyone. Maybe, it is short for us, so I will unpack for us both. I won't be long".

"OK, if you like. I'll sit here and read this 'Welcome Pack' on how to use the appliances. It's not gripping reading material, but it has to be done sometime. We can open the 'champagne', when you're finished".

Forty-five minutes later, Joy returned.

"All done. See that didn't take long, did it, and now we can live in our own house. Is everything all right?"

"Yes, you will be happy to know that I now know how to cook us a meal in this oven and wash our smalls in the washing machine".

"How unromantic of you, Frank! Why do you want me to wear underwear on our honeymoon?"

"You are the sexiest, most wicked woman I have ever met. Come here! You deserve a spanking!"

"Oh, Daddy, no! I'm sorry! I do like the idea of us staying in and eating a meal we have cooked together though".

"Yes, so do I, but since we haven't got any food in the place, I suggest we leave the cava for now and go outside for a reccy - a look around", he explained to her puzzled expression.

"I agree, but must I wear my bra and knickers?"

"If you keep talking like that, we won't get out at all this evening. Just come as you are, you look wonderful - you always look just so wonderful".

As they skipped down the flight of stairs to be ground floor, Frank warily looked up the stairwell thinking about the laughter he had heard earlier. Once in the exit hallway, Joy said:

"Look, Frank, our very first real letter to us!"

"That's funny, I didn't see it when we came in. I'm sure it wasn't there then".

"Perhaps someone picked it up by mistake and brought it back", suggested Joy.

"Yes, I suppose you're right. I shouldn't think that the postman has been since we've been here. It must have come this morning. Open it and see what it says".

Joy slit it open with the apartment key that was still in her hand and read aloud.

"Welcome chez moi! I bought this little place thirty-odd years ago, and it has been my bolthole ever since. A fantastic investment too. If you turn left out of the building and first right, there is a lovely bar with friendly staff and a barbecue chicken shop across the road. That is Comina de Coin. If you just turn left out of the building, walk to the end of the street and turn right, the bar La Teja is the friendliest, most typical bar in Spain. Keep on from there and you will come to de Coin again. Turn left, walk down the hill for five minutes and you will come across two of the best, and priciest, restaurants in town. I hope you have a great time, Michael. PS: by the way, keep walking down past the restaurants for ten minutes and you will be on the beach".

"That was nice of him, wasn't it?" said Frank before Joy could. He wanted to make amends for criticizing his generous benefactor before.

"Yes, it was", agreed Joy picking up a note in Frank's voice but dismissing it. "Which way then, boss?" she asked once on the street.

"I'm not your boss, Joy, not even in jest. Look the boss recommended left out of the building, then we have two choices. Let's get that far first and then toss a coin".

"Toss a coin for the Camino de Coin", she laughed. "I didn't really call you 'boss', Frank. It's just that the traditional Thai words for mister and missus are 'Nai' and 'Nang', which mean 'boss' and 'wife' It was only a Thai linguistic joke. Sorry. I knew you wouldn't get it. Anyway, now where?"

Frank felt in his pockets. I haven't got any coins".

"No, nor me. Oh, wait! I have an old Thai ten Baht that I carry as a reminder and for good luck. I don't like to gamble with the king's head, so you do it".

"Heads or tails for straight on to the La Teja?"

"Heads"

"Heads it is, here's your coin".

So, they walked up the gentle rise to the junction taking note of a minimarket and a bakery there, and walked the fifty metres to the pub. There were half a dozen men and women smoking on the pavement and enthusiastic banter could be heard from some distance away. The smokers on the narrow pavement gave way to the strangers to pass, but were struck dumb when they entered the strictly local bar.

They sat at the counter and Frank tried to order two beers when the barman approached.

"A pint for me, and what do you want, Joy?"

"I have always wanted a real San Miguel. They sell it in Thailand, you know. It is very chic".

Frank looked at the one pump and saw that it bore the San Miguel logo. They were in luck.

"Two pints of draft, please", he ordered.

"Pardon. No speak English", the barman smiled genuinely.

Frank hadn't been to Spain for a decade, but he looked around and spotted an advertisement for beer.

"Dos cervezas. Pints, er, grande, er, por favor".

"Si, señor. Dos pintas".

Joy was impressed, but she was much more the linguist that Frank would ever be.

"Will you teach me how to say that later? I'm going to buy a little book tomorrow and write down all the Spanish phrases that I have learned on our honeymoon. It will be a lovely reminder for when I am old, don't you think so?"

"Yes, I do. You are full of good ideas. You never cease to amaze me".

"Thank you, my darling. That is what a woman likes to hear, among other things".

As the barman put the pint pots down, they reached for them, clinked, and said 'Cheers'.

"You haven't got a bra on, have you? I just saw the left one jiggle a bit!"

"I am not wearing anything you can't see. You did say to come as I was".

"Yes, I did, didn't I?" and so saying he put his arm around her back, pulled her towards him, kissed her on the cheek and softly touched the side of her right breast.

"Oh, why didn't Michael leave us some food as well as wine? Then we could have stayed in!" he muttered. Joy smiled, kissed him on the cheek and put her hand high on his thigh 'to steady herself'. Then she tickled his crotch with her little finger as she did so and pulled away laughing softly.

"So, where shall we eat?" she asked.

"OK, let's walk down to the square and lave a look".

Of the two expensive restaurants, Michael had told them about, they chose the 'Vino Tinto' over the hotel for no reason at all. Joy had spare ribs in a soft cheese sauce and Frank had shoulder of Andalusian goat accompanied by a Rioja red.

Frank was not impressed with the scraggly thin chop that was put before him. He found it too salty. Joy thought that her meal had been over-salted as well, so they ordered ice cream to take the taste away.

"Ooh, that's cold!" said Joy holding her lower jaw.

"It's supposed to be, that's why it's called ice cream", he smiled.

"I know, but I have a problem with one of my back teeth. I should have had it fixed before we came away, but I am scared of dentists".

"OK, let's pay up and walk back", he suggested. "Did you think that was worth the money?" he asked en route.

"I have nothing to compare it with. I have never eaten in Spain before. Did you?"

In his new role of a happy, non-judgemental chappy, he told Joy that it was delicious, while vowing never to eat there again.

They walked back up the hill to their street, but as they were passing the Teja, they decided to stop in for a nightcap of a large glass of red wine each. That one glass each turned into three and they went home very happy, if a little wobbly, after almost everyone in the bar had got to know their names. They were still waving when they turned the corner into Calle Goya.

As he put the key in the street door lock and turned it, he remarked, as least judgementally as he could possibly muster, "It sounds like the neighbours are having a party". He pointed at the obvious sources of the loud laughter and music: the verandahs above and to the right of their apartment. The patio doors were open; shadows could be seen dancing in slow rhythmic shapes on the ceilings. "Live and let live", he muttered as they walked up the stairs.

As they opened their door and went inside, Frank was sure that he heard someone on the stairs above them again. He urged Joy inside the flat, but put a finger to his lips and waited. The automatic light in the passage clicked out, but Frank resisted the temptation to switch it back on. Footsteps and muffled voices approached from the darkness above, and then a face, a distorted face like a Halloween mask, appeared around the corner for a millisecond.

"Ooh-hahhh-ha", it laughed hysterically and disappeared. Frank looked up the stairs, but in the blackness, he saw only fleeing shadows and heard more childlike laughter.

"What was that?" asked Joy.

"Oh, nothing to worry about, my dear. Just a bunch of kids. On holiday, I shouldn't wonder... pissed, stoned and overtired. Let's just go inside and leave them to it. We can open that bottle of cava and see what Spanish satellite TV is like".

Joy tried to be enthusiastic, but the glimpse of that deathly-pale face had unsettled her. She took one sip of the wine and feigned sleep, although ten minutes later she was genuinely in the Land of Nod.

Frank just thought she had fallen asleep and continued to watch TV until the bottle was finished. As he was helping her to the bedroom, they passed the shower and Joy wanted to use it.

"Go and watch TV for fifteen minutes, my dear", she said, "I'll wait for you in the bedroom".

Frank agreed, opened the Rioja and turned the TV back on. When Joy called him, he switched the light and the TV off, stumbled to the bedroom, leaving everything else as it was.

Even in the state that he was in, he was able to make love to Joy, but then he quickly fell sound asleep. She was satisfied, but she was now awake and thinking. When he started to snore, she urged him onto his side, but as she did so, she froze. There was a noise coming from the bedroom veranda and the window was open, the curtain was blowing in the slight breeze. The party was still going on all around them, but there was one sound in particular that bothered her. She strained to listen, but the words above the laughter seemed plain enough: 'Can Mummy kiss it better too? Oh, thank you, Mummy, but don't stop massaging it, will you? It is so nice'. 'You're a wicked Daddy, aren't you? Making Mummy kiss it too. Shall I give it a suck?' 'Oh, I think it would help, Mummy...'

She didn't know what to do. She gingerly slipped naked out of bed and inched back the curtain.

Nothing.

As she began to relax and creep back towards the bed, she saw something move at the end of the corridor in the living room. It was a black shadow hunched over like a monkey, but, between cackles, it was repeating over and over again: 'Thai Mummy cocksucker. Thai Mummy cocksucker has big problem'.

Joy slunk into bed, but hid under the sheet shivering, rather than wake Frank to tell him. He continued to snore, blissfully unaware of the plight that Joy was going through alone.

The Ghouls of Calle Goya

6. THE BEACH

Joy hardly slept a wink all night what with the noise from upstairs and next door, the intermittent throbbing from her aggravated molar, and her husband's snoring. Sometimes, he stopped breathing for several seconds too and that was even worse. Once or twice, she thought she heard her name or their names being used upstairs followed by hoots of laughter, but none of it made any sense to her. Nobody knew them there and why would they be laughing?

At three twenty in the morning, Joy's heart leaped into her mouth when their buzzer rang. It seemed inordinately loud. She pulled the pillow over her head. Five seconds later, she heard two other buzzers and someone shouting from the flat above. There was a muffled reply in Spanish from the street below and the front door was buzzed open. Joy wanted to see what sort of guests they were having to their all-night party, so she wrapped a towel around herself and hurried to the spy hole in their exit door. She saw one thigh with a pistol strapped to it and then a police officer. Somebody had called the police, presumably because of the noise.

Joy went back to bed feeling a lot happier, especially when the music was turned off and she heard male and female voices apologising to the officers. It was three forty-five and Joy thought she might eventually feel safe enough to get some sleep, but not five minutes later, she distinctly heard someone spit out the words 'Thai cock-sucking bitch call the police, now Thai have big, big problem'.

"It wasn't me!" she called out loud. Laughter ensued and Frank stirred.

She attached herself to his back like a limpet, but he was already asleep again.

It wasn't until day broke that she dared to get up again. The house was completely silent, but traffic was starting to pass by the front in the street below. With her comfort towel firmly wrapped around her, she got out of bed, raised the raffia blind and opened the patio doors wide. The rapidly brightening sky was comforting, so she called Frank to come and enjoy it with her.

"Just another twenty minutes, dear. We're on holiday, I mean our honeymoon, don't forget!"

She opened the bedroom door inch by inch and peeped out. Everything appeared to be as she had left it, so she went to the loo and then into the living room. All was well. She pulled back the curtain. Other women were already mopping their balconies, so she thought she would do the same to try to fit in. One woman almost directly opposite called out 'Ola, señora' and some other phrases accompanied by a shake of her head. She had probably thought that Joy was a Filipina and was commenting on the noise of that night. Joy responded with a wave and a brisk 'Good morning!' picked up the empty wine bottle and noticed that the glass was half-full of a yellowish-green slime. She put the bottle on the draining board, and, assuming that Frank had been sick, she flushed the goo down the toilet and rinsed the glass.

It was comforting, like being back home in Thailand, mopping the tiled floors in the early morning, but she couldn't help thinking about the previous ten or twelve hours. Then she heard as if from the front balcony 'The cock-sucking bitch from Thailand has big problems coming'.

Her first thought was to run and see who was there, but she was too frightened and so told herself that she didn't want to walk on her clean, wet floor. Someone grabbed her from behind and she jumped, kicking the mop, bucket and its contents over.

"Morning, darling! A bit jumpy, aren't you? Did you sleep well?"

"Oh, Frank, it's you! You gave me such a fright!" she said spinning in his arms and clinging to him".

"My, my, you are in a state, aren't you? Whatever's happened? Come on, tell Daddy all about it".

As he led her to the couch, he noticed the wet glass and empty bottle.

"I don't think drinking so early in the morning is any good to you'.

"What?" she managed.

"You finished off the red. Don't get me wrong, I don't mind in the least, but it seems to have made you rather edgy".

"Me, drink red wine before breakfast?"

"You finished it last night, and you were sick in the glass. I just this minute finished cleaning it up!".

"Not me, love. I had one, max two glasses and I wasn't sick".

"You were drunk; you don't remember...?"

"I was drunk, I'll give you that but I have been a lot worse over the years and I haven't been sick for decades. I remember leaving the glass and bottle right here - I couldn't be bothered to put them away, went to bed without showering, we made love and then we went to sleep. See, I remember everything. I haven't got much of a hangover either.

"Look, why don't I help you clean up this water? Then we can have a shower, walk up to those shops we found last night, do some shopping, come back here for breakfast and then go down to the beach?"

"Yes, that sounds like a good plan...", but she knew in her heart that something was wrong.

"You didn't hear any strange noises last night then?"

"No... only that bloody party that seemed to be going on all around us. They wouldn't have been allowed to get away with it in Britain; someone would've called the police mucho rapido".

"Someone did call the police. They got here after three o'clock..."

"Just drunken kids on holiday, I expect. Any problems?"

"Er, what? Uh, no, I don't think so. They were only here a few minutes. Frank, I think that those kids think that we called the police".

"No... why should they? There are a hundred people living around here who could have done it. I don't even know the Spanish emergency number, do you?"

She shook her head.

"Well then, why should they suspect us? Anyway, who cares if they do? It is not a criminal offence to call the police when someone is breaking the law, is it?"

"No, but I don't want people to think badly of us".

"Nobody's going to do that. Do you want to shower first, or shall I?"

"You go first; I'll put my clothes out".

When Joy went under the shower, singing her favourite song, 'Ghost Riders in the Sky', Frank dressed and decided to give her a surprise. He checked his wallet for Euros, closed the apartment door quietly behind him and set off for the shops to buy some essentials.

The running water was soothing. Joy always felt uplifted by taking a shower. She turned her back to the shower head, and lifted her long black hair into the jet of cool water. She had always preferred a cold to lukewarm shower to a hot one, which was hard to find anyway in rural Thailand outside of a hotel.

She heard and then saw the bathroom door handle move.

"Come on in, Frank!" she called, but no-one came. She turned off the water, and called again. "Frank, come on in, I don't look that frightful without my make-up... Frank? Stop messing about!"

"Girl from Thailand have big problems", came a disembodied voice. "Thailand have big problems".

Joy began to cry, but she was defiant. She pulled her towel around herself, hopped out of the bath and wrenched the sliding door back. There was no-one there, but she heard her apartment door slam.

"Frank? Where are you, Frank?" She hurried to the door and opened it. She was almost sick when she saw the yellowish-green slime come off the handle onto her hand. She instinctively wiped the handle and her hand clean with the edge of her towel.

"That's what I like to see! My girl waiting for me at the door stripped and ready for action, but how did you know I was coming?"

"Er, I was on the verandah and saw you walking down the road" she lied. "Did you meet, er, anyone?"

"No, no-one we know. I'll start cooking this little lot and you get dressed. Then we'll go down to the beach".

∞

"All right, my dear, isn't that view fantastic? Beats London any time, eh? Where do you want to sit?"

"I don't know. Did you hear anybody say anything on the way down here?"

"Like what? I heard lots of snippets of conversations, but they were all in Spanish".

"I heard 'Thailand have problems'".

"No, I didn't hear that. Why has there been another bomb, a flood or a tsunami?"

"No, not that I know of..."

"So, where do you want to sit?"

"I don't know... anywhere".

"At the water's edge or at the back? With people or on our own? On the sand or under a parasol?"

"Oh, er, with people on the waterfront under a parasol".

"Right, now we're getting somewhere". Frank arranged for two sun bed loungers and a parasol, they stripped to their swimming costumes and lay down. "Isn't this just the life? I suppose you get a lot of this in Thailand, eh, Joy?"

"It's more on the coast... I come from inland, but yes, it's lovely".

An hour or so later, a boy came around with ice-cold beer in a polystyrene container, Frank bought two, handed one to his wife and continued reading.

"Are you coming in", he asked, "I need a Jimmy Riddle after that beer?"

"No, I'm OK, thanks. Have fun".

"Well, I don't know whether having a pee in the sea can be classified as 'having fun', but I'll try. Maybe, in twenty years' time, it will be all the fun I can have with the old boy. Anyway, must dash".

She flipped over onto her stomach and swapped ends so that she could watch him more easily. He seemed a good swimmer, thought Joy, although she wasn't, and then he disappeared under the water. A minute passed and she started to become concerned, but then he popped up twenty metres away from where he had dived. She held up a thumb and he did it again. He was showing off and they were both loving it. He dived again, but the head that appeared was not Frank's smiling face, it was deathly-white with streaks of red and green on it. A pale green arm pointed a long bony finger at her. It sent a shiver through her and she let out an involuntary yelp. Then the figure submerged.

"What is it, darling? You look as if you've seen a ghost".

"Oh, I'm OK," she whispered gripping his hand tightly. "I didn't see you come back up. I was worried about you"

"Silly mare! I'm not a bad swimmer and it is not deep where I was. You should come in and try it"

"No, not just now... Thai ladies do not like to get black skin. It is something that we avoid at all costs".

"Oh, I see. So, I suppose the beach is not your favourite place then?"

She only smiled and released his hand. "Perhaps we could go for something to eat now?" she suggested hopefully.

"It's not even three o'clock..." he began, but thought better of it. "Give my trunks thirty minutes to dry, or I'll have to go commando like you did last night".

She smiled weakly at his joke and buried her head in her towel in an attempt to block any further apparitions. She repeated Buddhist prayers under her breath that she had learned as a child.

They enjoyed a meal of tapas and red wine in the Teja and felt as if they had been going there for years. Joy was interested in the dominoes game going on at the back of the bar room. The noise was deafening and the excitement palpable.

"Can we go and watch?" she asked.

"Of course, you can!" replied Frank. "They won't mind. In fact, I'm sure they would be delighted to have a beautiful young Thai bird watching their every move".

"Come with me..."

"No, honest, they will love having you there. The easiest way is, next time you go to the toilet, yours is down a little past them, isn't it, just stop on your way back and smile? Trust me, just try it. If you wave your hand at me, I will come and rescue you".

Fifteen minutes later, Joy grasped the bull by the horns. She looked into Frank's eyes, nodded, slipped off her barstool and went over the top. It was a big thing for her. Frank knew it and he was immensely proud of her.

She was beaming when she sat down fifteen minutes later.

"They said I could play next time, if I am here before three".

"Really? That's great!"

"Well, I think that's what they said anyway. It was all in Spanish and I don't speak Spanish. They were very friendly though".

"Good, I knew they would be. Another drink?"

"Sure. That has put me in a good mood".

Frank didn't ask why she hadn't been in a good mood before, he just let it ride.

Sitting in the Teja, they noticed another small supermarket. The one closed at nine, the other at nine thirty. They missed the one that Frank had been to that morning, but bought more wine and plenty of cakes and biscuits to take home from the second one.

Sitting on the sofa nibbling, sipping wine and watching TV, Frank said, "You know Joy, I think I could happily retire down here. I just love the place and the people, don't you?

"Why the hesitation?"

"I don't know... I like everyone I've met face to face, but I am not sure about the others".

"Right, but you can't expect to like everyone, can you? Nor can you expect everyone to like you... and if you haven't met the ones you might not like, then you haven't got a problem, have you?"

"I don't know about that, Frank, I just don't know".

"What do you mean with 'I don't know'. Why don't you know? Look, if you don't yet know the people that you might one day have a problem with, how can you have a problem? What you are saying applies to every single person in the world every single day. You don't have a problem, do you?"

"I don't know, Frank, I just don't know".

"No, you don't know, and I don't know, but I do know that I am going to finish this bottle and either go to bed or open another one. Or from the other side, your side, I suppose I could say, I don't know whether I am going to bed straight after finishing this bottle or whether I will open another one. How's that?

"You are more than welcome to join me".

"I haven't gone anywhere, I'm still here".

Some moment while Frank's attention was on the screen, Joy started to sob quietly, slipped on to the floor and curled up into a ball. When he did notice, he assumed that she had gone to sleep, as she often slept on the floor Thai style.

"What can you do with pissed women?" he asked himself out loud as he looked at her small frame, but she didn't answer.

Some time later, Frank finished his bottle of wine, threw a cover over Joy, and left her on the cool floor in a pool of pale light from the street lamp outside and went to bed.

∞

A while later, she felt something touch her, no, brush against her and it woke her up. The room was completely dark except for a soft glow from the street lamps below. She opened her eyes, disoriented for a few moments until she remembered where she was. She could hear something scuttling about. It reminded her of rats back on the farm, but as she was about to get up, she caught the faint sound of a couple making love. She listened intently, it was so quiet, but she soon realized that it was she and Frank from the night before.

'Thailand have problems' was played intermittently over the grunting and sighing.

"Frank! Frank!" she screamed, as she watched a small, black, humanoid shape grin at her and then leap off their balcony.

7. FUENGIROLA SOUTHWEST

"That was some nightmare you had! I'm sorry that I left you alone on the floor last night, but you looked so peaceful. I thought, 'Might as well let her wake up by herself'. I didn't realise you were prone to bad dreams".

"I'm not. This was so real… I am sure that I was awake, but I suppose that it could have been a nightmare".

"Charming! You dream of us making love and describe it as a nightmare. You don't do much for a man's ego… Still, I suppose nightmares wouldn't be scary if they didn't seem realistic at the time".

"Oh, that is profoundly logical, Mr. Spock!"

"All right, no need to get sarky. I was only trying to help".

"Well, you didn't succeed".

"No, obviously not… Sorry. Why don't we try heading off the other way today? If that way is to the beach, up to the right might be older… or less touristic".

"Yes, OK, if you like, but there is something strange about this place. I don't know what it is just yet, but I don't like it".

"But you've already said that you like everyone you've met".

"Yes, I know, but there are some people I haven't met who are not nice…"

"Oh, we're back on that track, are we? Come on, shower, dress and back out".

"Are you going to go out while I'm in the shower this time? I don't like being left alone in this flat".

"No, I have no intention of giving you another nice surprise… I'll be here", he said sarcastically himself this time.

"Please, darling, don't be like that…"

"I'm sorry, but I just can't get my head around what is going on here. You talk about ghosts or black figures, but I've never seen them. You say that you have heard recordings of us 'in flagrante delicto', but I have never heard them. You talk about big problems that might occur, but every single person in the world can say that they might have a problem, even a big problem, soon. I understand that you want me to believe you, and I am trying to, but it is really difficult without any concrete evidence".

"OK, what about the wine you didn't drink and the vomit in the glass that you didn't put there?"

"Yes, but I left a bottle two-thirds full and an empty glass. When I got up, the bottle was empty and the glass was clean. I didn't see any vomit, and for all I know you or next door's cat could have drunk the wine".

"You think I drank it, don't you?"

"It is the logical conclusion, dear... or that I did. Look, this isn't getting us anywhere... Let's just get ready and go exploring. OK?"

"OK", she agreed reluctantly.

∞

They turned right out of the front door and left at the end of the street up onto the Camino de Coin again. They passed a casino, a fast food restaurant and a bespoke bakery called Rays They turned left over the crossing, and Frank wanted to sit outside a bar named the Sol de Mijas.

"Why stop already, Frank? We're only about two hundred metres from home?"

"I just want to sit, think and orientate myself. I have heard of Mijas and look at that manhole cover. It has Mijas stamped on it. That means that we are living right on the boundary with Mijas".

"Yes, and...?"

"And nothing, it is just nice to know. Let's finish our drinks slowly and then continue up there into Mijas..."

"If you like", she acquiesced, not having a better plan. They walked for an hour or so through streets of tiny terraced houses with Arab-style tiles on the front walls until Frank's back could take it no longer and they were completely lost.

"All these houses look the same and I haven't seen anyone for ages. The place is completely deserted. There isn't even a sound coming from any of these houses. No radio, no TV, no children playing, no cats, no dogs, nobody driving around... It's as if we've walked into a ghost town. Have you any idea where we are now, Frank?"

"Er, yes. I think so, but it's quiet because this is siesta time. Don't Thais have siestas as well? This looks like a much older part of town, as I though it would be. Traditions die hard. I guess that people here have been brought up not to make a noise in the afternoon. Anyway, look, we have been walking uphill in a westerly direction, so we have to go downhill in an easterly direction... or, we could cut across here and hope, I mean, and meet the de Coin over there..."

"No, not really... In Thailand, older people may have a snooze in the afternoon, but whole cities only go to sleep at night, not in the afternoon. Anyway, getting back to the point, you don't know that the de Coin is over there for sure, do you?"

"It sounds right..."

"Yes, but you aren't sure, are you?"

"My dear old Dad always used to say, 'If you're lost, stay where you are and someone will find you".

"So, we are lost! And anyway, no-one is looking for us, are they?"

"No, I didn't mean it like that. Why don't we have one in that cafe over there and get our bearings. I need to go to the toilet anyway?"

They sat outside and waited for some service, but then Frank went in to order a pinta and a cafe con leche. He was gone ten minutes, but when he returned, Joy was crying.

"Don't worry, darling. We know we aren't far from home and there's always a taxi. Anyway, here's your coffee and the barman drew me a map to get us home.

"What's up, girl?"

"Nothing..."

"That can't be true. What's the matter?"

"You won't believe me..."

"Yes, I will... this is becoming boring. What is it, Joy?"

"A black figure with a whitish face just passed on a motorcycle... it pointed at me and said 'Thailand have problem'. I am so scared, Frank, I don't know what to do... What must I do, Frank?" She sobbed and sniffled into her hands that were cupped as if in prayer.

He put an arm around her and looked up to the bright blue sky as she buried her head in his chest.

"I don't know what we must do, my dear, but one thing is for certain... you are not alone. I will always be with you. You will never face anything alone". As a last resort, he asked, "Shall I get a brandy for that?"

"No, please don't leave me!"

"Señor!" he shouted loudly, and the owner came out quickly to see what all the commotion was about during the siesta.

Whether it was the two brandies or Frank's kind attention or both, Joy slowly came back to herself and they followed the sketch back to the de Coin. Although they were far further up it than they had ever been before, or so they thought, in one instant they found themselves looking at the crossroads they had sat at earlier. They were coming from behind the Sol de Mijas. They must have made a loop in the backstreets and hadn't wandered as far away as they had imagined.

"There you are, my dear, I told you we weren't lost. All you had to do was trust my sense of direction..."

"You had a map!"

"Yerrrs, but I did know where we were anyway..." She looked him in the eyes with determination. "Roughly... I had the basic direction right... Anyway, who cares? We're here now... or at least, we're back on home territory. The casino is down there, then you get to the bar Michael recommended that we haven't tried yet, and around the corner from there is the Teja. Navigation is simple, if you have the aptitude for it".

She slapped the small of his back. "I believe you, but millions wouldn't".

With an eye to keeping his wife in a jovial mood, he suggested trying out the other bar that Michael had recommended.

Again, they were treated very well, even made a fuss of and Joy was her old self for a couple of hours. She didn't speak Spanish and they didn't speak English or Thai, but, a little tipsy, she had them eating out of her hands. Neither of them wanted to go when the bar closed at nine, yet they didn't want to go anywhere else and be disappointed, so they just went back to the flat.

This time, however, they made four bacon butties, drank a bottle of wine between them and went to shower and bed together, but it was a while before they got to sleep.

8. LOS BOLICHES

After a few days of feeling apprehensive and hearing voices, Joy was feeling a lot better one morning. She hopped out of bed at nine-ish and offered to cook them breakfast.

"It's a shame we haven't got any cava left", she shouted to Frank, as he was taking a shower, "we could have had Buck's Fizz with our fried eggs on toast!"

"I'll go and get some, if you like", he replied.

"No, it's not important, we can have it tomorrow", she answered thinking about what had happened the last time he had gone out and left her.

"This coffee is going down a treat anyway", said Frank over breakfast. "This is just what you need to set you up for the day. I was thinking that it might be nice to walk up the coast to Los Boliches, you said you wanted to go there, didn't you?"

"Yes, it's silly really but one of the girls at the embassy went there last year and she made it sound very pretty".

"Yes, well, here it is on the map... Look. It's about... oh, I don't know, but less than an hour away up the coast to the north. We'll be there in time for lunch, have a scout around, walk back and be back in time for tea".

"Or we could go with the flow and get back in time to go to bed", she said. "There's no work in the morning..."

"No, of course not, darling. Was I being too rigid again?"

"I don't know, were you? Let me check... No, it's still quite soft. Wait a minute... there is some life in the old boy yet!"

"If you keep doing that, we'll never get out. Go and shower".

"Spoil sport", she pouted in jest, took off the towel she had wrapped around her and trailed it to the bathroom behind her like a naked model dragging a fur coat down a catwalk.

"I said that you were the sexiest, most wicked woman I have ever met, and I love it", he said loud enough for her to hear.

"I do like to be remembered", she replied.

By the time they got to the beach, it was almost midday, later than they had expected, but it wasn't important to either of them.

"That's Los Boliches", he said pointing, "a couple of kilometres up around the bay. Are you still up for it?"

"Sure, but I couldn't find my sunglasses this morning, so I will need a new pair, and I want a wide-brimmed hat as well... one of those straw ones with a bow".

"No, problem. I imagine there'll be loads of shops selling those kinds of things on the way. We could probably stop off and have a cold beer, if it gets too hot as well..."

"You're a bit of an alki on the sly, aren't you?" she said toying with him.

"A single man has to find a way to keep himself amused, you know".

"Yes, and I can guess what you used to do too!"

"Ayyy, I was talking about drinking!"

"So was I! Why? What did you think I was talking about?"

"You know very well what you were talking about and so do I".

"Well, you're a merchant banker, aren't you? I'm sure I heard someone say that they were all tossers..."

"You didn't even know what the word 'tosser' meant until a couple of days ago. Anyway, I'm a Commercial Banker not a Merchant Banker".

"No, perhaps I didn't know what it meant, but I had still heard people say it... I just didn't know what it meant that was all.".

"You've got an answer for everything, haven't you?"

"I'm in the Diplomatic Service, I have to have. It's part of the training".

"All right, I know I'll never get the better of you with words, but I have my methods too... Look, hats and glasses, just what you're looking for".

After ten minutes of giving his opinion on various hats that all looked pretty much the same to him, his back started to ache.

"Look, darling; see that bar next door but two? My back is starting to hurt, so if we are going to make it to Los Boliches, I'm going to have to sit down. I'll wait for you there. We'll be able to see one another... I'll only be ten yards away and I'll watch you all the time to make sure no randy tourists try to chat you up".

"What about the randy Spaniards?"

"No, I can't go another round with you right now, I have to sit down". He kissed her on the temple, moved off and sat down, all under her watchful eye. He waved at her and she went back to her hats.

Frank ordered a beer but kept watch as he had promised. He was idly watching the passers-by, many of whom had hardly any clothes on at all, when he spotted what looked like a commotion some fifty yards off. As they drew nearer, he dismissed them as students or actors from the local theatre promoting their latest production. There were two witches in black complete with pointed hats, warty noses and broomsticks and two demonic black familiars with tails. He thought that they were trying to act like cats, but he wasn't sure. They were interacting with people and the 'cats' had collection buckets, into which people were tossing coins.

He started rummaging through his pockets for when they got to him. When they were about to reach Joy, she went into the shop to pay for her items and missed them. As she left the shop, she saw them dancing around her husband and him giving them money. She cowered behind the windbreak of the shop trembling, hardly daring to peep out lest they saw her. A few minutes after they had gone, she came out wearing her straw hat with its large pink bow and Ray Ban style sunglasses. She looked like a film star in disguise and Frank said so.

"I didn't want those horrible creatures to recognise me".

"Which horrible... those students?"

"They were witches and demons... not students".

"They were local students collecting money for something... I didn't catch what. They were good though, I'll give you that. Hey, what am I saying? You don't believe in all that stuff, do you?"

"Yes, and I have seen them before... in our apartment". She pulled a 'so there' expression with her face and poked out the tip of her tongue".

"Come on! You're kidding me, right? This isn't the Dark Ages".

"No, it isn't, but they existed then and they still exist now. You can believe me on that score".

He studied her beautiful face for a few seconds and could see that she was serious.

"Promise me, Frank that you will have no more to do with those things".

"I only gave them fifty cents between the four of them. I didn't have anything to do with them".

"Please, Frank!"

"Yes, all right. Let's move on".

They walked on in silence, each considering what had just transpired, but both were coming to very different conclusions.

They stopped twenty minutes later outside the Yaramar Hotel. "This looks all right. If we come back, we could stay here, it's a lot handier for the beach and the things that holidaymakers do..."

"Let's move there tonight, Frank".

"No, come on. Why would we want to do that? We have a perfectly good apartment, and it's free".

"And it's haunted..."

"What? Now where are you coming from?"

"Our flat, Frank, it's haunted. I've seen horrible black figures like those four earlier in there at night. I've heard them too... they call me names... and they drank your wine then spat in your glass. It was a foul, smelly vomit from Hell".

"I've had enough of all this crap for one day, Joy. Let's turn up this alley and see what's behind the hotel".

The first thing they saw was the "Uppa Crust'.

"Shall we stop here, Joy? I could murder a full English. I haven't had one for ages... well, not cooked for me anyway and they're always better".

She agreed, but ordered Calamaris and Chips. Both the meals were scrumptious and great value for money. They chatted with the friendly owners Sean and Debbie for a while, which made Joy feel a lot better.

"We'll have to come back here again", said Frank.

"Did you hear what that man just said, Frank?"

"No, which man?"

"He went down there..."

"What did he say?"

"Thailand have problems".

"Why would he say that? It's not even grammatical".

"I don't know, but he said it. Didn't you hear him?"

"No, when was this?"

"A minute ago. I can't believe you didn't hear him."

"Joy, this has got to stop", he said taking her hand. "If we continue up this way and then take the first or second left, we should find a couple of nice bars and we'll be heading back in the right direction too. What do you think?"

He was hoping that a few brandies would have the same effect as they had before.

"OK", she agreed not sure what they ought to do.

The second place they liked the look of was a karaoke bar and it was having a two-for-one Happy Hour.

"We've got to go in there, Joy, you love karaoke, don't you? What's that song you often sing in the bath or the shower?"

"Ghost Riders in the Sky..." she said slowly, for the first time realising how inappropriate it sounded in her current predicament.

"That's it. Unusual choice for a Thai woman, I would have thought, but you do do a good job of it".

She was still considering the irony of her favourite song as they were entering the dimly-lit, half-full bar. They ordered a couple of double brandies with coffee and waited to become acclimatised to the lighting and the atmosphere of the bar. There was no shortage of singers. The format was for a would-be singer to fill in a slip of paper with his or her name and preferred song, hand it in and await their turn.

"This is a bit of all right, isn't Joy?" asked Frank ordering a second round. "That's two good places within a few hundred yards of each other. We'll have to come back this way again. It looks a lively part of town. Do you want to sing your song, dear?"

"Maybe later", she said begrudgingly still thinking about the group of witches.

"All right, well, no pressure. It's up to you. 'Scuse me; must go to the Gents".

While they were sipping their third round and starting to get into the swing of the place, they heard the disc jockey say:

"Joy and Frank. Let's hear it for, er Joy and Frank", he said checking the slip of paper. "Joy and Frank, are they still here? They want to sing 'Ghost Riders in the Sky'. That's a great choice, folks, a real classic."

"Go on, that's us, it has to be. Go on, Joy. You do it so well… for a girl…" he goaded her. Frank pointed at his wife's head, as the disc jockey was scanning the audience.

"Come on, don't be shy, is there a Frank and Joy still… Ah! We have our Joy, but it looks as if our Frank - Oooh, Betty, the cat's done whoopsie on the carpet! - sorry, Frank, only kidding. It looks like Joy is going to sing alone. Come on, Joy, don't be shy, your public awaits you with bated breath. That's it! Give her a big round of applause! Over to you, Joy".

The video started up, but Joy didn't need to read the words from the large screen where a video with words was played to accompany each track. She had been singing this song since she was about ten. By the time the second chorus came around, she was well into the act she had developed to accentuate her party piece - she was slapping her thigh, dancing and wailing 'Yippee eye ooooh, yippee eye eeeh, Ghost Riders in the sky…"

Suddenly, some people were wolf-whistling and shouting 'Get yer kit off, darling!'

She was confused; she had never experienced that reaction before. She tried harder, but Frank was running towards the stage waving his arms about. She turned to look at the six by nine-foot screen and saw herself naked riding Frank in their bedroom. She froze, then started trembling, and sobbing as Frank arrived and escorted her off the stage to some calls of 'Boo, spoil sports'.

The tape was stopped and Frank demanded to see the boss.

"How the Hell could this have happened?" he asked enraged, his arm around Joy, who sat just there, a shivering, nervous wreck.

"I've no idea", said the owner. "I've spoken to the DJ, and he says that some guy handed him the memory stick and asked for it to be played as a surprise for 'Joy and Frank'... We took him at his word... we didn't have a clue what was on it; though to tell you the truth, the videos that some people play of themselves would be banned in the West End... Some girls are shameless, and the blokes are starting to go the same way. I'm sorry and all that, but no-one will even remember it tomorrow, trust me".

"My wife will and so will I, trust me! What did he look like?"

"I don't know. Mikey, that's the DJ, said that he was tall and thin; dressed in black with a Halloween mask on. Bound for a fancy-dress party, I shouldn't wonder, though you get all sorts of nutters here these days.

"Like I say, what can I do? I'm sorry. I can see that you're both genuinely upset, but the horse has bolted, as the saying goes... the milk has already been spilled. It's a dangerous game, videoing yourselves on the job. You never know when it might get out".

"But we didn't..." Frank stopped himself. "OK, thanks for your time and thanks for the video. Bye. Come on, Joy. I don't think that this gentleman had anything to do with it".

"Thanks for being so understanding, can I get you another complimentary drink each?"

"Joy?" She shook her head, still sobbing.

"No, thank you, but can we get out without going through the bar?"

"No, I'm afraid not. It's the only way in or out".

Frank walked out of the bar with his head on Joy's and his arm around her shoulders. She was still studying the floor and quaking. They stopped the first taxi they could and went straight home.

Joy cried herself to sleep within an hour, probably helped by the four double brandies, but Frank was not so lucky. The events of the evening just baffled him, and baffled him completely. He spent until well past five a.m. trying to find a connection between what had happened and what Joy had told him, but nothing presented itself to his logical mind, except the memory of her crying, which was breaking his heart.

9. PARANOIA

Frank showed the first signs of being awake the following morning. He looked at Joy, assumed that she was still asleep and started to get out of bed.

"Where are you going?" he heard in an anxious voice from behind him. "Don't leave me!"

"I'm only going to the toilet. I won't be long".

"OK", she replied, but he could tell that she was crying again.

As he was standing before the toilet bowl, wondering what to do when he had finished, he heard Joy scream his name. There wasn't much he could do to stop what he had started, but he grabbed the glass that held their toothbrushes, threw them into the sink, and waddled back to the bedroom peeing into the tumbler and hoping that it would be big enough to hold the contents of his bladder.

"What's the matter?" he asked in the doorway

"They're here again", she said turning around to face him. She almost laughed, but the way she felt was too strong to be mollified even by the ridiculous spectacle before her.

"Why are you peeing into a glass?"

"You called me, I couldn't stop, so I came running..."

"Watch out!"

The glass overflowed onto the floor"

"Oh, shit!" he muttered, turned and hurried back to the toilet wetting his underpants. Joy stepped over the puddle and followed him.

"You just threw that pee into the sink over our toothbrushes".

"Sorry, I had other things on my mind. Why did you call me like that?"

"I was lying in bed and I heard someone or something say 'Thailand have problems'. I turned and saw a black thing jump off our balcony".

"Just wait there a minute". He flushed the loo, took off his underpants, threw them into the bath, got in after them and turned on the shower. Three minutes later he was drying himself.

"Come on, let's go and have a look". He stooped, picked up the drip mat he had been standing on and took it with him. He dropped it onto the puddle of urine on the bedroom floor and said, "Come on, show me".

"You do the weirdest and most disgusting things", she said watching the mat turn yellow as it soaked up his body fluid. "I was lying in bed watching you walk away, when I heard 'Thailand have problems' from behind me on the balcony, so I rolled over, and saw something jump off the balcony. Then I called you".

Frank stepped onto the balcony; studied the floor and the railing and then looked up and down.

"I can't see anything..."

"Why would you be able to, if they are not from this world?"

"Well, you did... 'They'? I thought you said that there was only one figure".

"Yes, this time, but I think there are more of them. Perhaps you can't see them because I am psychic and you are not".

"Eh?"

"Perhaps I am psychic and you are not, so I can see them but you cannot".

"Hey, that rhymes..."

"And I'm being serious!"

"Yes, sorry... That may or may not be the reason".

"You don't believe that I saw them... it, do you?"

"I don't know, I want to believe you, Joy, but I just wasn't brought up that way. I don't have any experience with ghosts and the supernatural".

"I'm so frightened, Frank. I can see and hear them in my head all the time. I see them on the street too and they laugh and point at me. Why only me, Frank? I have never hurt anyone as far as I know; my Karma should be good. What have I done to deserve this? Please help me, Frank".

He pulled her to him, hugged her trembling body to his and looked up at the ceiling. He didn't have the slightest idea what to do. They eventually went through to the lounge to escape the smell of decaying urine and sit down.

"If this place frightens you so much, would you like to go out?"

She shook her head, which was buried in a cushion on her knees. She was still sobbing and shaking.

"The thing is, we can't just sit in here; we haven't got much food. Shall we just go up to the shop and get some supplies?" She shook her head.

"Do you just want to stay here?" She shook her head again.

"Which one are you least frightened of doing: going out or staying in?" Joy shook her head again without looking up.

"This is silly. You can't answer a choice question with a 'No'! It has to be one or the other! So, which one: stay in or go out?" Again, she just shook her head, but the sob that accompanied it was louder.

"Oh, this is ridiculous! We can't go out and we can't stay in. So, what are we supposed to do... vanish? Shall I call you a doctor?" he suggested, and then realised that he didn't know how to do that. Joy shook her head again, which let him off the hook, he thought, although perhaps only temporarily.

As he held her around her back, he wondered whether a doctor was the only solution... or to call the rest of the holiday off and just go home.

"Do you want to go home?" he asked. Joy nodded. As you sure? I can book us a flight back to London on my laptop". She shook her head again.

"Joy! Can we have a bit or sense here, please. First, we can't go out and we can't stay in; and now you want to go home but you don't want to go home! Which is it, darling?" He wanted to add 'for Christ's sake', but stopped himself. His level of frustration was rising too quickly for his own liking.

"Go home to Thailand', she mumbled into the cushion.

He felt like an idiot now, of course that was where her home was. Where her mother and family were.

"OK, my dear. Well, there's only a week or eight days left to the flight..." he looked up to the ceiling again, wondering how they were going to be able to last another week of this. He had an idea.

"I'm just getting my laptop, darling".

He removed the computer from its bag and switched it on, then looked in the bag. He found his travel sicknesses pills. They always made him feel drowsy, so he reckoned that a couple might help Joy relax. He fetched a glass of water and passed her two pills.

"Here, darling, these will help you relax". She took them and the water without question and Frank went online to look for a pizza delivery shop in Fuengirola. There were plenty, one was not two hundred yards away on the de Coin. It would be quicker to walk there and get it himself, but that was out of the question. Frank ordered two large pizzas and three bottles of red wine. He had a feeling that this was going to be a long, hard day for both of them.

Joy was asleep when the pizza boy arrived thirty-five minutes later. Frank opened the street door by remote and took the delivery at the apartment door. Joy would not wake up to eat, so he put the TV on and started alone - especially on the wine.

Frank fell asleep at about three and they both stayed that way until Joy awoke with a start. It was dark outside and the curtain was flapping in the light, cool breeze from outside.

"Look!" she urged, "There's something on the balcony!" However, Frank did not respond very quickly in his groggy state and didn't see anything. He closed the patio door, pulled the curtain and switched the light on.

"I didn't see anything, sorry, my dear". He looked down at the half a bottle of wine and a quarter pizza on the table before him and decided to carry on where he had left off. He poured himself some more wine and a greenish-yellow goo flopped into his glass. It floated on the deep red wine like a gone-off egg yolk.

They stared at one another; she with a look of vindication on her face and he with one of horrified amazement.

"But I only dozed off for a while, it's not possible that someone could have... er..."

"Not someone, Frank, something. Their time is not the same as ours..."

Frank ordered six more bottles and opened the third.

∞

When Frank opened his eyes very carefully the following morning, he saw Joy's legs halfway up the wall. He followed them up.

"What are you doing, love?"

"I'm painting out the security cameras so that the ghosts can't film us any more".

"Oh, good idea", he heard himself saying to his surprise. "Where did you get the paint from?"

"It's nail varnish".

"Ingenious... What time is it?"

"Gone eleven".

"I think I'll open another bottle of wine and order some more pizzas. I'm starving".

They went through to the lounge together and Joy climbed onto the arm of the sofa to reach the other camera.

"No, sick today, was there?"

"Not inside the house, I made sure the door and windows were locked before I took you to bed last night. There was some on the balconies though. I've cleaned that up already... and your mess, that you forgot about".

"Sorry, darling... What are we going to be doing today?"

"If we have to stay here another week, I want to make this a ghost-free zone. So, when you order those pizzas, ask for extra side dishes of garlic, onions and rosemary, if they've got it... better get two of garlic".

Frank opened the wine, poured two glasses and looked up 'garlic, onions and rosemary' on the Internet. He placed the order and included four more bottles of wine.

"That should keep us going until this evening", he said only half in jest. Joy spent the afternoon threading cloves of garlic and rings of onion, there was no rosemary, onto threads of cotton from her emergency sewing kit, and hanging then in front of the door, the windows and the ventilation grills.

"That should keep the monsters away, Frank, shouldn't it?" He didn't like to voice his true opinion, so answered, "You know more about it than I do, dear".

They remained huddled inside their protective square of vegetables with the windows closed and the curtains drawn for the rest of the day, but it didn't stop Joy from hearing the voices outside the apartment and inside her head. That night, in her drunken stupor, she started to talk to them, or not so much talk to as remonstrate with them.

Frank was woken up several times during the night by her thrashing about and the sound of her saying such things as: 'What have we ever done to you?'; 'Get out of our lives' and 'We don't want to know you, please go away'. Sometimes, she was crying as well, but every time she looked so incredibly sad... like a refugee who has just lost everything, family and home, in a bomb raid.

And all that Frank could think of doing was putting his arms around her or opening another bottle of wine. He had never felt so useless in all his life.

∞

By the fourth day of being under siege, both of them had given up on their appearances. They lived and slept in the same clothes, slept wherever and wherever they could and drank bottles of red wine, ate pizza and watched TV whenever they couldn't.

One afternoon, Joy burst out laughing.

"It was so funny to see you in the bedroom peeing into a glass and it running over onto the floor. Oh, my Buddha!"

Frank was a little worried that she sounded hysterical, but there was nothing he could do about it. His travel sicknesses pills had run out the day before, so he just laughed with her and topped up their glasses.

After six days in their fortress, in a bleary daze, Frank realised that something had to be done and be done quickly.

"Joy, this is crazy! We came for a dream honeymoon and walked into a nightmare. We're flying from Malaga on Thursday, so why don't we go there tomorrow afternoon and have two nights there for a change. It's not as if we've seen much in the last ten days, is it? I can go online now and find us a hotel near the airport. What do you say?"

He looked at his poor wife. Red wine stains down her T-shirt and shorts, dishevelled hair, partly worn-away make-up and he was certain that he didn't look any better.

She looked him steadily in the eyes, took a gulp of wine and said: "Do you really think that they will let us go?"

"I think so", he replied holding her gaze. "I think they've probably had their fun with us by now".

"All right, if you think it's worth a try".

They phoned up another two pizzas and six bottles of wine and sat down to discuss their escape plan.

The next morning, they began packing with a glass of wine each on a bedside table. When they were done, they finished off the pizza, put the three unopened wine bottles in their luggage as gifts, took showers and smartened themselves up.

"OK, here I go", he said dragging one suitcase out of the apartment. You lock the door behind me, then take out the key or I won't be able to let myself back in. Don't open the door to anyone, I won't be long".

He kissed her, and then dragged the case to the Teja.

"Can I leave this here for ten minutes, Salvador?" he asked the kindly landlord and showed him a piece of paper with the Spanish translation.

"Si, si, amigo", came the reply. They clapped each other on the shoulder and Frank returned to the flat.

"That's the first one, are you ready to go?"

"Yes", she replied, "emptying the bottle into the two glasses. Let's go for it".

He smiled, touched her glass with his and drained it.

"Bpai!" It was one of the few Thai words he had learned - it meant 'Let's go!'

Joy opened the door, Frank took the case outside and Joy pulled the door to.

"Urgh!" she simpered holding her hand up and locking the door with the other. "Vomit! Green and yellow sick! They know that we're going, so they can follow us! We'll never be free of them now". She was crying again, holding her upturned hand out, snot, mucous and bile dripping between her fingers. Frank took out his handkerchief, cleaned his wife's hand and threw it on the floor in disgust.

"And good riddance!" he said addressing the flat once outside. Joy noticed him looking up at their balcony; her eyes followed his gaze.

"Oh, no! Will it never cease?" Dangling by a hangman's noose from their balcony, looking like a grotesque female Guy Fawkes, was a crude head meant to resemble Joy's. It had her new hat on it with her old, expensive sunglasses on the brim. A used condom was hanging out of the slit of a mouth. Below that hung a two-foot wide card with 'Bye-bye Frank and Joy' written on it in capitals. Before comforting his wife, who was on the verge of collapse, he had the presence of mind to take a photo of it with his iPhone.

"Come on, dear, these people are sick!"

Salvador and another working there, Jesus, welcomed Joy with a big smile as they always had, but they could see that something was very wrong.

By sign language, a translation app and a bit of English, they explained that they were going to Malaga early because of certain unspecified problems. The kind-hearted Spaniards didn't ask which and they were not told. Salvador's wife was preparing for a family party in the kitchen, but she came out to comfort Joy, woman to woman, even though they could not speak to each other in words. Joy cried inconsolably and the landlady patted her on the back making cooing sounds as if to a sick child. When Joy had calmed down a lot, the lady gave her one of the 'special potions' that she took when she had a hot flush. It was a gesture much appreciated by both the honeymooners. Frank had a pint and a double brandy with coffee. Joy had a large glass of red wine.

Frank typed into his translation app, 'May we leave these keys with you, please. I'll phone the landlord to tell him". Salvador agreed, so they were all set to go, they just needed a taxi.

There was only one incident. Joy went to the Ladies and returned crying. Salvador wanted to know the reason and Joy managed to explain that while in the toilet, she had heard 'the dominoes-player in the blue shirt' say 'Thailand has problems'. They relied heavily on the app. Salvador sent Jesus to fetch the man. He was a large burly man with a beer gut and resembled the stereotypical truck driver. Salvador explained the accusation and he denied it. Everyone but Joy believed him and Frank shook his hand and apologised, saying that his wife was upset as an excuse. It was accepted by the gentleman who was concerned about the obvious state of distress that Joy was experiencing, and hopefully forgotten.

Two hours later, forty minutes before the family party was to begin, Jesus called the taxi and it was there. Forty-something kilometres and fifty Euros later, they were in their new hotel near the waterfront in northern Malaga.

The Malaga Beachside Hotel was a disappointment to Frank. He had allowed Joy to choose the place on the strength of the advertising, name and photos alone, whereas he usually went deeper into things than that before booking. Joy seemed happy enough though and that was all he wanted. It was four-ish when they arrived and the area was a ghost town, but they put their bags in their room, walked down to the nearest restaurant on the sand and ordered. Or at least Frank did. For the first time since they had met, Joy 'wasn't hungry'.

"Just a small bottle of mineral water for me, please", she said to the waiter. Frank had a pint of beer, a dozen large prawns fried in Garlic and fresh crispy bread rolls. The drinks arrived immediately. Joy looked around.

"They've given me a litre of water, not the half that I asked for" she whispered.

"So, what? It's just a mistake. Five hundred cc's or a thousand, who cares? It'll only cost pennies. Don't worry about it".

"No, Frank. It's a marker - a beacon! Look around... I'm the only one with a large bottle of water. He's pointing me out to the ghosts", she whispered, looking about her furtively.

Frank looked and she was right - the only one out of forty or fifty diners.

"Perhaps they ran out of small bottles..."

"No, I'm a marked woman. We have to go now before they get here. Come on quickly or I'll have to go alone. I don't want to lead them back to the hotel and then on to Thailand".

Frank reluctantly abandoned his fried prawns in garlic olive oil with farmhouse bread, paid the bill and rushed after his wife who was hurrying down the empty pavement like someone looking for an opening in heavy traffic so she could cross the road during rush hour.

"Don't you think that you're taking this a bit far now, Joy? You're behaving as if alien abductors are after you".

"No, I don't think it's that", she said obviously considering the prospect. "I definitely think it's ghosts or worse... demons". He took her arm to slow her down. Then he realised that he was going to have to explain to his boss why there were threads of garlic and onions hanging every six inches from the ceiling in his apartment.

"Oh, shit!" he said out loud.

"What is it? Can you see them?" she asked urgently.

"No, I was thinking about something in work. Don't worry about it. Where are we going now? Back to the hotel?"

"Yes, but I want to find a greengrocer's first".

"And I want to find an off-license" he muttered.

They ate in the room with room service that night and when the boy came to take the trolley away, Joy invited him on an all-expenses paid, free holiday to Thailand. "It is very nice there, you will love it... I promise you!"

The boy had looked at Frank and hurried out of the door, probably wondering what sort of odd-ball couple they were. After he had left, Joy started putting up her vegetable trimmings and Frank opened yet another bottle of wine.

Frank hung the 'Do Not Disturb' sign on the door before curling up with

Joy so that the chambermaid would not get a sniff of what was going on in the room.

∞

They were getting ready to go down for breakfast, but as Frank was showering, Joy called out they had to go 'right now'. "I can't go right now, love, I'm soaking wet!"

"I'm taking the luggage downstairs and checking out". She was closing the door behind her when he came out of the shower naked. He looked down the corridor and called her name.

"Don't try to stop me, I'll be back for the other bag in five minutes. Get dressed. They've found us!"

Five minutes later a member of the hotel staff was knocking on the door.

"Your wife wants to check out, sir. I think you ought to go now".

He allowed for English not being her mother tongue, but said:

"I don't give a shit what you think. I have paid for another night and another night I will stay. Now, please, sod off, the sign on the door says 'Do Not Disturb", and he closed the door in her face.

Ten minutes after that, a different female member of staff, an older woman, brought his wife and her bag back.

"I'm dreadfully sorry, sir. There seems to have been a mistake. Your wife thought you were checking out today, but you are booked in until tomorrow".

"My wife may have been mistaken, but a member of your staff came here telling me I had to leave. I would call that an even bigger mistake since she has a book she can check in, don't you?"

Joy was standing in the corridor with her bag still sobbing and the woman turned on her heels and strutted off. He felt a little better after taking some of his frustration out on someone who deserved it.

"Come on in and sit down, dear. Let me make you a nice cup of tea. Now, tell me, what that was all about?"

"When you were in the shower, I heard a Thai woman down the corridor telling me that they have found me and that we must leave..."

"Did you see this Thai lady?"

"No, I heard her through the walls... she's three rooms down and has an English husband. She said that they are always fighting. I want to thank her for the warning and tell her that she must try harder because my English husband is a very nice man. Shall we ask them to have a drink with us later?"

"Yes, if you like, dear. We'll look them up later". He cŵtched up to Joy and she put her arms around his waist. When he could hear her breathing deeply, he reached for the remote and put the TV on.

'Now what the Hell was going on?' he thought.

He realised that the hotel manageress hadn't commented on the onion and garlic decorations, and found that inexplicable, unless she thought them mad.

Joy woke up in the early afternoon and wanted to go and see her 'new friend' down the corridor. Frank had been hoping in vain that she might have forgotten about her, but he managed to delay the meeting by insisting they shower first, then he tentatively led the way to the room three doors down.

"Are you sure you want to do this?" She nodded.

"OK", he tapped the door, but to his complete relief there was no answer.

"Why don't we go to the supermarket across the road to buy your family some presents, then sit in the bar downstairs for an hour to see whether your friend turns up?"

Joy agreed. When they were sitting in the bar, Joy seemed almost like her old self. She was a little too wary, skittish even, but she was telling jokes and being sexily wicked just as she had used to be. It warmed his heart and he dared to think that she had turned a corner. However, as the hours passed and it became increasingly unlikely that her friend was going to turn up, Joy's mood began to change.

"Do you think he's killed her and moved on?" she asked.

"Who's killed her?"

"Her husband, of course! She said they were always arguing! I'm going to ask the hotel management to check her room. Perhaps there's a corpse in there".

"Oh, come on now, Joy. We've had a lovely afternoon, now let's go for dinner. If she doesn't turn up by the end of that, we'll go to bed, check out at eleven and warn the reception to check her room. I'm sorry, but that's all I'm prepared to do for a woman neither of us has ever met and you spoke to once through three walls. All right, dear? That's it! Finito! Bpai!"

After their meal, they drank another bottle of wine, and he tried to coax her to sleep, but as she was drifting off, he heard her mumble:

"I'm sorry we never met in person. Thank you for the warning. I hope that your husband has not harmed you... That's good... My husband is a very nice man as well".

His heart sank.

He reached for the bottle and sleep.

10. THAILAND

When they woke up in the morning, Joy was morose about the fate of her new 'friend', but Frank chivvied her along with the prospects of breakfast, going back to Thailand again and giving the ghosts the slip. She was encouraged by the first two, but seemed doubtful now that the third would be easily possible.

"I'm sorry, my husband, but I do not believe that it will be easy to shake off the demons that are plaguing me... and you. It will take someone strong to convince them to leave us in peace... and of course, the flipside of them leaving us in peace is that they will attach themselves to someone else, because that is how these things survive... They thrive on other people's torment... It is not only how they get their kicks; it is also how they get their sustenance. My fear, because I see that you are too ignorant to be afraid, is what they feed off. It is like us salivating when we see a big fat roasted chicken. We, or I, am no more than a big fat roasted chicken to them, so if I am denied them, they must find another meal elsewhere... I want to lose the demons, but I don't want to give them to someone else... Do you understand, darling?"

"Er, yes, I think so, but it is all new to me. You just keep telling me what you think, and I'll keep listening. Who do you think will be powerful enough to deal with the demons?"

"In the end, everyone has to face their own demons", she said looking at him with the utmost seriousness, but who will be powerful enough to help me do that, I do not know yet. However, the only place that I know to look for that help is back home... I do not know anyone in Britain or Spain who can help. All the people I know in Europe only think about money and possessions. It is getting that way in Thailand too, but we still have some people who follow The Path".

Frank had some recollections of a Path, and wanted to look it up later, but for the moment was just concentrating on getting his wife fed and to the airport. He booked a taxi at reception for twelve thirty.

By the time that they had found out where baggage check-in was it was one thirty and they had two hours until it opened. Frank was fine with that. He would get a few gifts of his own, buy some more travel sicknesses pills, have a beer or two and go through to departures, but that didn't take into account what Joy might do. He was frightened that someone might deem her unfit to fly. So, they put their bags in Left Luggage and meandered around. He tried to keep her mind occupied by pointing out pretty things and asking what he could expect to see in Thailand.

His strategy worked and at three forty-five they walked through to the Departure Lounge arm in arm. Joy wanted to buy some Duty Free and Frank wanted to buy some beer. He didn't know whether to trust her alone, but he chose a bar where she could see him at all times, if she wanted to and they went their separate ways.

He was just on his second pint when he spotted her walking towards him. She was beaming like a Cheshire cat and looking like the woman she used to be just two weeks before... less even. 'How quickly things can change?' he thought, 'And ruin your life and that of others around you'. She waved at him and he waved back wanting his old wife back. It suddenly dawned on him that the opposite of what they were going through would be winning the lottery or having a long-awaited child.

"Hello, darling! Did you find anything nice? Can I get you a drink?"

"No, drink, darling, I think I spent too much".

"It's your money, love, you can spend of it what you want... Go on, have an orange juice. How much did you spend then?"

"OK. 949€... it is a lot, eh?"

He looked in her sealed bags - a couple of bottles of perfume and two bottles of Champagne.

"Yes, it is quite a lot, but as long as you are happy... That's the main thing", and it really was for Frank, because he foresaw a long and arduous journey before them. Nineteen hours' worth, to be precise.

They boarded the plane and Joy was in high spirits, but that bothered Frank too. He wanted to see her on an even keel, neither too manic nor depressed. It was taking feats of magic on his behalf to accomplish that, he thought.

As the plane was about to take off, Joy leaned forward, tapped the woman in front on the shoulder and said:

"My husband is a very nice man". The kindly fellow-passenger turned around to look at them and replied:

"Yes, dear, he looks like a very nice man".

It satisfied Joy - and Frank was thrilled to bits too. He hugged his wife to him, as much to prevent her accosting anyone else as anything, and told her that he loved her. As the aircraft left the runway, he was hoping that she would soon be asleep after consuming the three travel sicknesses pills he had slipped into her orange juice at the bar.

Joy was indeed dozing off, but an attendant offering in-flight drinks brought her around.

"Two brandies, a coffee and a cocoa", said Frank quickly and Joy didn't argue. She was asleep less than fifteen minutes later and Frank felt that he could relax for at least an hour or so.

He must have dozed off himself, because he was awoken by a flight attendant asking him what his choice of evening meal was.

"Er, chicken for me, please. Joy, what would you like?"

"Chicken for me too, please. Can I ask you something, please?"

"Certainly, madam".

"Are we going to have any problems on this flight?"

The attendant looked at Frank with a puzzled expression and then back at his wife.

"No, madam, no problems, I can assure you that they are very rare".

"Thank you, it's just that I was told that there might be..."

Both men could see people turning to look at them. While the flight attendant was wondering what to do, Frank said:

"It's all right, dear, there's no need to worry. I'm sorry, but my wife suffers from travel sicknesses and the tablets make her a little nervous. Sometimes, she imagines things on them. There's nothing to worry about".

"Very well, sir, but I can call one of the female attendants, if you like?"

"No, that won't be necessary, thank you... Joy, you can't go around saying things like that... You'll frighten people".

She looked around her and said in a normal voice, "Don't worry, everyone, nothing's going to happen. I'm sorry if I worried you..."

"Yes, all right, Joy", said Frank for her ears only, "its better if you just let the matter drop". She nodded sagely and put a finger to her lips as if they were sharing a secret.

"Would you like a drink with your meal, sir?"

"Yes, two bottles of red wine, please".

"Certainly, sir".

"...and one for the wife".

The attendant nodded and handed them over.

They got through the flight to Istanbul without too much of a problem by drinking more wine every time she woke up, but Frank did have to rescue a few passengers from Joy's unwanted attempts at being friendly. She wanted to tell people that Bangkok and Thailand were wonderful places and that there were no problems there. Another time, she was wishing people a very happy holiday in her country and handing out her Thai phone number so that they could contact her if they experienced any problems in Thailand.

People were kind to her, but it was embarrassing - she was behaving childlike rather than badly. Frank was wondering whether it was just the travel sicknesses pills or the fact that they were mixed with alcohol as he fell asleep.

They slept near their boarding gate at Istanbul, where they had to wait two hours for their flight on to Thailand, so there were no incidents there, but Frank had to be careful that she didn't wander off and cause a nuisance of herself.

They duly disembarked in Bangkok and headed for immigration passport control.

"This is where we are going to have problems!"

"Why?"

"I don't know. Can't you hear the ghosts telling us that we have big problems?"

"No, Joy, I can't. Sorry, dear".

They were standing on the large, red-carpeted floor space before the long row of passport control points. "This is where the big problem is... You won't get a visa... You're going to be deported and I will be detained for helping an illegal immigrant".

"What are you on about? You said that all British visitors get a thirty-day visa on arrival. I checked and that's true. Why would they think I'm an illegal immigrant?"

Joy was looking around as if wanting a taxi on a busy street and Frank was trying to calm her down, when an airport assistant approached them.

"Can I help you, sir?"

He looked at Joy. "I work at the Thai Embassy in London..." The young woman glanced down at the diplomatic passport in her hand.

"Yes, madam, the exclusive Diplomat Channel is right there", she saw Frank's red passport and continued, "and the visitors' channels are right here. Please join the queue, sir", and walked off.

There was no-one in Joy's queue, but about five hundred in Frank's. His heart sank.

"See, the problems have started already, they are trying to separate us. Don't leave my side. I'll do my best to get you through this". Frank thought she was overreacting, but did as he was told to humour her.

"What now then?"

"I don't know", she whispered, "just wait".

Another assistant approached them. "Can I help you, sir?"

"I hope so, my wife and I are wondering..."

"Thai wife, sir?" she asked looking at Joy. He nodded. "Please use the Priority Thai Spouse Visa Channel over there, sir".

Frank thanked her effusively, and she gave him a perfect example of the famous Thai smile and waaied him back. "My pleasure. Welcome to Thailand, sir, madam", then she walked off.

"There you go, Joy, that was easy enough and there are less than a dozen people in those three queues. Let's hurry before another plane comes in.

Joy allowed herself to be led away, but she wasn't convinced. She was visibly shaking and it got worse with every step they took towards the immigration officer. In a last-minute rush, they filled in the long, narrow, blue immigration cards they had been given on the plane, but forgotten about.

When it was their turn, Joy pushed him forward. "I'll wait here in case they don't let you in". It was the last thing he wanted the officer to hear. He stepped up to the desk, smiled and handed over his passport. The officer eyed him suspiciously and looked through it carefully.

"No stamp for Istanbul, sir?"

Joy squeaked.

"Er, no, officer, it was a stop-over from Malaga".

"I see, and the purpose of your visit?"

"We are on our honeymoon, I've come to meet my wife's family and see some of the country".

"Very well, sir. Please toe the yellow line in front of you for the camera. Your passport is almost full, sir. Keep an eye on that. Have an enjoyable stay in Thailand", he said pushing the passport back. Mrs. Jones... please".

They spoke in Thai, but Joy gave the impression that she was at an important job interview - she looked so wooden. When asked to toe the line for a photo, she came to attention like a corporal on the parade ground. She was waved through though

"See, no problems..."

"Show me your stamp".

"Why?"

"I think it's a fake. They have given you a fake visa so they can arrest you whenever they like". She held out her hand.

"No, I am not showing it to you. I have been travelling for nineteen hours... twenty now and I want to get where we're going. I've had enough. You are just looking for problems now. Well, I am not looking for them and I haven't got any and neither have you, so let's just get our bags and get out of here. Come on! Now", he demanded, "right now!"

She shook her head and held out her hand.

"Joy, as much as I love you and don't envy you your pro... er, confusion, I swear that if you don't stop this nonsense and come with me this instant, I will get my bag, take the nearest taxi to the Red-Light District and book into a hotel without you. I've had enough, understand me? Up to here. I want to relax somewhere and that is not in an airport!"

She was crying again but her arm dropped and she took a step towards him. He put his arm around her shoulders and led her away to collect their luggage.

They put that on a trolley and headed for customs. Joy was pushing the trolley. She stopped before the red and green channel's. "Please!" she implored him holding out her hand. "Please don't go through there into Thailand with a fake visa!"

They were within a few yards of the nearest customs officer - easy hearing distance.

"That's it!" he said, taking his case, "You're on your own". He walked calmly through the green channel and no-one stopped him or asked him for anything. He was feeling bad about leaving Joy and wondered how long it would take her to get through when she appeared drying her eyes. They headed for the light and the world outside behind the large sliding doors in front of them.

Frank had never been to a hot country at its hottest time of the year before. It was like opening the oven door to take out the Sunday roast.

"Phew, Joy, I wasn't expecting this, love. It's got to be at least thirty-five degrees". She said nothing, but just pointed at the digital L.E.D. display over the door, which gave the time, the date and the temperature in a continuous loop.

"Wow, forty-two! Right, what now?"

"I don't know", she mumbled inaudibly.

"Pardon? I can't hear you".

The same again, her lips barely moved.

"Are you sulking?" Nothing. He dragged his case to two empty seats by the roadside. A taxi driver motioned him to sit down, wiped his brow with a two-foot towel, smiled and said something in Thai - presumably something about the heat. Frank smiled back and mopped his own brow with his hanky. It had about one percent of the absorption capacity of the Thai's towel and would soon be saturated. The man smiled at him again probably thinking the same thing.

Meanwhile, Joy was standing where he had left her four or five yards away staring down at her case or her feet. He called her over and she sat down.

"What now, my darling, it's very hot here for a pink Englishman, you know?"

She looked at him as if he were a stranger.

"Where are we going?"

The mouthing of what looked like 'I don't know' again. He started to lose his temper big time now.

"What do you mean you don't know? You have dragged me five thousand miles to sit on the side of a smelly airport access road where it's forty-two in the shade and you don't know what to do next? Is that what you're telling me?"

"I don't know", he gathered from reading her lips.

"Well, if you don't fucking know, then who the fuck does? This was your idea and it's your country... GET UP AND ACTUALLY DO SOMETHING!!"

He watched her stand up and walk around fingers to her lips. After a few minutes, she sat down again.

"What was that? Did you actually do anything?" She looked up at him like a small frightened animal and he instantly felt ashamed of himself for browbeating her.

"All right, Joy, let's start again. I'm sorry for shouting at you, but we have to do something, girl. We can't just sit here, can we?" She was sobbing again and people were showing concern. "Look, this man here with the towel, oh, most of them have got towels, this bloke here with the green one. I was just talking to him... he seems nice enough. Ask him to take us to a hotel nearby...- Any hotel. Please do that".

She leaned over Frank and spoke to the man in Thai in a whisper. He had to lean in to hear her, so they ended up having a conversation about nine inches above Frank's genitals.

"What did he say?" asked Frank, relieved that they had finished since he had been travelling in those clothes for two days and wasn't certain that they didn't smell.

"He says eight hundred Baht".

"What? I can't hear you". She repeated it a little more loudly.

"Great! Take it! I don't care whether it's expensive or not, just say 'Yes'. Do you have enough money?"

It took her several rather annoying minutes to find a bundle of about ten thousand Baht. It took Joy another seven or eight minutes to arrange for the prepay service, but then they were on their way rolling along the motorways outside the airport and eventually into what Frank assumed was Bangkok, but it was actually thirty-one kilometres from the city centre. They passed scores of hotels and Frank could feel the anger starting to build again.

After a thirty-minute ride, Joy spoke to the driver and pointed into a narrow side street. Children and adults with white-powdered faces were throwing water at the taxi and each other. The taxi slowed to a crawl to avoid injuring anyone. Despite everything that he had said about ghouls and demons, he couldn't help thinking that they had arrived in some Hell hole. The people looked happy enough, he thought, perhaps manic even. Most of them were dancing to sources of loud music. He noticed that many of the teens and adults were drinking whiskey from bottles. Some of the revellers slapped white powder on the car's windows, others threw water at it, but even more just smiled at the travellers inches from the glass.

"I'm glad that you're with me Joy, if I was travelling alone right now, I think I would turn this taxi around and get on the next flight back to Europe. Are Thais always this intimidating?"

"They are not trying to intimidate you!" she replied rather testily. "It is Songkran, the old Thai New Year. It lasts three days or more and people get a bit carried away. They probably think that you have come especially for it, many foreigners do".

He was amazed. He had never seen anything like it before and wondered how something like this could have escaped the attention of a man of the world such as he considered himself to be.

The car moved slowly down the lane, called a 'soy' in Thai, giving the residents and Frank plenty of time to look at each other. Joy had the taxi brought to a halt outside a small two up and two down. They got out, thanked the driver and opened the gate. A child threw a bucket of water over them and ran away laughing. A woman rushed out and spoke with Joy; she smiled at Frank and waaied him. He reciprocated and they were shown inside, where she offered them towels, but they weren't too wet so refused them. As soon as he could do so politely - he lasted only three minutes - he held his arms out like a plane, walked about a bit and slapped his legs.

"Must have exercise", he said. "We sit long, long time. I go walking. Joy sick from flying". He imitated someone vomiting. "Joy, some money, please. I saw an old bloke in a bar-cum-cafe up the road. I'm going to join him for a couple of hours. Come up later if you like. Bye". He waaied them both but only the sister reciprocated and he got out before anyone could try to stop him.

By the time he reached the shop he was soaked through and covered in white powder, which he discovered to be talcum powder mixed with water. Some smelt very pleasing, while the menthol talc that some were using was cool and refreshing.

The place he had spotted turned out to be a noodle shop. A place where a hearty bowl of noodles, vegetables and a few scraps of meat could be had for sixty pence, but like most shops and restaurants, they also sold beer. Frank had his first Chang - Elephant Beer - and then a few more. It was empty and the owner spoke no English, so he had plenty of time to think. The owner's son tipped a bucket of iced water down the back of his neck, which brought him back to his senses with a jolt. The boy ran away laughing, but seemed to be hoping that Frank would retaliate in fun, but he only had his beer and he was not about to waste that.

He still loved the woman he had married only sixteen days before and he felt terribly sorry for the crazy lady that he had just left with her sister, but what was he going to do about it?

He couldn't even contemplate leaving her after just sixteen days, but then he couldn't go on like this either. He could not understand what had altered the balance of her mind so rapidly. OK, he thought, there were a few things that couldn't be explained and the video and the head in a noose were cruel, but surely humans, sick people, had to be responsible for that? Why did Joy assume it had to do with ghosts or demons? It was all beyond him, so he ordered another beer.

After three hours or so, as it was getting dark, he ordered three beers to take away and trudged to his new temporary home getting another soaking along the way. He opened the gate, but stood in the frame of the open front door.

Joy was lying on the floor moaning softly to herself and her sister, Gail, was kneeling by her side dabbing at her forehead with a damp flannel.

She motioned him in and he sat down, on the floor. It was obvious that his first night in Bangkok, the nightlife capital of the Orient, was not going to be a barrel of laughs.

11. JOY'S SISTER

"So, Mr. Frank, why my little sister like this?" she said passing him a towel again.

Frank looked at Gail and felt rather silly for having acted out his words a few hours before. She was perhaps four or five years older than Joy, but other than that, they looked a lot alike except that Joy smiled a lot more and wore sexier clothes. Gail struck Frank as a frump of an old Maiden Aunt, who could look a lot better if she tried.

"I'm sorry, Gail, I didn't realise that you could speak English. I feel such a fool about earlier. Please just call me Frank… no 'mister'.

She nodded. "It is not problem. My English is not strong. If you go in the kitchen there, you will find something to open your bottles on the fridge. Put two inside, if you want. It very hot now in Bangkok".

"Do you want one?"

"No, thank you.

"Now, my sister", she reminded him when he had sat down again.

"I assume you know the story until we got married". She nodded. "Well, we went to Spain as the first part of our journey here and Joy started to hear voices. She became really weird, paranoid…"

"And nothing happened to cause this?"

"The Norwegian boys, er, young men upstairs and in the apartment alongside us were rather noisy, er, loud, even a little aggressive, but I didn't find them threatening. Joy didn't like them, but she never even spoke to them and she didn't blame them for what happened".

"What happened?"

"Joy saw ghosts or demons in our apartment several times. There was also some vomit left a few times and…er…"

"Please, everything".

"While she was singing 'Ghost Riders' in a karaoke bar, they, er, played a video of us making love in our bedroom. They said that someone had handed it to them to play as a surprise for us. Then, the day we left a hat and sunglasses of Joy's were put on a dummy and hung from our balcony, but Joy was far gone a week before that". He took a large swig from his bottle.

"We stayed in the apartment for a week and then moved to another city for two days, until Thursday, but nothing changed".

"Do you believe in ghosts and demons, Frank?"

"No, I can't say that I do".

"Do British people in general?"

"I don't know... None of my friends do, or at least, if they do they wouldn't talk about it to me".

"Why, Frank, because you would laugh at them?"

"I wouldn't lau... well, maybe so, yes, but I hope not out loud".

"In Thailand, there are many, many people who believe in such things. Probably much more than half, would you laugh at all those millions of people, just because they do not believe the same as you?"

"I hope that I wouldn't..."

"But you might, eh? Stupid Asian peasants; bloody Buddhists..."

"Oh, come on, be fair..."

"I am trying to be fair. I always try to be fair - I have my Karma to worry about. You in the West don't think that you do; you think you can do what you like and Jesus will make it all right for you. I try to understand why people think, believe and do what they do".

Frank started to speak, but he could see that he had seriously underestimated Joy's sister. He took another swig of beer instead.

"I take it that you are still in love with my sister, since you only got married the other week, so what do you think we should do about her?"

"I don't know. I have given it a lot of thought, but all I can suggest is that poison from her bad tooth is causing the auditory hallucinations - the er, voices".

"So, you suggest a tooth doctor?"

"Yes, a dentist, a tooth doctor, as you say".

"OK, very well. It is past my bedtime; you must take over now. If you want more beer, the shop two doors to the left is open until nine thirty. There is no need to walk back up to the main road, unless you need more exercise. I gave her a sleeping tablet earlier, so she should be quiet until the morning. There are English-language channels on the TV if you wish. Good night, Frank, and thank you for bringing my sister back to us".

They waaied each other and she went upstairs. It was eight o'clock.

∞

When he awoke at ten thirty-five, he noticed that Joy was gone. Since he couldn't locate her sister either, he assumed rightly that they had gone to the dentist together. He felt like a three-week old dirty rugby shirt, so he looked for the shower, availed himself of it, changed and sat back down. Five minutes later he put the TV on and five minutes after that, he switched it off again, and took his last beer out into the front of the property. There was a round concrete table with four curved concrete benches to match. He plonked himself down like a sack of spuds to await their return. He had to buy another three beers for that though because they didn't get back until almost three o'clock.

"Hello, darling, how's your tooth?"

Joy squeezed her lips together tightly and held her forehead in reply.

"The anaesthetic will wear off in an hour or so and you will be back to your old self by tomorrow, you'll see". Tears dripped from her eyes and she hurried inside.

"She hates going to the doctor's and dentist's", he confided in Gail.

"Yes, I know, she has done for the last twenty-four years, but she wouldn't see the dentist. I told the dentist what you told me, and she gave us these antibiotics. We have been for lunch, but Joy hardly spoke a word and the gist of what she say was that demons are following her. Excuse me, please, I will give her her tablets now".

Frank sighed long, hard and loud as he flopped back down. Then he came to a decision and went to buy three more beers. He returned to Gail's soaked for the second time that day, but was getting used to the mad New Year's party antics.

Meanwhile, Joy resumed her position on the floor and her sister administered tablets, love and comfort. She was soon asleep again, the morning's activities and jetlag having drained her. At seven o'clock, Gail called him in for supper. They had various dishes that Gail had bought earlier, but she was feeding Joy with rice soup the consistency of porridge. It was the Thai equivalent of chicken soup.

"I have given her her antibiotics and a sleeping pill. Tomorrow, we will try again, but she wants you at her side when she meets the doctor. Please make sure you can do that tomorrow, I could not wake you this morning. Good night now, I am feeling very tired myself tonight".

Frank was left feeling bad about leaving the care of his wife to others, but he had been through a lot over the last ten days and needed to recharge too even though his method was not approved by the PC brigade.

He propped his head on an arm, put the other around Joy, and tried to go to sleep.

It came surprisingly easy, but he dreamed that cackling demons were pursuing Joy and him around the world.

∞

He heard Gail taking Joy to the shower at just after nine. They had already eaten. When they returned, they waited for him and they were off in Gail's car.

Frank and Joy hadn't had a conversation since they had arrived at Gail's. Joy simply showed no interest in him and hardly spoke at all anyway. Anything she wanted, she pointed at or mouthed it in Thai. It irked Frank no end. He felt like a paramedic in an ambulance, who having delivered the patient to hospital was excluded from any further decisions in the case.

Gail pulled up outside the front doors of a large hospital. "Take her in there and wait for me. I must park car".

Frank did as he was told. When someone offered Joy a wheelchair, Frank refused it, but the man put Joy in it anyway. They were left standing there like a statue, until Gail came hurrying up.

"OK, follow me", she commanded, but as Frank started pushing, the man gently eased him aside. It was obviously his job to push wheelchairs and no untrained foreigner was going to do him out of his job. The signs were in Thai and English, which Frank took as a good omen.

"It's all right, my dear, the dentist will sort that tooth out in no time and we'll all go out for a slap-up meal at your favourite restaurant. That's something to look forward to, isn't it?" he asked stroking her temple as they moved through the hospital. They went up three floors in a lift and proceeded past various signs, until they turned off at 'Clinic of Mental Health - Psychiatry'. Joy was looking around confused, but she was not the only one, so was Frank. He took her hand.

Gail spoke to the nurse behind the desk and they helped Joy into a chair where they monitored her vital signs. Frank could see that the readings were phenomenal: 175/135 with a pulse of 145. Then they checked her height and weight.

"My wife hates hospitals... er, white coat syndrome?" The woman smiled and tried again. The readings were lower, but not a lot. "The doctor will see you now", said the nurse taking Joy's arm and leading her down a short corridor. Gail urged Frank to follow to a door clearly marked 'Psychiatrist'. They went in. The session lasted barely fifteen minutes then they were off to 'Neurology'. The young doctor was very pleasant and even asked Frank's opinion about his wife's condition, but dismissed his abscessed tooth theory with a brisk 'No, symptoms do not match your prognosis'. From there they went to 'Radiology', where she underwent an MRI scan. On their way out, they had to pay at the desk to receive their prescription.

18,750 Baht, about £400.

Joy didn't have the currency to pay for it, and Frank didn't think that it would be a good idea to claim it off her government health insurance policy in case having been to a psychiatrist affected her prospects of promotion, so he paid for it with his own credit card.

"Why did you take me to see a psychiatrist, Frank? Do you think I'm crazy?"

"No, darling, I don't. It wasn't my idea. Ask your sister. She lied to both of us. I thought that we were going to the dentist". Gail looked at him in the rear-view mirror.

"It was the easiest way to get her to a doctor. My conscience is clear. I did the best I know how for my sister. If it is the money you are worried about, I will repay you myself".

"It is not the money, Gail, it is the deceit. I am legally responsible for my wife's health as her husband, not you. I demand to be consulted in future on all matters concerning my wife".

She looked at him in the mirror again and smiled. "This is Thailand, we are family and you have no chance. Husband come and husband go. Can have three four in one life, but she only have one mother, one father and one sister. Take me to court".

The matter was closed, he could tell that. Gail would tolerate him, even be nice to him for her sister's sake, but allow him to take charge in matters related to her family? Never in a million years!"

And in an odd sort of a way, he knew that she was right.

They arrived home via a take-away and ate on the concrete table in the front yard. Joy was still not speaking, especially not English, but she ate a dozen half spoonfuls of food and Gail gave her her tablets: eight new ones and three from the day before and then put her to bed on the living room floor after having had a shower.

Frank bought some more beer and waited to see what would happen next. Gail came out with a glass of iced tea. She sat down opposite him at the round table.

"I understand your frustration, even your anger, at being left out of the decision-making process. I really do and I will try to include you more. However, do you see my point of view?"

"Yes, I do, but I don't want to be made to feel like an interloper – an outsider". The translation app played a large role in their conversation.

"Good, we understand each other. The fact is that I work in that department, psychiatry. I do the same job as the nurse who took Joy's blood pressure today. However, I want to progress and Joy helps me with that. I take examinations every year to better myself. When I was young, I only wanted to be a mother and get married. That finished many years ago, but left me with a beautiful baby girl. Bew is preparing for university now and she has Joy to thank for that.

"I owe Joy more than you can imagine".

She was steely faced and Frank wondered whether that was her way of stopping herself from crying. Her eyes were moist, but no other emotion was evident. His first encounter with an Asian on their home territory who wanted to remain inscrutable. He felt sorry for her, much like he felt sorry for himself. Neither of them wanted to lose the wonderful entity in their lives that they called Joy. He put his hand on hers, then stood up to put an arm around her shoulders.

"We're in-laws now", he reminded her. This is our problem, not just yours". She nodded ever so imperceptibly and took her glass inside.

∞

The following day, they had to go back to the hospital for the results of the MRI scan. The same doctor of neurology congratulated them that there was no tumour, but pointed to minor lesions, which he said could have been caused by Joy's hypertension. He recommended stopping taking the antibiotics and offered them a CD of the scan as a souvenir. Frank took it and smiled. On their way out, Gail called Frank over to the cash desk.

"You have to pay a bill", she advised.

"What, you have to pay for the results of a scan as well? Jesus!" However, the £40 bill was for the souvenir CD.

Later, sitting in the front garden again, Frank voiced his opinion.

"So, Gail... all that we've been through and paid for in the last two days has resulted in what? They say that the cure lies in reducing her anxiety and her blood pressure. Hell, I could have told them that as soon as I saw those first blood pressure readings. OK, I'll admit that I was wrong about the tooth, but I didn't know about the hypertension and you don't need a psychiatrist, a neurologist and an MRI scan to tell you that sky-high blood pressure needs to be reduced. I feel as if we have been put through the grinder to help justify and pay for some hospital's expensive, but very prestigious equipment. How much does an average Thai earn?"

"Perhaps six to ten thousand per month. I can see where you are coming from, but many of those will have insurance plans to cover these costs".

"Yes, so has Joy, but we don't want her employer to know she's been to a psychiatrist, do we? So, the insurance is useless. We spent more than an average Thai earns in three months in one afternoon to find out that Joy's super high blood pressure has to be brought back to normal and that she shouldn't worry so much about the voices that she hears, because they are probably the result of the hypertension anyway. No certainty there, the neurologist said only probably.

"That sounds like a rip-off to me, sorry".

"But we do know that she doesn't have a brain tumour".

Frank looked at her in disbelief. "No-one ever thought that she did have a brain tumour, but you can clearly see the hypertension and the anxiety!"

"Some tumours grow very slowly, others very quickly. It is good to know that she has neither".

"OK, Gail, I'm glad she doesn't have a tumour of any kind too, but we are going to have to disagree on that one. Oh, what about the most expensive, and useless, CD in our collection? Two thousand Baht for something that no-one will ever see again?"

"You asked for it... You could have said 'No, thank you' and walked away".

He could see that she was a company woman who would not tolerate criticism of her hospital or department. Later that night, lying next to Joy, he wondered whether he was the same about the bank he worked for. They, indeed all banks, had been up for a lot of criticism for years, but he had always found a way to defend them.

∞

There followed three days of daytime isolation for Frank while Gail was at work and on the fourth she brought Bew back with her.

"Bew has been celebrating Songkhran in Pattaya. It lasts a week there, so she has been staying with her father. Say hello, Bew. That is Frank, Aunty Joy's husband".

Bew waaied and then leaned over Joy to shake his hand. "Nice to meet you", she said. "How is Aunty Joy?"

Frank made a face, which he hoped conveyed that she had seen better days. Bew dropped to her knees, hugged Joy and said something in Thai. Joy opened her eyes and her arms and they both embraced and cried. Frank actually felt as if he were intruding, so he slipped out the front, bought a beer and sat at the table.

12. BEW

He didn't stay there long though, he felt bad for leaving his wife and anyhow, Bew intrigued him. He left the full beer outside and resumed his place on the floor next to Joy. Gail excused herself to go cook the evening meal.

Bew was still on school holidays, because March and April were deemed too hot to work in, being Thailand's summer months. She was preparing to go to university later that year, but already looked like every boy's dream of the stereotypical female undergraduate. She was tall for a Thai, about five ten with long shiny black hair down to her thighs. From the back, she looked like an expensive wig on pencils, no clothes could be seen. From the front, she was thin and flat-chested. Frank suspected that the small bumps on her chest were more bra than breast. It was probably her biggest concern in life, he thought, that and verging on anorexia. She had a high forehead, a winning smile and big brown eyes. She spoke English even better than her mother too.

She was sitting mermaid-style at Joy's side a body's width from Frank stroking Joy's hand.

"What happened?" she asked.

Frank gave her the three theories as he saw it: the ghost/demons theory; the hypertension theory and his now deprecated tooth theory. He tried to lay more emphasis on the hypertension and much less on the tooth.

Her eyes lingered on Frank and then Joy several times as she mulled the hypotheses over.

"Joy thinks it's demons, doesn't she and you don't believe her?"

"Yes, I suppose you could put it like that..."

Joy suddenly came to, saw Bew, burst into tears and threw her arms around her. Bew hugged Joy, started crying herself and laid her aunty back down. They were murmuring things to each other in Thai and rocking a little. He began to wish he had stayed outside for all the attention he was getting.

Eventually, Bew let Joy go, put her finger to her lips and went to see her mother. She returned with a cold, damp flannel from the fridge for Joy's forehead.

"Aunty Joy says that demons made the people upstairs and next door want to harm her. Why would she think that, Frank? Oh, I suppose you've my Uncle Frank now".

"Technically, yes, but just Frank will do nicely. I don't know how many Norwegian neighbours we had, but they lived above and alongside us. They were rowdy, noisy and antisocial, but they were just young people on holiday. I think. I only met two boys once. The guy next door had locked himself out and he wanted to climb from our balcony to his own, I refused in case he fell because he looked drunk or stoned. Another time, the boys next door were making so much noise on their balcony, that we couldn't hear our TV, so I asked them politely to 'keep it down a bit, please'. I did get dirty looks for that and a 'Why, what are you doing?' then they both started laughing. Drunk and stoned again, I think. Besides those two instances, we probably had twenty or so people we didn't know ringing our bell from the street. I wouldn't let any of them in. Joy did become irrationally scared of these Norwegians, but they never touched or threatened us".

"Joy said there was, er, mess, er, vomit and slime".

"Yes, there were a few instances of a yellowish-green slime or vomit in and around our apartment".

"In? Actually in your apartment?"

"Yes..."

"And you didn't stop to wonder how it got there?"

"Well, we were both drinking quite heavily and I assumed that Joy had made it and was too embarrassed to admit it or just didn't remember doing it... I know that she blamed me for the first lot".

"Anything else?"

"Er, yes...". He told her about the hat and sunglasses first and then reluctantly about the video. Or he feigned reluctance, because he actually found it quite arousing to talk to this young woman about their video. She seemed to sense this and cut him short.

"Yes, I get the picture. Aunty Joy must have taken that pretty badly".

"Yes, it hurt her very badly, er, both of us..."

When Gail came in with supper, Bew helped Joy to sit cross-legged to eat. She found it much easier than Frank or her mother had ever done, but perhaps the tablets and familiar friendly faces were having an effect.

However, Joy ate less from the eight communal dishes than would constitute a handful and refused to eat more, so they gave her her tablets. Much to everyone's surprise, she remained sitting with them.

"Spain people are lovely people", she said looking around and nodding, "and the country is beautiful". She kept nodding her head as if agreeing with herself as she stared at her fingers, which she was knotting and unknotting repeatedly in her lap.

"Yes, they are, aren't they, Joy? You liked Spain and the Spanish, didn't you?"

She gave him one quick look and nodded more vigorously. He took her hand. There was more of the old Joy in her at that moment than the whole time since they had arrived in Bangkok. He smiled at no-one in particular.

"Did you make any friends in Spain, Aunty Joy?"

Joy looked at Frank and creased her brow.

"There was Salvador and Jesus in the Teja... the one you called 'The Black Man' from Morocco... and the English man and woman. Remember? Er, Martin and Abbey... Remember, darling?"

Joy looked up, nodded and looked back at her fingers.

"My head hurts", she sobbed putting her fingers to her temples, "I can't stop thinking I have big problems... Keet maak, mi penha yai!"

Frank and Bew reached to put an arm around her shoulders simultaneously and they overlapped. Bew moved her arm lower.

"Come on, my dear, you did meet some nice people over there, didn't you? We both did". He thought she said 'Yes', but it was too quiet to hear.

"They are here now", she murmured shaking. "I can hear them".

"What are they saying, Joy? I can't hear them", said Frank.

"I have big problems", she cried, picked up a pillow, buried her face in it and pushed herself back down to the floor. Her sobs were muted, but still audible. Frank shrugged his shoulders, which Gail and Bew took as a bad sign.

∞

Frank awoke to the sight of Bew in a thigh-length, baggy T-shirt, probably her night-shirt bending over at the waist to help Joy to her feet to go to the bathroom. There was not much left to the imagination, but when she spotted him looking, she bent from the knees. "I thought you were asleep", she said without any warmth. "Mum has gone to work and I am taking Aunty Joy in to see the doctor in twenty minutes - at eleven. We have had our breakfast, you were asleep. Are you coming with us?"

"Yes, of course, I'll just go and shower... Look, is there somewhere we can wash our clothes. They are pretty smelly now".

"I know. I have already washed Aunty Joy's things and hung them out to dry. Mum and I have lent her something to wear until then".

"I see", he said not realising that a Thai woman would never touch the soiled clothing of a man she didn't know very well, even if he was an uncle. He took offence. "I'll be right with you".

From the taxi, Bew led them the familiar route to the psychiatrist's office and fifteen minutes later they were back out. No-one spoke to him and he didn't understand a word. They saw Gail, but she only gave him the briefest of smiles before talking with her daughter and then going about her duties.

Frank was called on to pay another 3,750 Baht or £75 for the consultation and fourteen yellow tablets. The writing on the label, the instructions and name of the drugs, he presumed, was in Thai and so illegible to him. He was still out of the loop and funding the hospital, as far as he was concerned.

He grew sullen and followed behind as Bew led Joy outside by the forearm. They stopped off at a deliciously smelling take-away and went home. After the meal, Bew gave Joy one of the new tablets.

"What about all the others?" asked Frank.

"They are no longer necessary. Today's tablets... er..." she checked her phone, "yes, today's tablets supersede them. Only the hypertension tablets and these, need to be taken now".

That meant that they were ditching about eighty tablets he had paid for.

"No refund?" he asked with a smile, "On old tablets?"

"No, are you a Cheap Charlie?"

"No, it just seems a waste. If we had another appointment anyway, why give us tablets for days after then, which might be no good?"

Bew carried on tending to Joy, disregarding his questions.

"Bew, your mother and I have an agreement. We are working together to make Joy well. This is not Thais against Brits or your family against me".

"Mum, didn't mention it to me".

"We all want the same thing here, for Christ's sake!" Bew nodded about a quarter of an inch. "Well, let's get on with it then, together..."

She nodded again. "We are going to the village tomorrow afternoon when Mum has finished her shift".

"Thank you for telling me. I appreciate it". Again, the short nod.

Joy was beginning to have brief flashes of lucidity, but for hours on end, she was either asleep or half mumbling and half crying about problems - sometimes in English but increasingly more often in Thai. These times were very difficult because Joy was not listening or at least not responding. She often had a pillow over her whole face, or just up to her eyes, which were usually closed, but if they were open, they were filled with terror. Frank was loathe to mention it, but he was frightened that they would put her in an institution. Not that he had ever encountered a person with mental health issues before and not that he had any idea which conditions were serious enough to warrant being sectioned and even then, he didn't know whether the little he thought he knew applied in Thailand.

It was a mess, and despite the family's help, he felt as if were dealing with Joy's problems completely alone.

"How are we getting there and how long will it take?"

"Mum will drive us there; it should take six or seven hours, if we can leave at three and avoid the rush hour traffic".

"We'll be ready", he said rather pointlessly. There was no reaction from Bew. "Bew, have I done anything to upset you?"

"Er, you told me about your sex life; you put your hand on mine; you tried to look up my skirt; you do this with your shoulders to say that you don't care about your wife and you sit around all day feeling sorry for yourself drinking beer Chang. How could any of that have upset me or my mother?"

He decided that honesty was the best policy with this intelligent young woman.

"OK, the worst one first, yes, I did try to look up your skirt, but you are a beautiful young woman and I am not yet senile. It was an automatic reaction, and I apologise, but I dare any man who is not gay not to want to see more of you. Next, touching your hand, it was not done on purpose, we just made the same instinctive response at the same time. It was a coincidence, that is all -I wasn't trying to touch you. Third, drinking beer all day and feeling sorry for myself... I suppose that is true, but you have only seen Joy for two days. I have looked after her alone for two weeks except for our time in Bangkok, and brought her eleven thousand kilometres. I have watched my beautiful young bride being terrorised and sink into... er, the state she is in now. Yes, I do feel sorry for myself and I feel sorry for Joy and you and your mother and yes, the way I am handling it is by drinking, and it may not be your way, or even the best way, but it is the only way I know how. I'm sorry if that makes me stupid and selfish in your eyes, but where do you get the idea that I don't care any more?"

"You did this the other night", she said shrugging, "Do you remember?"

"Yes, I do remember, that meant that I don't know what to do any more".

"In Thailand, it means I don't care any more, I give up".

"So, you were willing to condemn me on a gesture?"

"Perhaps you should be more careful with your gestures when you are in a foreign country? Anyway, in combination with the other things I mentioned, it was a logical conclusion".

"I can see what you are saying, but it was still the wrong conclusion. Can we start again? Give me another chance, please".

"Yes, all right. Joy must have seen some good qualities in you. I will try to do the same".

He was going to hold out his hand but thought better of it. He waaied instead and said 'Thank you'.

∞

The following morning, after Bew had taken Joy to the bathroom and helped her shower and dress, she sat her down at the table outside and went to fetch breakfast.

Joy looked at him. "You need a clean shirt and a shave before you meet my mother. I don't want her to think that I don't look after my husband". It was the first time that she had shown any concern for him for at least two weeks. It brought tears to his eyes. He cupped the back of her head in his hand and kissed her cheek.

"I'll see to it after breakfast", he promised, "I've let myself go these last few days, I know".

Joy remained lucid throughout breakfast and the three of them had a fairly normal conversation, but she was soon tired, so after taking her tablets, she wanted to go back to sleep. Frank wanted to go with her to help, but Bew beat him to it. From behind Joy's back, she held up a thumb and smiled at Frank. When she returned to clear away the dishes, Frank spoke.

"That was a good sign, wasn't it?" Do you think that the medication is beginning to take effect, or the thought of going home to see her mother brought it on?"

"I don't know, Frank, either or both, but I like to think that the tenderness we have shown her has also contributed".

"Oh, yes, I'm sure that it has... That goes without saying. I just meant in addition to the kindness she has received here".

Bew cleared the things away without coming back, and he was left to wonder whether he was included in the group that had shown Joy tenderness in this house.

13. GOING UP COUNTRY

"We are ready to go to the hospital", said Bew at twelve thirty, "are you coming with us or going to wait for us here?"

It seemed that Gail had forgotten their agreement and that Bew hadn't taken it seriously.

"Sure, I'm going, but why didn't you tell me about it earlier? I would have been ready and waiting".

"I thought my mother had told you".

"No. Is this how it's going to continue?"

"We only want the best for Aunty Da".

"Who?"

"Your wife, Joy".

"Yes, I know the name my wife gave me to call her, thank you very much, but I have never heard her called Da before".

"That was her nickname in the village, before she went to university and chose to be called Joy. People in the village all know her as Da, not Joy. Up there, no-one will know who Joy is".

"I see. Thanks for telling me that at least".

The taxi took them back to the same hospital and Bew led them back to the psychiatric ward, pushing Joy in a wheelchair. She still wasn't saying much and looked frightened. Frank stooped to comfort her, but it had little visible effect. When they went in, Gail was behind the receptionist's desk and took Joy's vital signs after greeting them. She phoned through and asked them to follow her into the psychiatrist's office.

Joy sat at the desk immediately in front of Frank who sat on a large leather sofa. Gail sat next to Joy, but Bew chose to stand. There followed a chat in Thai for fifteen minutes, which went completely over Frank's head, but at the end of it, the psychiatrist spoke to him in English.

"I have given your wife new tablets, please incinerate whatever you have remainder of the old ones. When these are finished in two weeks, please come back".

"We won't be here, doctor".

"Oh, and where are you going?" she asked.

"Er, I'm not sure, but north to visit Joy's family and then back to the UK". A rapid conversation in Thai ensued and then:

"There are good hospitals in Phitsanulok, take her to one in two weeks, and come to see me again before you book your flights home. Bye-bye. Enjoy the beautiful Thai countryside".

"Thank you", he managed as they walked out of the room. Gail's replacement was already at her station, so she said something to Bew and Bew led Frank and Joy away.

It cost another 3,750 Baht for the consultation and new tablets. While Gail was handing over, showering and getting changed for the journey, they waited for her in the coffee shop.

"That wasn't so bad, was it, darling?" he asked Joy. She looked at him and mouthed something.

"I can't hear you, Joy. What?" He wanted her to repeat aloud what she had said, although he guessed what it was. She hadn't disagreed with anyone since Malaga. "It was all right?"

"No, telak. When are we going home?" He didn't know which home she meant, but replied:

"We will be in your village this evening". He looked at Bew for confirmation and Joy followed his gaze. Bew nodded.

"We'll be there by eight thirty or nine o'clock". Joy smiled for the first time in ages and it warmed the cockles of Frank's heart. Gail was not long, then she brought the car around to the side entrance for them.

"You get in the front", said Bew, helping Joy into the back, "you have longer legs than me". A driver behind them beeped impatiently, so he jumped in, just as he realised that their legs were about the same length. He looked at her in the rear-view mirror. She was cuddling Joy's torso and smiling.

"Seat belt", barked Gail as they took off on their long journey.

Still in Bangkok, he saw Joy looking in her bag.

"She wants her travel sicknesses pills", suggested Frank. Bew found them for her and was about to pop two when Frank asked to see them.

"She can't take these. It says on the label, 'Not to be taken in conjunction with prescription medication without the permission of the doctor concerned'. Look, there's some Thai alongside". Bew reluctantly confirmed that it was true. All three were very well aware that Joy would not be able to hold out long without them.

Their tactic was to stop at each motorway service station they could find to take a few minutes' break. Mother and daughter went to the toilets each time, but Joy just groaned on the back seat puking into a plastic bag.

They tried to ply her with food, but she would not eat, and they didn't try too hard because it was all coming back up. The smell was pretty bad. Frank wondered whether the smell was contributing to the nausea in a vicious downward spiral. He certainly didn't feel too well either. He tried to keep Joy's spirits up by talking to her, but he wasn't getting anywhere. She was probably using all her willpower to be as little sick as possible, he realised after a while and just put a hand on her knee.

It was easier all round.

It took a little longer than they had predicted, but they duly arrived in the village a short time after nine in the pitch dark. Frank hadn't been able to see anything after they had turned off the main road onto the slip road that led to the village, but when they arrived there all he could see by the dim lights from houses were wooden constructions and dogs lying in the road. Gail approached them slowly, giving them plenty of time to wake up, stretch, register their annoyance and move slowly aside. It was their job to be there, they were earning their keep by guarding the village from strangers as their ancestors had done for thousands of years. The car stopped again, Bew, hopped out, opened the gate and Gail drove them in.

Frank could see four people sitting on a large square table near a side entrance to the house. Bew opened a rear door and spoke to Joy.

"Are we nearly there yet?" asked Joy rubbing her eyes.

"We're at gran's house. Come on everyone is waiting to say hello".

Joy sat up, ran her fingers through her hair and spotted her mother sitting on the table. She checked her face in the rear-view mirror, looked at Frank who was holding out his hand to help her, and slid across the seat towards him smiling weakly.

"Welcome to our house and our village", she said quietly as he helped her out. Then she stood next to him and put a hand on his forearm. "What are we going to do, Frank?" she asked.

"How do you mean, darling?"

"About all our problems?"

"We don't have any problems. We are in your village, eleven thousand kilometres from Spain; we have money and we have return flights. What possible problems can we have?"

She looked him in the eyes, rubbing his forearm, then she sank to her knees. He managed to grab her hand as she offered it up to him. He had never seen the look she had in her eyes, in anyone's eyes before. It reminded him of soldiers in war films who had been shot by a sniper. It was a mixture of incredulity and shock, then her hand slipped through his grip and she hit her head on a kerb, but only from a few inches.

Frank thought that he had witnessed his wife's death and had no idea what to do. Gail quickly slipped between her sister and the raw soil driveway. As she stroked Joy's temples, she shouted to Bew. Smelling salts from a First

Aid kit in the boot of the car appeared under Joy's nose in seconds and she opened her eyes. They still had that bewildered look as she beheld him and he started to cry. He had never seen anyone faint before.

"Are you all right, dear?" Her reply was a blank expression as she waved a hand before her face. He interpreted it as meaning 'not now'. He offered a hand to help her up, but Gail waved it away. He was just so happy that she wasn't dead, that at that moment, he would gladly have given all his possessions to charity.

Before her mother was able to get to them, Bew was helping Joy to the table. This time, Frank was so thankful that Joy was reprieved, that he didn't feel jealous.

Bew placed Joy's backside against the table, but she couldn't quite get onto it. Willing hands helped her up, but she was exhausted by the miniscule effort. Frank stood before her smiling encouragement, but not knowing how to behave. Joy took his hand, turned forty-five degrees and introduced him.

"This is my husband, Frank. He's a lovely man". Joy shuffled around another forty-five degrees to face the others. Frank sat awkwardly on the table and put his hands on Joy's shoulders, smiling and nodding at the strangers before him.

Frank presumed that the one that Joy had addressed was her mother. She was the only one of the four with a full set of teeth. There were two men and two women, but he didn't know whether they were partners, married or related. Joy had said that her father had died some time ago, but perhaps her mother was thinking of remarrying. No-one thought to introduce him to any of them. To his tired eyes, they were all too thin, all had decent heads of hair, dark brown skin, could still sit in the lotus position, and had very few teeth, except for his mother-in-law.

Not one of them seemed to laugh or smile. The men wore old clothes, and the women had a sort of blue rinse and wore long, traditional Thai skirts called sarong with Western blouses. All of them wore some gold around their necks.

When Gail and Bew had taken the luggage in they joined them on the table.

"She was sick all the way here", said Bew. "We kept telling her she had to eat something or she'd be ill, but she wouldn't. You know what she's like on long car journeys and not being able to take the travel sickness tablets… well, something like that was bound to happen, wasn't it?" People started nodding and talking among themselves and mostly at the same time.

If Frank hadn't been so happy that his wife was still alive, he would have realized that with everyone speaking Thai, he had never been so lonely in his life, but he didn't. He busied himself watching Joy's every movement and surreptitiously observing how the family interacted. He was a keen observer of people.

He couldn't work out though, why no-one was taking any notice of him. He had just married their daughter and flown eleven thousand kilometres to meet them, yet no-one paid him more than a cursory glance. It crossed his mind that perhaps they blamed him for her illness. Perhaps they were thinking that this would never have happened, if he had taken better care of his wife.

He couldn't see what he could have done to prevent it happening, but he certainly knew that he would have done anything in the world to protect Joy.

When the new arrivals had had their fill of food, drink and chat, the whole party, except Frank and Joy, waited for their turn to shower and went to bed. They were shown to a single-roomed upstairs, where eight mosquito nets hung. They crawled into theirs, Joy put bedding and their outer clothes over the net where it met the floor to stop bugs creeping in, and they went to sleep. At least Joy did. Frank was too excited to sleep. He would have rather have had a few beers and a chat, but he was pleased overall and stared into his wife's smiling, sleeping face until he too succumbed.

14. BAAN LEK

Frank woke up alone, soaked in perspiration. He was hotter than he had ever been in his life, yet he was not even under any covers and was wearing only the short trousers he had arrived in. He slid under the mosquito net and looked around the large wooden room. It seemed like someone was on the veranda that ran all around the upper storey, so he tentatively walked towards the outside light and the table he could see with a glass of something on it.

The occupant of the high-backed wicker chair was concealed, but she looked behind her when a floorboard creaked. Joy had a surprised expression on her face, she had obviously been expecting someone else, but she motioned him to pull up a chair and sit with her.

He did so, saying, "What an impressive improvement, Joy... I'm so pleased. How are you feeling this morning?"

Joy put a finger to her lips as she pointed for him to sit down.

"You look a lot better than you have for ages. Do you feel it too?" He watched her intently.

Her eyes began to fill up, as she mouthed the word 'No'.

"I can't hear you, love, sorry, you'll have to speak up. You know I'm a bit Mut". He was hoping that his use of Cockney rhyming slang would bring a smile to her face, but it didn't. She just shook her head and pointed to her temples.

"I'm not a mind-reader, Joy. Talk to me".

She glared at him. "I can still hear them", she said barely audibly and directed her gaze before her again.

"Oh, I thought you were looking so much better. I mean, in Bangkok, you spent all the day and night lying on the floor either crying or sleeping and now look at you. Don't you feel any better, now that you are back in your village?"

She held up her right hand. The index finger was about half a centimetre above her thumb. She shot him the briefest of glances to see whether her had seen her gesture and looked forward again.

"I see. It's going to be like that, is it?" Joy didn't reply in any way.

Bew appeared behind them as silently as a ghost. There is breakfast for you downstairs, Uncle Frank. I'll sit with Da now".

"Thanks, but if I can't have it with Joy, I don't want any. You go and have yours and I'll sit with my wife".

"We all had ours at six o'clock, before the sun came up. We always do at Grandmum's. It goes back to the farming days. I suppose the heat woke you up, neh? There is a power cut. They happen quite often up here".

"It was getting warm in bed, but it was OK", he replied, not wanting to give her the satisfaction by telling her the truth. As if on cue, a fan started to turn a few metres to Frank's right.

"Ah, it's back on again. It usually only lasts an hour or so. All right, if you're not that hungry, I'll bring you up some iced tea". She turned and left, leaving the husband and wife in an awkward silence. At least, it was awkward for Frank, because he didn't know what to say to someone who responded in sign language, if she replied at all. So, he just sat there looking at her, trying to think of something to say that she would find stimulating enough to reply to, and she just stared ahead at what appeared to be a boundary wall of tall bamboo.

Their position was roughly equal to the top of it, but many shoots were a few feet taller again. Frank found the sight interesting, but then he had never seen it before. He imagined that Joy had grown up with it, so reasoned that she must be looking with her mind's eye... but what was she seeing? He couldn't guess, and she wasn't telling. Sometimes, she would shake her head as if she were arguing with herself or someone that he could not see. His emotions were being stretched to the limit of his endurance, but there was nothing he could do to improve their lot.

After drinking his tea, showering and getting changed, Frank re-joined his wife with his Kindle. There was absolutely nothing to do, so he thought he might hitch onto Bew's Internet connection and download a book to read. He was pleasantly surprised to find that he didn't have to ask Bew for any favours because there was an open, unprotected connection called Thamafuang Free. He logged on without needing a password, and turned to Joy.

"Hey, there's an Internet link here called Thamafuang Free. Who are they, Joy?"

She didn't respond, so he repeated himself.

"Eh?" she eventually said looking annoyed for having been disturbed. "Oh, local government. It gives free Internet to our villages".

"That's wonderful, isn't it?" he asked trying to start a conversation. "You wouldn't get that in the UK, would you? Imagine the local authorities destroying BT's broadband business! I should coco. Think of all the taxes they'd lose". But Joy wasn't biting, so he settled back to read the book he had chosen *Tiger Lily of Bangkok*. He had searched on 'novels about Thailand, and the cover had intrigued him.

∞

A few hours after lunch, he tried another tactic to get Joy to actually do something. "Why don't you show me around this village of yours? It's lovely and quiet. Not like London or Bangkok, eh? I could retire here one day, couldn't you, Joy?" She nodded. "Come on then, let's go for a walk". She tightened her lips and shook her head. She must have been agreeing with the suggestion of retirement.

"OK, I'll go on my own. Should I go right or left?" Joy held up her left hand, so he got up and left her there. As he passed before the family table of the night before, he waaied to the five people seated on it and walked out of the gate, but not before he noticed Bew rushing to replace him at Joy's side.

He was glad that someone had.

∞

Baan Lek was a very quiet village, but only during the day, when the children were at school and most adults were at work in the fields, because it was predominantly a rice-farming village. There appeared to be two concentric irregular circles of houses. It took him just fifteen minutes to walk around the inner one. On a brief reccy, each of the houses in the outer circle seemed to be connected with the small fields across the road from them. Everyone who saw him stopped what they were doing as he passed by and stared. Two children in their gardens burst into tears and many dogs barked at him from a safe distance until he was outside someone else's house.

However, he found three examples of shops that he was looking for. They were all grotty like the one in Gail's street, but he sat in the nearest one to Joy's house and ordered a pint bottle of cold beer Chang in sign language. He was glad that he had brought his Kindle, so he sat back and began to read only slightly aware of the people who suddenly realized that they had to buy something in order to get a closer look at him. He spotted them from time to time in hushed conversation with the shopkeeper pointing at him.

When he was on his second bottle, about an hour and a half later, and the interest in him had faded, the old shopkeeper sat opposite him; it was obviously where she too took her breaks and gained refuge from the relentless sun. He looked up and smiled at her for a second. She was already studying him and smiling broadly.

She was short, roundish, seriously overweight, but old enough not to have to worry about it, since Thais, being Buddhists, believe in reincarnation. 'Why struggle in this life to be someone you were not cut out to be, when you can come back again and start from the beginning in the next one?' Joy had asked him once. He was watching the philosophy in action.

"Ankit?" she asked, but to no avail. "English? You English or American or Germany?"

"Oh, sorry, English. London", he elaborated trying to reward her with a conversation for trying. "Husband, er, boyfriend, friend Joy", he said pointing up the road to Joy's house. "Sorry, Da friend Da from London".

"Ah", she replied sagely holding her index and forefingers tightly together in front of her, which Frank correctly interpreted as a sign of marriage. Of course, he realised, the whole village would have heard of Joy's marriage to an Englishman. He returned her friendly smile and held out his right hand. She knew what he was doing, she had seen it in films on the TV, but she had never done it before, and held up her left hand. Frank took the back of her hand in his and shook it. She looked most pleased.

"I, er, me, er, Frank. And you?" he asked pointing to his own heart and then to her.

"Frank, neh? Chan cheu Elle. Elle".

"Elle, eh? That's easy to remember... 'She' in French... and She as in the film" he mumbled and then to himself only "after she came out of the flame". He smiled at his own cruel little joke, which Elle took as a good sign and held out her left hand again. Frank extended his left too this time and the Boy Scout shake worked well. He noticed a few customers watching. He surmised that that was probably why she wanted to shake the second time and was correct again. She pointed at the bystanders with her chin, let go of his hand and stood up. "One more?" she asked him mimicking the phrase he had used twice previously.

"Yes, please, Elle". She grinned like a Cheshire cat as she breezed past her customers, some of whose jaws were literally hanging open.

Frank finished that third bottle slowly, bought three more to take home and took his leave of Elle.

During the evening meal, which lasted from about four thirty until bed time at eight thirty, Frank tried to relieve his own tedium and engage Joy, since she wasn't speaking unless spoken to, by telling her about his adventures in the village.

"Most people here have only seen white people in films", she explained. "Did they stroke you?"

"What do you mean? I'm a respectfully married man!" he quipped, hoping that he had caught a glimpse of the dirty 'old' Joy in her remark.

"You will notice that Thais do not have hairy bodies like Falang. So, the old ones often take a Falang's arm and stroke it like a cat".

"No, that didn't happen to me today", he said disappointed in Joy's remark. "Perhaps, I'll be luckier tomorrow. Why am I a Falang and why do toddlers cry when the see me?"

There was a hint of a smile as Joy explained, but it looked as is she was struggling to get the words out.

"There is a lot of crap talked about the word 'Falang' and some Falang take offence at the word, but there is no need. The first white people here were French and we called them Falangset. It is actually spelled with an 'r', not an 'l', but that is how most people pronounce it. Anyway, Falangset meant French, and still does, but Falang has come to mean any white person. It is easiest to think of it meaning Caucasian".

"So, how can that be offensive? White Europeans, Americans, Canadians, et cetera, are Caucasian".

"Yes, silly, isn't it? Some people who know too little, see a word like 'manfalang', which means potato, and think that we are calling them 'potato men' or 'potato heads'. It's all very silly and just goes to prove that every country has its own share of idiots".

"And the babies that burst into tears as I came into sight? Am I that ugly to Thais?"

"No, far from it. Most women would give up their virtue to have white skin like yours. Brown skin means you are poor and stupid, so have to work in the sun; white skin means you have passed exams and have a good job. Watch Thai TV for as long as you like - you won't see a dark face on it. Look in Thai bathrooms, they all contain bottles of skin whitener... It is very sad, but we are all affected by this prejudice... Even I protect my white skin - I worked and still work hard for it. I won't go outside when the sun is strong.

"As for the kids, that's easy. Traditionally, when there were tigers, huge snakes and kidnappers roaming the villages at night, parents frightened their children not to wander far from the house with stories of wicked ghosts, pi pob and many other creatures. They were all big, fierce and white. Again, watch Thai TV, you will see a story like that every week. Now, never having seen a white man before, they assume, quite naturally, that you are one of these monsters come to eat them.

"It's not you, my dear, it is our culture. Don't worry about it, just be yourself and smile. When they realize that you haven't come to eat their intestines or suck their brains out of their noses, they will come around".

"OK, my love. I believe you, but millions wouldn't. That old shopkeeper, Elle. She seems all right".

"Yes", she smiled, "we have known each other all my life. She has a good heart, jai dee, but she is also the hub of all the best gossip in the village…"

"Da," Frank heard a stranger say, and with that his wife's attention was distracted away from him and he was a silent, as good as deaf, onlooker again.

∞

As everyone lay asleep in bed later that night, Frank was still alone. He felt that there had definitely been an improvement in Joy's behaviour since arriving in the village or taking the new tablets, but he couldn't discuss it with her for fear of disturbing the others in the room, and because the last pill that Joy took every day was a powerful sleeping tablet.

He lay there thinking and listening to the animals of the night - birds, dogs, reptiles and insects - until he fell asleep, which he assumed was his normal time of between twelve and one o'clock.

15. LIVING WITH MUM

When Frank awoke the following morning, his wife was already gone again, but at least the electric was still on. Knowing what to look for now, he saw Joy sitting on the veranda the same as the day before.

"How are you doing, my darling, you get up early these days?"

"OK", she mouthed and waved him into the seat opposite. There was food on the table; she pointed at it and pushed a few of the dishes in his direction. He sampled one, so that he could have something to talk to her about. However, he knew as he put half a spoonful to his lips that he wasn't going to enjoy it. It was at least three times hotter than any dish he had eaten before. Joy recognised the splutters, looked at him and saw his eyes and nose running and almost smiled. "You must eat with rice", she said pushing the bowl of rice towards him.

"It is very hot. Is that what you eat for breakfast?"

"Not first course, maybe the second", she allowed him.

"I'm sorry, darling, but I can't eat food like that at the best of times, but certainly not first thing in the morning. Jesus! Why do you get up so early, this is our honeymoon?" She only shrugged and continued her long-distance stare at or through the bamboo.

At eleven o'clock, Joy was crying for her tablets and Bew was pleading with her with tears running down her cheeks to eat something first, as the doctor had ordered. Joy refused and became argumentative, but Bew held her ground. Frank had missed all these tantrums and realised in a flash why Joy got up early - so that she could have her tablets and stop the voices. It was a grim realisation. He had thought she was getting better, whereas all she was doing was relying on medication to get her through the day. It hit him like an unexpected divorce as he realised that she was no better than weeks ago, it was just that tablets were keeping her afloat.

He stood up and kissed her on the top of the head, but got no response. He looked at Bew with new eyes, realising how much strain the young woman had relieved him and Joy of. Seconds later, he surmised that they wouldn't be going home anytime soon. It also dawned on him that that was a problem only he could solve.

With his new-found respect for Bew, he allowed her to lead his wife downstairs to eat, so that she could have her next batch of tablets. He followed on behind like an obedient puppy. It did not come naturally to a high-powered, big-earner like him, but he was clever enough to know who knew more than he did and give them their head. It was what he was paid to do at the bank. The only problem for him was that neither his job nor his life-long experience had prepared him for seeing the person he loved most in the world losing her mind.

He didn't know whether to drag her away from the obvious comfort she derived from being with her family and take her to Bangkok or even to London. He was used to problems that money could solve, but that didn't seem to be the point in this case.

He was well and truly flummoxed, for the first time that he could remember in his life.

He felt belittled and that annoyed his ego. He wanted to shake Joy and tell her that they had to go back to the UK soon, so get well, but he knew that that was selfish and wouldn't work anyway. After Joy had eaten and taken her tablets, she wanted to stare at the bamboo again, so Frank went to see the nearest and closest friend he had for five and a half thousand miles, Elle.

∞

The days passed and Frank began to sink into the same depression that his wife was in, although they couldn't find each other there in the valley of despair.

∞

Frank was nothing if not a methodical man. He made lists on Outlook computer calendar and set reminders. The latest one reminded him that he had to check his tickets and passport, because they were due to fly out in two days and go back to work in four. It was unthinkable for Joy to make such a journey in her condition, but he made his checks anyway and was glad that he did, because he had forgotten about his Thai visa. He had received a 'free thirty-day visa' at the airport on arrival, so it was still valid for seventeen days, but that was cutting it fine for a man like Frank. For his own peace of mind and to give him something to do, he set about finding out how to get a new one, because with all the goodwill, prayers and tablets in the world, he could not see them being able to go home on April the 29th or even May the 14th. He was cautiously hoping for May the 29th, which meant getting a new Thai visa, postponing the return flights and phoning their respective employers. He also thought that it was about time he phoned Mike, his immediate superior in the bank, to give him advance warning about his impending delayed return to work and to thank him for the use of his apartment.

'His apartment!' he thought, 'Oh Hell! What a state they had left that in and they had forgotten to leave a tip for the cleaner'.

He looked at his phone for the time. Just gone three and he noticed that the battery was seventy-five percent charged. It was time to go and see Elle; he could research the visa, and phone Mike from there. He asked Joy to go with him, as he always did, and when she refused, as she always did, he kissed her, patted her on the shoulder, promised to return at sixish and left.

As he walked past the table, he waved and smiled at Bew and Mae, Mum in Thai, which he had learned was pronounced in the same way that lambs call their mothers, and kept walking. None of the six people took any notice of him. As he turned to close the gate, he saw Bew's behind disappearing into the house, presumably to take his place with Joy.

He sighed loudly and heavily, and trudged his way to the shop.

"One more, Mr. Frank?" she asked, as he sank down onto the hard concrete bench.

"Yes, please, Elle", he replied noticing that whatever English she had learned in her life was slowly returning to her, or possibly that she was actively trying to learn a few more words every day. He thought of correcting the 'mister', but couldn't be bothered. It would keep for when he was in a better mood. He checked the time again: three thirty, nine thirty in the UK. It would be one of the busiest times of the day in the bank. That suited him fine, he would drink a beer first and think about how to make his apologies.

"Here, Mr. Frank! Bia Chang yen yen wan nee. Beer Chang very cold today. Elle put on ice for you in night".

He put the ice-cold bottle to his forehead, which made her laugh out loud for some reason, then he took a mouthful and filled his glass, which had ice in it. 'Why not?' he thought; drained the large pot and filled it up again. Elle brought him a bucket of ice and a pair of tongs, which she proceeded to show him how to use to pick up ice and drop it in his glass. He got the message, nodded and smiled and took out his Kindle to make notes for his apology.

It wasn't that he was frightened of Mike. No, he was embarrassed. They were quite good friends and often socialised together when his wife, Jocasta, would allow it. She was highly strung and subject to strange mood swings, which demanded Mike's presence, although everyone who knew them had noticed that they never occurred during office hours. Mike was easy-going, loved his wife and tolerated her possessive nature - some even suspected that he liked being in such high demand, because it made him feel indispensable.

He took another gulp of beer, checked the time again and pressed the speed dial. Number two, one was for Joy, three was for his mother. Nothing happened, so he checked the time again. It was ten forty. 'Number Unavailable' flashed onto the screen. It was unthinkable that Mike would switch his phone off. They joked in the office that he probably listened out for it when he was making love with Jocasta. He tried again, but the same error message appeared. He clicked 'Edit', added +44 to Mike's number and tried again.

The video call was answered in two rings. He was slipping. "Hello, Frank! How's the honeymoon going, you lucky old dog? You look exhausted. Hard at it, eh? Honeymoons can be strenuous when an older man has a young wife, eh?" At fifty-nine, his handsome face was beginning to show signs of aging despite regular visits to the gym and the masseuse. He smiled easily and most of it was his own natural warmth coming through.

"Er, things are not going quite as expected, to be honest, Mike. Have you got ten or fifteen minutes - this call is partly work-related".

"Sure, what's the problem, old boy; I've always got time for my friends and colleagues, you know that. Let me get behind my desk. Now, what can I do for you that that lovely Joy of yours cannot? Is she well... enjoying the old Motherland or Fatherland or whatever they call it over there?"

"Well, no, er, not exactly... that's one of the reasons why I'm calling you. First, I want to thank you for the use of the apartment and apologise for the state we left it in..." Frank gave him a précis of their time in Spain, during which Mike did not interrupt.

"I see. Consuela, the manageress, did mention something about onions and garlic, but then you expect that sort of thing from the southern Europeans, don't you?" Mike laughed, but Frank did not. "Why, what was that all about? Some sort of Thai wedding night tradition? Or were you trying to keep away vampires?" He was laughing again.

"I don't know if it was vampires exactly that she was trying to keep away, but she was having trouble with, er, let's call them 'Creatures of The Night'".

"Creatures of the Night? What the Hell are you talking about, man?"

"I know. It sounds crazy, but Joy is convinced that she saw ghosts, ghouls or spectres, call them what you will, creeping around the flat at night. I didn't see them myself, but some weird things did happen".

"Like what?"

"Well, someone drank our wine and left vomit in a glass - several times - and a few items of Joy's went missing". He didn't want to mention the video.

"Someone, or one of you? We've all had more to drink than we expected, been ill and misplaced things. Jesus, man, there probably isn't an adult, or teenager for that matter, in the whole of Europe who hasn't done that... even Jocasta and I have".

"Yes, I agree, but there's more. I'm sending you a photo... and someone filmed us on the job and played it in a local bar and put it on the Internet... Joy doesn't know that bit yet".

"You're not sending me your homemade honeymoon porn video, are you?"

"No, of course not".

"Thank Heaven for that! I know that we are mates and all that, but some things are beyond The Pale, aren't they? Private issues and the like. Ah, I have your photo. Rather cruel, isn't it?"

"Yes... it really upset Joy".

"Still, I can't see ghosts or ghouls drinking wine and taking porno films, can you? And how would they get them played in a bar and on the Internet?"

"I know about the same as you do, Mike. However, this whole affair, however you want to explain it, has caused Joy to suffer some kind of a nervous breakdown. Nobody speaks English over here and those that do in the family are not telling me anything. They don't include me in the decision-making and don't share doctors' conclusions with me. For the last few days in Spain and on the flight, she was raving. Then for a week in Bangkok, she was asleep or crying and now she is either catatonic, begging for tablets to stop the voices, crying or asleep".

"I see... Well, my heart goes out to you both... I wouldn't wish this on my worst enemy. You are in a tough situation. What can I do to help?"

"I don't think there is anything, Mike... except keep my job open for me, because I can't fly her back in this state. It's going to take at least another fortnight, but maybe a month... I have no idea".

"I take it you are all right for money, and you have insurance, eh? Your job will be safe, at least until you get back and hand in your report and supporting evidence... The bank's family insurance policy is one of the best in the land, and I should think Joy's embassy has good cover arranged for her too".

"Yes, we're OK for money, thanks, but the insurances have failed. I didn't get around to adding Joy to my policy and we don't want the embassy to know about her mental health... Still, medical care, the best available, is very cheap compared to Europe, so that's not an issue anyway. No, I would pay anything to have Joy back the way she was a month ago, but these things take their own sweet time, don't they?" He wished he hadn't said that last part as soon as the words had left his mouth.

"Yes, that's true", he replied as if deep in thought. "Look, you just get that lovely wife of yours better and give her my love and if there is anything I can do for you here, just let me know. I will make a note on your file that you have rung, but please keep me informed of developments... and I mean that as your friend as well as your manager".

"OK, Mike, thanks. I'll ring you in a couple of days. Bye for now... say hello to Jocasta for us, won't you?"

"Sure. Bye for now and hang on in there... All nightmares come to an end some time".

Frank clicked the video link off and a tear came to his eye.

Elle brought him another beer and poured it for him before he could get any ice in his glass. She held the glass towards him so that he could drink a couple of inches to make room for the ice. His suspicious nature told him that he had just been tricked into drinking his beer more quickly than he otherwise would have done, but he didn't really care. It was only a pound a pint bottle and he was used to paying three, four or even five times that amount in London.

As he contemplated a fourth bottle and was deciding in favour of it, he typed 'how to obtain a visa in Thailand' into the search engine. He selected the one that looked most relevant, right-clicked it and opened it in a new window. Being in northern Thailand, it seemed to him that he could either go to Nan, an even more northerly Thai province, or leave the country altogether and go to Vientiane, the capital of Laos. He would try discussing the pros and cons with Joy later.

He bought three more beers to take home and bade Elle a good evening.

There were eleven people seated at and on the large wooden garden table when he arrived home, including Mae, Bew and Joy, who were also the only ones not drinking. Joy said something to Bew, and she hopped off the table. She placed a chair for him to sit with them, took his beer inside to the fridge and returned with an open one.

"Do you want a glass and ice?" asked Joy so quietly that he barely heard her.

"No, this is fine as it is, thanks. How are you doing, my dear? What's this a party?"

She described circles with her index fingers at her temples by way of reply, but Frank couldn't make out what she was trying to tell him.

"Oh, I see... like that still, is it? I spoke to Mike this afternoon. He sends his love". He realised that he was the only one talking and that he had probably interrupted their conversation. Joy seemed to confirm his suspicions by dropping her chin to her chest, closing her eyes and putting her hands over her ears.

"We are discussing Aunty Da's health", explained Bew.

"OK", he said, "sorry I'm late, but I didn't know - again". As soon as he put the bottle to his lips, they started talking again - in Thai. Neither Bew nor Joy translated for him, although Joy only spoke if asked a direct question.

Frank soon began to wonder whether just three beers was going to get him through the evening as it appeared to be unfolding. Many times, he saw Joy shaking her head slowly and putting her hands to her ears. She was on the table immediately in front of her husband and he frequently rubbed her back to remind her that he was with her. He was getting the impression that they were trying to get her to do something, but he had no idea what it was.

He had realised that he normally drank a pint of Chang in an hour, or an hour and a half, if he was doing something else as well, but he had finished his three beers within two hours, he was so bored and frustrated. However, the amazing thing to him was that Joy had counted the number of bottles he had brought home and how many he had consumed and sent Bew to buy him three more. It was a display of more awareness than he had seen from her in nearly two weeks. "Thank you, my love, that is very thoughtful of you", he said to her, rubbing her back. "Thanks, Bew", but Bew only raised her chin in acknowledgement.

The discussion continued until gone ten and then they either went home or took their turn in the shower. All except Frank and Joy who went to bed as they were. Frank had one more beer in the fridge, but he was none the wiser about what had transpired that night. He had been hoping for some enlightenment from Joy, but the sleeping tablet that Bew gave her knocked her out.

That night, Frank prayed for the first time in forty-something years. He asked God to transfer all his strength to Joy to make her well regardless of the consequences to himself. It was all that he could think of doing. He couldn't even remember all of the Lord's Prayer. As he tried to remember it, he gazed at the back of his wife's head and laid a hand on her shoulder as he cried himself to sleep almost silently, his wife's name on his lips and in his mind. "Oh, Joy, please come back to me... I love you so much... I will die without you... I would want to die without you..."

16. COVENTRY

As was becoming part of his daily ritual, Frank found his wife on the balcony with half a plate of partially stained rice beside her. Bew obviously insisted that Joy eat some meat or vegetables with her rice before she would administer the tablets. It was like watching a junkie. When he sat across the table from her, she barely acknowledged his existence, but Bew backed off to allow them some privacy.

"How are you today, my dear?" he asked hoping against hope as had become the norm. She just shook her head and turned circles with her index finger by her right temple.

"Listen to me, Joy, I am getting a bit fed up with this. Tell me what the matter is, so that I can help you work it out!"

She turned and glared at him. "Chan kiet maak! Kiet!" He shrugged.

"I don't speak Thai..."

"I think a lot... I cannot stop thinking a lot! I worry! Do you understand?"

"No. What do you think about?"

She hesitated. "I don't know".

"Look, love, you can't be thinking about something, let alone worrying about it, if you don't know what it is... Can you? Come on, be fair... Tell me the problem and we will work it out".

"I don't know what the problem is! Can't you understand that, you idiot?!" she spat out at him.

Frank was shocked, but recovered his composure quickly, and countered.

"No, actually, I cannot understand that! how can you worry about something and not know what it is? If you are worrying about not having any money, you know that money is the problem. If you are worried about your health or your kids' education, you know that that is the problem... but I have never heard of someone worrying and not knowing what they are worrying about... How can you think about something that has no form?"

"Will you just shut up and go drink more beer in Elle's? Leave me alone! I have enough problems without you starting as well..."

Frank was hurt. He had tried a new approach but it hadn't worked.

"OK, have it your way. I'll go and get drunk. I'll see you at six or so". It was nine o'clock, and he hadn't been out drinking so early since a friend's stag party at university. He walked past the garden table without acknowledging anyone and turned the opposite way from Elle's shop. This was going to be a pub crawl; he couldn't face sitting in one grimy shop for nine hours. As George Thorogood sang, he had to "make it three'.

The first shop was nondescript, to the point that the middle-aged male shopkeeper seemed to resent his presence, so Frank sat there for four hours reading his book and only had two beers just to spite him. The second shop was better, but the twenty-something year-old shopkeeper was jealously guarded by her equally young husband every time she tried to show Frank any attention. He got the impression that she was only trying to upset her husband. He didn't want to get between man and wife and certainly didn't want to get beaten up as a pawn in their game, so he had two and read his book for three hours.

As he was 'completing the village circuit' and heading, a little light-headed towards Elle's, he passed a shop that he had overlooked on his first tour. The middle-aged woman cleaned the concrete benches and the table before gesturing him to sit down. He smiled his appreciation, asked for a 'bia Chang' and waaied her, which she reciprocated, although he had broken protocol without knowing it. He liked her attitude. He even fancied her, and felt that she liked him too.

However, his beer arrived with a smile and the shopkeeper left and nothing happened, which Frank, even as tipsy as he was, realised was for the best, so he just read his book. However, he did feel relaxed there and it wasn't so far from Elle's or home.

At four forty-five a bus stopped outside and a load of children of various ages got off in a noisy gaggle. Many of them stopped in the shop to buy a drink or a cake before going home, but not one of them didn't stare at him as if he were from another planet.

Three giggling girls in their mid to late teens sat opposite him at the only table in the shop. He couldn't understand them, but he knew that they were talking about him, because he heard the word 'falang' often. Sometimes, he would look up and smile at them, trying to imply that he knew a little of their language.

When the initial excitement had died down, the pupils, in their sky-blue shirts and navy shorts or skirts drifted off home, but one remained sitting opposite him. She was staring at him and sucking on a straw in a small carton of soya milk.

He tried to ignore her but couldn't. She aroused him, but he fought hard not to speak to her. He guessed that she was somewhere between sixteen and eighteen. When the carton was empty, she started making slurping noises with the straw, which were beginning to annoy him. He looked up into her large brown eyes.

"My milk is finished", she said.

"So, I hear", he replied and then was stunned to hear himself say, "can I get you another one?"

"Yes, please..." she replied. "Are you English?" He confirmed her guess. "I want to live in London, England, one day. Where do you come from? Manchester United?"

"No, I come from London. I don't know how to order your milk, will you do it, please, and ask for a beer Chang for me too".

"I go get. It is not problem". She returned with the drinks and sat next to him. "Cheers!" she said, "tapping his bottle with her carton. "That is correct, no?"

"Yes, that is correct".

"I learning English in school. May I see what you read?" She placed her hand on the bare part of his thigh between his knee and his shorts. "It is nice, no?" she asked kneading his leg, but pointing at the book on his Kindle.

"Yes", he managed in a calm voice. "How old are you?"

"I am nearly eighteen. I want to go to university at the end of the year".

"Oh, good for you! Where?"

"In London, if I can find a sponsor, or otherwise in Bangkok". Her hand moved up his leg and he didn't try to stop it.

"I see... What is your name?" was the only thing he could think to say.

"My name is Boo... Khun poot passa Thai, mai?" From his expression, she guessed that he did not. "Not speak Thai? Oh, I can teach you! My name Boo... the crab. You know crab? He walk like this" and she walked her hand down to his knee and then back up to his trouser line. He likes to hide under stones and in holes... like this..." Boo put her hand up his baggy shorts and grabbed his engorged cock. "Oh, you have big chang like elephant. People tell me that falang have big cock, but I don't know before. I want to see him".

Frank looked around as she pulled the front of his shorts down. She withdrew her hand from his trousers and grabbed him from the top. Five seconds later, he came in her hand.

"English man come quickly!" she giggled. She inspected his seed, raised her skirt and wiped her fingers on the outside of the back of her white knickers. Then she swang her legs up and over the bench between them, making sure that he got a good look at the patch of knickers over her crotch, laughed at his expression and stood up. She called the boss over and a wave of guilt spread over him with the speed and force of a Tsunami. Was she going to report him?

"Deo! Deo! Quickly, please! Frank wants me to help him with his big, er, chang".

He felt impending disaster: humiliation, a long court case, compensation, dismissal from the bank, divorce and imprisonment.

"Mai poot passa ankit, dek! (I don't speak English, child!) Ao alai? (What do you want?) Eek Chang neung? (Another Chang?)"

"Chai (Yes)", she said pointing at him, "Chang yai (a big Chang)". They both walked off together, leaving Frank with his pessimism. He knew that 'chang' was the Thai word for elephant and the slang word for penis, but in his state of shock and panic, he forgot that it was also the name of the brand of beer he was drinking. Yai, he had known for some time, meant 'large'.

The two ladies appeared at his table suddenly.

"I have your big, big chang in my hands again, Frank, but this one is very cold, yours was very hot". She put it down in front of him, laughed at his obvious discomfort and said, "Bye-bye, Frank, see you and your Chang, er, beer again tomorrow, I hope". He could hear her laughing as she walked up the street, but he picked up his new bottle, toasted Deo with it and gratefully took a long swig. He had never been so frightened in his whole life, not even by Joy's current illness, because he was confident that she would get over that.

His eventual sigh of relief was a long time coming, but it was a sign that his pulse had returned to normal and that he was probably in the clear. He paid up and left for Elle's. He was glad to see her; he felt more at home there than at Joy's mother's house.

However, after two there, he staggered home with three in a bag. Bew relieved him of them as before and he took a seat at what he was beginning to think of as the Council of Elders.

"You have a stain", said Joy, pointing at his crotch with her chin unobtrusively, "you must take more care when you go to the Gents' or people will begin to laugh at you and call you a dirty old man".

"It's probably just beer that dripped off the bottles I've been drinking", he said.

"Condensation from cold beer bottles is clear water, it doesn't leave a stain. Other things that chang does do leave stains".

He was beginning to wish that he had just accepted her warning and not got her thinking about 'other bodily fluids'. He tried to make amends quickly.

"Yes, I'm sure you are right. I'll take more care in future. How are you and what do all these people want this time?"

"I feel a bit better, but it comes and goes. One minute, I'm thinking about our wedding and I want to describe it to everyone, and the next my mind clouds over and I feel that massive problems are going to befall us any moment. I feel fifty percent better than yesterday and this morning though. How was your day? Meet anyone interesting?"

"I'm so pleased you're making progress, Joy. That's great news... the best I've had for weeks. Me? Meet anybody interesting? How can I do that? Nobody speaks enough English to even discuss the weather!"

"Most of the younger people have learned some English at school - especially the most recent schoolkids. The girls always tried harder at English that the boys when I was at school. I suppose they still do".

"Why's that?" he asked starting to become worried again.

"Well, the boys want to become farmers like their Dads and drive big tractors and one day, they will inherit the farm, so English is of no possible use to them. The girls, on the other hand, look at their mothers, either pregnant or up to their knees in mud all the time and don't want the same life. They see English as a route out of the village and the drudgery that is the life of a farmer's wife here. They dream of meeting a rich Thai businessman or a wealthy falang tourist in Bangkok or one of the tourist cities like Pattaya, Hua Hin or Koh Samui... there are quite a few in the south and in the north. Like Chiang Mai, a few hours north of here. It's probably what I would have done, if my family hadn't helped me get a good job after university".

"I see. Why do I feel as if I'm getting dirty looks from these people? Did I interrupt anything?"

"Yes, but I am happy that you did so. It was boring. They are just saying the same things as last night. They want me to go to see another doctor".

"And you don't want to?"

"No, I don't want to!"

"Well, that's good enough for me. You still have about ten days' tablets from the doctor in Bangkok and your health has definitely improved since Bangkok, so I am with you. Keep taking the medication you are on now until they are gone, and then decide what you want to do. Any doctor would advise you to complete the course of medicine you're already on, before trying another, especially if you start seeing an improvement. And you are a lot better this evening, my darling. This is the first sensible chat we have had since our lock down in the apartment in Fuengirola, isn't it?"

She nodded and was about to speak when her mother said something to her and the debate started again in Thai without him.

He opened the bottle that Bew handed him and noted stern looks from some of the people he didn't know. He held up the bottle to them and smiled just to spite them. The discussion became heated, and as it did so, he noticed that more fingers, chins and icy glares were being directed at him, with a few at Joy as well. Bew was the only one who looked vaguely sympathetic, but she wasn't really taking much part in the pow-wow. Perhaps they thought her too young, he rationalized. When he saw Joy put her head in her hands, her hands over her ears and begin to rock back and forth shaking her head, he thought that all the day's progress had been lost. He tapped her on the shoulder and asked what was being said.

"They are saying that I should go to see a more local doctor because that is the majority family decision. They are saying that if you were a real man, you would make me go and that you are going against the family, but since you're a foreigner, you wouldn't understand our ways".

"Well, they are probably right on the last part. However, you can tell that fat cow over there, that toothless git there and those two laughing jackasses there, that I do understand: one, that it is rude to point and sneer and two, that I do understand that it is an adult's own choice whether he or she wants to go to se a doctor or not especially when they still have a bagful of tablets from the first doctor, which seem to be helping! Explain that to the gormless yokels!"

"Frank, please! Please! You are not helping" She was crying again and rocking still. "Please, will you all just shut up! Yoot! Nyep, ka!"

Nobody stopped talking, not even Frank.

"The fucking bastards ganging up on you like that and making you cry. How dare the shits call themselves friends and family! You don't need enemies with friends like them, do you?"

"Frank, please... please... please, stop... just stop".

"OK, for you, but what does this 'hamore' mean that I keep hearing?" Joy would not answer.

"Bai ha more' - 'Go and see a doctor" whispered Bew. Frank heard her and nodded, but it started another round of 'Bai ha more' almost like a rhythmic chant from the others".

Frank was ready to hit a couple of them, as opposed to violence as he normally was.

Bew led them both upstairs and gave Joy her tablets before returning to the table below. Joy was soon asleep, but Frank could hear the voices for hours.

Frank didn't get up until gone eleven and made his way over to see Joy. "How are you today, my dear?"

"Oh, I've been much better and a bit worse", she replied. "How about you?"

"I haven't had a hangover like this since I graduated. My mouth feels like the armpit of a very sweaty gorilla that has just woken up from a very long nap".

"You were very drunk".

"What do you expect? The amount of food they give me to live on would leave a sparrow hungry".

"That's my fault. Sorry, they don't know how to keep a falang".

"You make me sound like some exotic animal".

"You might as well be. You don't eat the same food as we do, don't eat the same quantities and don't even eat at the same times we do. We graze, all day, but you gorge on two large meals. My mother wouldn't know what carrots, peas, mashed potato and gravy were if you put them in front of her. I'll bet she has ever seen a steak or a lump of cheese in her life either. Nor eaten bread, butter, jam or Marmite.

"You turn your nose up at what she eats, but that's all she knows. What can she do about that? Until I'm well or we can sort something else out, you'll just have to live off beer, cake and biscuits like you did when you were a student".

"How do you know what I ate..."

"All students eat too much cake and biscuits and you like beer".

"OK, you've got me there, but I like wine too".

She gave a thin smile, but it was the best he'd seen for some time.

"That's my girl!" he offered in encouragement. They were interrupted by Bew when she shuffled her feet halfway across the room to announce her presence. She placed a plate, with a bag of small cakes and a few leaves on it, and a glass of tea on the table. "It's all I could find", she apologised to Joy and left quickly.

"You'll like the cakes, they're made with bananas, and these are traditional Thai sweets". She unfolded a leaf that had been pinned with toothpicks into the shape of a three-dimensional triangle and filled with a kind of pink blancmange".

"It is made from over-cooked rice or rice flour", she explained on seeing him examining it. He tried one.

"Very sweet... not like blancmange, but nice". He liked the cakes too and ate the lot when Joy refused the one he offered her. "Well, there are two things I can eat".

Joy refused all future attempts at conversation and went back to contemplating the bamboo. Frank took out his Kindle and read.

When three fifteen came, he felt the need for a hair of the dog, so asked Joy to accompany him to Elle's, but she refused. So, he went down waved at the people on the table, but got no reply. He felt guilty passing Elle's, but he held up two fingers and hoped that she would divine that he would be back in two hours or after two beers. He hurried on to Deo's, wondering whether that delectable girl would be there again, although he had convinced himself that they would never have any physical contact again.

He greeted Deo, ordered a beer and started to read. Ninety minutes later, he saw the same three girls as the day before on the point of sitting at his table. They smiled, giggled, put their packages on the table, waaied him, and sat down.

"Hello, girls. Can I get you a drink?" The one he was starting to think of as 'his girl' translated for the others. They giggled and went to the fridge to make their selections, then returned to sit with him, waaied him again, and just stared at him, while sucking on their straws.

"My name is Frank, what are your names?"

They looked each other again and giggled, then the one to his left opposite said, "My name is Ma. How do you do?"

"Very well, Ma, thank you. Nice to meet you" and they shook hands. The other two used exactly the same routine, so he guessed that it was a set piece that they had learned in school. His girl was called Boo, but he didn't let on that he already knew and the other one Din. They were all pretty, but Boo had a twinkle in her eye and a wicked sense of humour that aroused him like no other had - even more than Joy, although he hated to admit it to himself. The three of them were 'still growing', but they were already head-turners. As he was studying what he could see of them above the table, Boo broke his reverie.

"We have been shopping. We like prick, don't we girls?" She repeated it in Thai and her friends nodded enthusiastically. "I like hot and spicy prick", she breathed sexily licking her lips. Her friends were still nodding and smiling. "Yes, I like all kinds of prick... the small ones in this country and the big red ones like you have in your country. Would you like me to prove that we can suck a red prick here? All three of us?" He didn't know what to say, but sensed a trap. "We especially like prick juice, don't we, girls" she said raising her eyebrows and licking her lips.

"We don't have any prick juice to eat... unless you have some for us, Frank. No? I think I remember you had some yesterday?"

He wasn't saying anything, but he was rock-hard.

"OK, if you cannot give us any prick juice to eat, we will just eat a prick for you". She rummaged in a bag under the table, put something in her friends' hands and said something to them. They stood up as one and started sucking and nibbling on the red, one-inch chillis between their forefingers and thumbs. There wasn't the slightest sign of discomfort on anyone's face but his. He was relieved.

"We have to go home now. Our mothers are waiting for the shopping, but if you give us some prick juice tomorrow, we will eat that for your too, won't we girls?" Boo translated and they nodded enthusiastically. They departed laughing and giggling leaving him in a mess both down below and in his head.

Boo was the sort of woman that could get a man into trouble. That much was obvious to him.

So, with his mind in turmoil and his dick bouncing around in his trousers, he went to Elle's, calmed down over two beers, bought two to take out and went home.

Everybody but Joy completely ignored him, although it was fairer to say that Bew just looked down at the hands in her lap, whereas most of the others did look at him, but did not acknowledge him.

He didn't care. "Can I put these in the fridge?" he asked Joy. She pointed, but he knew where it was anyway. When he returned, Joy spoke to him.

"You have broken the family code, so none of them will speak to you right now. I will explain it better tonight or tomorrow, but for now, it would be easier if you drink your beer upstairs on the balcony. I will come when I can. Sorry".

It wasn't as if he wanted to talk to any of the older people on the table, or that he could even if he did want to, but being ostracised did hurt him. He didn't think that he had done anything bad enough to warrant being sent to Coventry. He sat on the balcony, put some mosquito repellent on and read his book alone, but not much of the story was sinking in.

17. AWKWARD TIMES

The additional stress caused by Frank being sent to Coventry by her family sent Joy into a relapse. All the progress that she had made over the past week was wiped out. She was back to sitting on the balcony after being bribed to eat food in exchange for her tablets. She rarely spoke, at least not to him and that had nothing to do with his ostracisation. The only person she was interested in was Bew, and that was only when she wanted more tablets. She was back at the junkie level as Frank thought of it.

He could not believe that a family would jeopardise the health of someone they said they loved in order to hurt someone they obviously despised.

Bew gave him his cake and tea and squeezed his shoulder. "I cannot talk to you", she whispered, "but I do agree with you and Joy", and with that she hurried away.

It was absolutely certain that they would not be flying back on schedule now. The thought crossed his mind that that was why the family had reacted like they had - to keep Joy with them. If that was what had happened, it was a twisted form of love that this family had for one another. However twisted and unfathomable it was though to him, they still had one another, whereas he had no-one, just the shell of a wife... and Boo, he thought.

She made him smile, frightened him even, but she made him feel alive. Joy had joked before that she was only half his age, but that would have put him at fifty-eight. Boo was actually a third of the age he would be on his next birthday. On a sudden whim, he checked the age of consent in Thailand and found that it was variable, but generally considered to be sixteen. He knew that he was heading in the wrong direction, but he couldn't help himself - not yet. He struggled to return to reality.

The tickets... he had to postpone the flights, but by how long? He wanted her well, so that she could take the travel sickness pills, although it looked as if that was still a month off, but he didn't want to stay too long because of the effect the ostracisation was having on her. He decided on a fortnight, but without conviction. However, that would make it necessary for him to do something about his visa. He had sixteen days left, but another delay would put a lot of stress on him. He wanted a visa for another two months and then he could forget about that irritation.

At three, he went through the vain ritual of asking Joy to join him in Elle's; she just shook her head; he kissed it, said see you at sixish and left. This time though, he did go straight to Elle's and postponed the flights back to London until the last day of his current visa, giving them fifteen days to put their house in order. Then he phoned Mike.

"I'm sorry, Mike, but bad news. Joy's family decided to send me to Coventry the other day and it sent Joy into relapse. The stupid bastards have put her back at least a fortnight and she was starting to do so well. I have put the return flights back to the fourteenth, when my visa expires, but to be honest with you, I reckon that it will be another two weeks after that before we can fly out of here... and in the meantime, I need another visa. It's all gone tits up, Mike, our dream honeymoon is just a nightmare".

"Hold on in there, son. You will get there and don't worry about this end. I've got you covered at least until you get back, but don't forget, keep all your receipts and doctors' reports... It helps establish where you were and what you were doing".

"OK, thanks, Mike... I'll see you when I wake up and I hope to God that it's soon... honest to God I do... I even started praying the other night... and you know me and God, we've forgotten where each other lives, it's been that long".

Mike sensed a note of desperation in Frank's voice and hung up with a heavy heart.

Frank's next phone call was to the Thai Embassy in London. He had got on well with one of Joy's colleagues and looked up the embassy's number on his own phone. This time he remembered to edit in the country code before phoning. The switchboard operator remembered him and tried to be friendly, but he deflected her and asked for his contact, Somchai.

The customary greetings over with, Frank got down to business. "I'm sorry, Som, but we won't be able to fly back tomorrow, so Joy won't be in work on Monday... and neither will I, unfortunately". He did not go into details, but left it that Joy had fallen ill, was with her mother and under the supervision of a doctor.

"I see", said the kindly Somchai, 'Er, I really hope that Da, er. I mean, Joy, gets better soon. I will pass this information up and inform you of the correct procedure to take. Possibly, I will phone you back, or perhaps the head of personnel will".

"Yes, that's fine, Som. Just one thing. Use Da's number if you like, but please use mine between nine and one UK time - three and seven in the afternoon Thai time. Thanks very much... We will meet up again soon, yes... and go out for a drink... We will look forward to it. Bye for now... Yes, I'll keep you informed. Bye". He clicked the "Cancel Call' button.

He was exhausted and checked the time. It was four forty-five. He might still catch her, if she really wanted to see him. He finished up and left.

Boo was still sitting at 'his table' - and she was flanked by her two usual girlfriends.

"Hello, ladies... may I join you?" he asked sitting down opposite them without awaiting an invitation.

"Yes, sir", replied Boo, "do you have any prick sauce for us so that we can prove our skills to you?" The three girls laughed this time, Boo's friends behind their fingers. Frank guessed that Boo had let them in on some private joke.

"Deo, a beer Chang for me and whatever the ladies want". Boo translated for him and it promptly arrived.

"Cheers, girls", he said. "Now, Boo, what is all this prick nonsense about?"

"Oh, it is not nonsense... You have a Thai wife, no? I thought you would know that prick means chillis and that 'naam prick' means chilli sauce or chilli juice. You did not know? I am very sorry if you think I led you up the garden path. No, I do not want that!"

He didn't quite believe her, but her story was plausible, if prick meant chilli in Thai. As he was talking to them on random matters, he looked it up and it did mean what she said it did.

They all chatted for a while and Frank was thinking of enlisting Boo's help with his visa, when she said, "Would you like to suck our, er, er, nom? I forget the word in English... Your Chang is finished and it is hot'.

Sensing another trap, before answering, he looked the word up. It meant 'milk' or 'breasts'. They were each drinking soya milk out of a carton.

"Let's put it this way, Boo. You are very clever with your words... I don't want a suck of your milk, but I do want to suck your tits!" He tried to convince himself later that he had been trying to shock her into silence, but it was an uphill task.

"No, problem", she said calmly, "on Saturday afternoon". Then she and her friends got up and left him to his own devices.

'What have I done now?' he thought, as he ordered another beer Chang.

It was five thirty, or eleven thirty in the UK. He wished the embassy would ring and get it over with so that he had some news for Joy. He went to Elle's to be that bit nearer to 'home', ordered a beer and phoned Joy's number. Bew answered. "Da is in the shower", she informed him without emotion.

"OK, just tell her I will be an hour late. I am waiting in Elle's for a phone call from London", and he hung up trying to be equally cold to her.

When Elle brought the second beer over, she lowered her large, shabbily clad frame down opposite him with a heavy sigh and a smile. He eyed her suspiciously hoping that she only wanted to take all that weight off her feet and not wanted to chat. He wasn't in the mood, so he pretended to be busy with his phone. The awaited call eventually came. "Mae London! - My London mother!" he lied proud of his first attempt to speak Thai. Elle smiled broadly and leaned in closer. She believed that all good sons were close to their mothers.

"Frank? This is Somchai. Good news. There is no problem at this end with Da having extended leave due to illness. However, the regulations state that she must provide written evidence from her doctor within one week of not showing up for work. Full details will be sent from Bangkok to her registered address in, er, Baan Lek... that is where you are, right? ... Good. The letter will recommend the Pitsanuwed Hospital in Phitsanulok.

"It is the best hospital nearest to you and is used by the local government staff in that city. We have an arrangement with them... Da should know all about it. Anyway, any problems and give me a ring".

"Thanks, Somchai. That's a big help. All the best..."

He hung up cursing under his breath because he hadn't thought that they might insist on a medical. Of course, they would! Any employer would, even his own. "Idiot!" he said a little louder and lowered the phone. He was confronted by Elle's puzzled look from less than two feet away. "Mae London sabbai? - Is your London Mum well?" she asked. He knew the word 'sabbai' meant health or healthy, because it was a greeting that could accompany a waai - 'sabbai dee' - 'Good Health'.

He thought that the best defence was avoidance, so he ordered another beer and took out his Kindle to read.

∞

He sat with Joy the following morning as usual, but she still wasn't speaking. Halfway through his breakfast of tea and cake, he tried again.

"Joy, my dear, we have some very important things to discuss. Please try hard, I need you to understand me and give me your advice". She spared him the briefest of glances, but her expression was not the one he had expected. It was bitter and resentful - her eyes and lips were drawn narrow. It shocked him, but he continued anyway.

"Today is the twenty-ninth..." She shot him another of those looks, but held it slightly longer. He was still puzzled, "do you know what day that is?"

"Friday!" she sneered.

"Yes, we were supposed to be going home today, but you cannot travel for twenty hours in your condition, so..."

She cut him off, tears in her eyes, "So, you are going to leave me here and fly home alone".

He was beginning to understand. "No, my darling! No", he said pushing the table out of the way and shuffling his chair up tight to hers. He took her hand. "Whatever gave you that idea?"

Through many sobs and tears, she managed to get out, "I just thought that you have a good job and a nice life n London... You don't want to be stuck with a crazy Thai wife who hears voices in a house where people won't talk to you in a village where no-one can talk to you eleven and a half thousand kilometres from home. It makes sense for you to divorce me and find a good, new lady..."

He put an arm around her shoulder and squeezed her hand. They were both in tears. "Is that what you think I've been planning?" A sob, a nod and a glance were his reply. "I wouldn't give up on you ever and we've only been married a month - a month ago tomorrow! Jesus! Marrying you was the best thing that ever happened to me and yet these last three weeks have been the worst in my life and yours too, I'm sure".

She nodded and squeezed his hand tightly. Tears dripped onto their clasped hands like rain.

"No, I am not going anywhere without you, my darling wife", and then he remembered that he might have to break that promise, "No, I have something else to discuss with you. I rescheduled both of our flights yesterday for the fourteenth, the day my visa expires. I also phoned Mike, my boss, and told him and today I phoned Somchai at the embassy and told him. He said that you should get a letter here from Bangkok on Tuesday or Wednesday".

"You are not going to leave me?"

"No, it never crossed my mind... Why ever would I want to do a thing like that? I love you!" Joy lifted their hands to her heart, pressed them to it and kissed his.

"Oh, thank you, thank you, thank you, my love. I love you so much, I die without you..."

He put his forehead to the side of her head. It didn't seem the appropriate moment to say that he might have to go to Nan or even Laos in ten days or so.

When Joy had recovered sufficiently, she fed the remainder of the cakes to him and handed him the glass of tea as and when she thought that he needed it. She appeared to be deriving great pleasure from behaving like his handmaiden.

"Is that what your relapse was all about? How stupid of me! I thought it was because you were upset about your family ostracising me".

"That did upset me, but when they reminded me that our flights were due soon, and I knew that I couldn't go with you... well, that just made it worse".

"What? The bastards suggested that I would leave you behind? What a low-down stunt to pull".

"No, it is not like that... It was their duty to think of all the possibilities. Let me try to explain.

"Usually, when you, or we Thais, have a problem, we try to sort it out for ourselves with advice from a spouse or possibly a friend, like you do in the West. However, when it is a big problem, one that you cannot solve on your own, or one that may affect the whole family, you take that problem to the family and ask for their advice and help.

"That is effectively what you did by taking me to my sister's and bringing me home here. You, and I, if I was sane, involved the family and they were grateful, because it was the correct thing to do. It was what they would have done. However, once you involve the family, you are expected to abide by their majority decision. Otherwise, you are effectively saying that you know more than all the wisest people in my family put together and that is insulting.

"Do you follow?"

"Yes... So, why did Gail ignore anything I had to say in Bangkok and keep me out of the loop?"

"I don't know anything about that... No-one has ever mentioned that. If that was what she did, then she was wrong and I apologise for her disrespectful behaviour. You are not Thai, but as my husband, you have the right to speak your mind where it concerns me.

"These people don't know Westerners; they only know the traditional Thai ways. You broke the family code and so you are being punished. It is why Bew cannot be seen to be friendly with you. She was the only one, besides you and me, who voted to complete the first doctor's course before consulting a new doctor. We lost, but we have to go with the majority. You started shouting. Raising one's voice, especially in an argument, is considered very bad manners and loses a lot of face for the one shouting. Very bad

"We Thais need our families. When times are hard, there is no social security; when you are sick, you must pay to go to a good hospital. Only a few have insurance. This is not the West. Without our families, whether we agree with them or not, many poor, sick Thais would die.

"Most Thais simply do not have the money to be individuals like Westerners yet. Some people see that as a good thing, others do not. If Thais had more money, we wouldn't need such close families, and if we didn't need them, perhaps the bonds would weaken, and we would become more like Westerners, less Thai. Many are frightened of that, seeing it as the break-up of our traditional society. It is a national debate that rears its head more and more often.

"Our society is deeply unfair, but we still have each other. Yours is also unjust, but your family bonds are weaker. Who knows which is the better?"

"Perhaps, you will one day, my love, after we have been married for thirty years and not only thirty days".

"Perhaps", she said, "but I like the idea of being married to you for thirty more years". He squeezed her hand and looked into her face.

"So, do I", he agreed and winked. She winked back, then closed both eyes and was asleep - a knack that many Thais have, but he suspected that the relief of knowing that he was not intending to abandon her, and the concentration it had taken to deliver her explanation about the family code, had exhausted her.

He kissed the top of her head, went for a shower, a walk and a beer, despite it still being early.

He resisted the temptation to wait in Deo's for Boo to come home from school. It didn't seem right to talk to and lust after her, when his wife had seemed so much better just now, so he just sat in Elle's and drank a beer slowly. He had finished his book, and had seen the advert for the sequel, *Tiger Lily of Bangkok in London*. It seemed appropriate, like a good omen, so he downloaded it from Amazon. The Lily in the book was a feisty young woman who reminded him of how Joy had used to be, she was also crazy, which was an unfortunate parallel with how Joy was now. He hated himself for making that latter comparison. She was much better today, he told himself. It took him four beers to reach six o'clock, then he bought three more and went home.

He was pleasantly surprised to see Joy standing at the gate, but then Bew ran up behind her and took her by her shoulders and other, less pleasant scenarios presented themselves to his mind.

"Were you coming to join me?" he asked hopefully?"

Joy shook her head, started crying and walked towards him arms outstretched. "I think she thought you had gone for your plane".

"Silly mare", he soothed kissing the top of her head. Bew took the bag of bottles. "My case is inside and my passport is in your bag. I couldn't go anywhere even if I wanted to, and I told you this morning that I am waiting for you".

"An old lady told me over and over again laughing that you had left me by the back door".

"Which old lady? I'll knock her and her old man out… and kill their dog, if they've got one".

Joy pointed at her head. "She's in here…"

"Oh, that old lady", he said looking at Bew. "Well, just tell the old bag to shut up…"

"She won't shut up… I've already been terribly rude to her, but she takes no notice".

"I wish I could give her a piece of my mind, because I'm right fed up with her, I can tell you. Come on, let's go inside. I'm also fed up with being stared at by those old farts on the table too. By the way, thanks for voting on our side, Bew. Joy told me all about it". She turned and led the way inside.

She took them up onto the verandah, settled Joy in and scuttled off, returning minutes later with a bottle of beer, a glass and a bucket of ice for Frank. "I have seen you drinking it with ice in the village", she said looking down. "Aunty Da, you have a surprise for Frank, don't you?"

Joy looked around as if she needed reminding. Bew mouthed something in Thai. "Bread", said Joy. "maybe bread, butter and ham, but no cheese, I think".

"That's fantastic, darling, how did you manage that? A ham sandwich would go down a treat, especially with a cold beer". His mouth was genuinely salivating just at the thought of such a luxury.

"Er, Mae asked the mother of one of the local girls who goes to school in Phichai to look in the 'Seven - Eleven by the station. No guarantees, but people say they think they have seen such items there before". She spoke to Bew in Thai. "The girl is late. She should have been here before you got home. I am sorry, my dear".

"You have nothing to be sorry about… No-one has, everyone has done their best. If it doesn't work out, it doesn't work out. That's how it goes. It was a lovely idea anyway".

Bew heard her name, curtseyed, and dashed away. She returned a minute later and spoke to Joy in Thai. "The girl is here, but she wants to meet you. Will you do that, please?"

"With pleasure!" he replied grinning, "No sacrifice is too great at the moment for a ham sandwich".

"Thank you, darling. You know what young girls are like; they are very curious. Bew, tell Boo she can come up for a minute".

His heart leaped into his mouth. He didn't know whether to hope that it was the same one or that it wasn't, but he didn't have long to think about it. The pretty woman who bounced into view with collar-length blue-black hair, twinkling eyes, a sky-blue blouse and calf-length pleated navy skirt was 'his' Boo.

He watched her walking towards them flicking her skirt with her free hand, but she gave no sign of having met him before. She spoke to Joy, handing her the carrier bag and then fishing in her deep skirt pockets for the change. It looked as if it was about six Baht. Joy thanked her in Thai and told her to keep it, then said, "Frank, do you have something to give Boo? She gave up her lunch hour to get this for us".

"Sure, what shall I give her?" Boo swivelled on her hips to look at him, her face pointed at his groin, but her eyes were on his.

"Er, twenty Baht". He looked in his wallet, removed a twenty and handed it to her. She curtseyed, waaied him and took it.

"Thank you, Aunty, Da, thank you Khun Frank", she said.

"Ah, that's right... Your mother said that English was your best subject. Why don't you come around here sometimes and you can get some conversational practice with Frank? He's very bored, because he doesn't know anyone to talk to but me and Bew, and we're often, er, busy. You wouldn't mind would you, Frank?"

"Er, no, of course not, not if you don't, dear".

"Why should I mind? That's settled then. You can sort the details out with Bew both of you".

"Thank you again, Aunty Da and Khun Frank. I'm sure I will learn a lot. I had better go home now". Joy turned to face the bamboo, interview over, but Boo held out her hand to shake Frank's. "See you soon", she said transferring a piece of paper into Frank's outstretched hand, "Good night".

"Good night", he repeated watching her bottom sway away from him, and putting the piece of paper into his pocket to be savoured later.

After a couple of ham sandwiches.

The Ghouls of Calle Goya

18. BOO'S DEN

Later that night, just before going to bed, Frank sat in the toilet and read Boo's note. It said in English, 'If you want to see me tomorrow, walk towards Elle's, but take the first left. Turn right and take the third left. It is a path between rice fields. Walk for 300-400 metres to some trees. Sit on a log and wait. I will be there at three. Boo x'.

He lay it on his hand, took a photo with his phone and saved it to a secure folder. Then he tore it into tiny shreds and added it to the mess beneath him. He had no idea whether he would go or not, but he finished his business, took a shower and went to bed. Joy was muttering in her sleep in Thai, but he thought it best not to wake her.

∞

Joy was still complaining to the old lady in her head when he got up at ten. Apparently, Joy had given Bew instructions on how to toast the bread and the squares of processed ham. She made a good job of it too, but the women insisted on scraping the few square millimetres of black off lest he 'get cancer'. 'Everyone' knew that burnt toast gave cancer, they agreed. Frank actually liked a small bit of burn, but considered it puerile to argue under the circumstances. He was also given freshly squeezed orange juice for the first time, and felt that it was one of the best breakfasts he had ever eaten. It was brunch by the time he had finished it. Then he went for a shower and put on his only remaining clean clothes. He asked Joy to ask someone to do their laundry and she agreed. Frank only wondered whether she would remember to do anything about it.

Two o'clock seemed a long time in coming, once he had decided to look for Boo's den. He went to Elle's first for some Dutch Courage. Had two swift ones and then followed the route that was ingrained into his memory.

The path between the small fields was narrow and crooked. But he could clearly see the copse that she had mentioned. It appeared to be about fifty yards wide and he entered it cautiously. It turned out to be about fifty yards in diameter. It was almost impossible to see into from the outside because of the perimeter bushes that were taking advantage of the sunlight, but once inside that natural fence, there were plenty of shaded, almost barren patches.

It was like a clearing in a forest, although it was not large. There were several fallen trees to sit on. He chose one and took out his phone, but there was no signal. He started to play a game, but it was spoiled when he considered that he might be in a trap. He could easily be killed and robbed here, buried in a field and nobody would ever be any the wiser. Joy would probably assume that he had abandoned her and might even end up in a mental home as a result. He was a sitting duck.

He wished that he smoked to give himself something to do but be frightened every time the breeze or a small animal made a noise. All of his senses were on edge.

The tension was worse than his university, bank, or Masonic interviews. He checked his phone, it was three seventeen. He would give her until half past and then never trust her again. As the time dragged by, he tried to appreciate the beauty of the glade. It was cool, airy and green and he had a log to sit on. He tried to remember the pranayama yoga breathing exercises that he had learned from a girlfriend in university, but breathed deeply and slowly anyway, because it seemed to help. He had chosen a place on the log from where he could observe the path that he had travelled for at least a hundred yards and maybe twice that. He stared down the path and counted the seconds down.

When he heard an engine approaching, his first reaction was to hide. He hid behind a tree opposite from where the sound was coming, which was the other side of the copse that he had approached from. He assumed it was a farmer checking his crops. The engine stopped and he prepared an excuse for being there. He tried to look innocent... He decided to say that he was 'just exploring' or 'looking for wildlife... snakes and crocodiles would do it, he thought. Then he realised that no farmer here was likely to speak English. He decided to just walk back the way he had come and say that he was lost. As he left his hiding place as nonchalantly as he was able, he heard a voice behind him.

"Hello, Frank, are you leaving so soon?" He looked over his shoulder and was ecstatic to see that it was Boo. She was wearing a loose T-shirt, shorts, a huge smile, and had a Seven-Eleven carrier bag in one hand.

"What do you think of my den?" she asked.

"Er, it is very, er, nice", he replied guardedly, "but what if people come?"

"Why should anybody come here?" she asked. "All this land belongs to my parents, and if they do come, what are we doing wrong?"

He nodded in agreement, but had been thinking that the whole point of being there was 'to do something wrong'.

"OK, you're the boss, what are we doing here?"

"We're going to have a barbeque", she replied holding up the carrier bag, "you are going to give me some lessons in English, and I will teach you some Thai. Is that all right?"

"Yes... great! I'm looking forward to it. What do you want me to do?"

"Right. First, we should move over there... and then you can make a fire on those ashes... Can you make a fire?"

"I can lay a fire, but I don't have a lighter..."

"OK, you do that; I have one on my motorcycle. I'll go get it, and you make a fire".

There was already a pile of wood by the fireplace; he only had to find some kindling, which was not difficult. As he was arranging his materials in place according to his memories from his Scouting days, hands were placed over his eyes.

"Guess who?" came a familiar female voice.

"The wicked witch or the woods", he said and put his hands over his shoulders. He found two naked breasts. He squeezed them over and over again and groaned even as she did. He pulled her onto his lap, kissed her once on the mouth and then sucked her whole left breast into his mouth. He squeezed her buttocks and felt for her pussy. She wriggled to pull her shorts down so that he could do what she wanted. He pushed his thumb into her, rolling it back and fore until she came noisily. He was scared that her cries would attract attention, but he was so turned on that he could not stop. Her fluid was dripping off his hand onto his lap and he was loving it.

After coming several times, she pushed herself up. "Come on, take your clothes off. It's not fair that I am the only one naked". As he unbuttoned his shirt, she pulled his shorts and underpants down in one swift movement. "That's better!" she said as she started to suck on his hard cock. He let the side down again and came in her mouth within two minutes. She showed him his spunk on her tongue and then swallowed it.

He was exhausted, but Boo looked as if she had only just started. "You get the fire going, and I'll make our love nest more comfortable". He watched her lay out a blanket as he started the fire. "Did you like that bread yesterday?" she asked.

"Oh, it was the best food I've had for weeks", he replied.

"Did Da or Bew have any?"

"No, I don't think Thais like bread... or dairy".

"I'm glad, but it's funny you should say that about dairy... The reason I was late bringing the shopping to you, was because I opened the bread and rubbed each slice on my breasts just for you, and then repacked them. I rubbed this bread in my pussy because I knew for sure that only you and I would be eating it. You can think of it as my own special spread!" she laughed. He was getting another erection, and it didn't escape her attention.

"Shall we do something about that for you, before you dangle it in the fire?" She led him to the blanket by his dick. As they began foreplay, he asked, "Doesn't anyone else ever come here? It's quite hard for me to, er, relax..."

"Have no worries, Frank. I've been wandering around here naked for at least four years... since I was about eleven anyway..."

"Four or five years since you were eleven! Christ Almighty! That makes you fifteen!"

"Yes, but I did say at least four or five years".

"You also said that you were nearly eighteen".

"Yes, well, that was a slight exaggeration, but it is the direction that I'm heading in".

"Really? I don't know anyone who is heading in a younger direction, do you? So, how old are you, honestly?"

"Sixteen and a half, but I am on the pill. My mother noticed my interest in boys a long time ago and had this contraceptive implant put in my forearm. Strange place to put it, don't you think? Anyone who knows what that blue mark means, knows they can shag me and there will be no babies. It's like giving them the green light to chat me up... not that I mind... I like boys, that's why my Mum had it done. Boys like girls, so why shouldn't girls like boys? That's what I think". She threw her right leg over him and inserted his cock. "There, what could be nicer than that?"

He had no answer to her logic, so just got into rhythm and tried to last a little longer this time, but it was so very difficult.

After they had toasted bread on the fire, eaten it, washed it down with a bottle of beer that Boo had provided, and made love again, she suddenly announced that she had to go. She took his boxers, wiped the excess fluids from herself, threw her three items of clothing on in a minute and pulled the blanket from under him, like a magician pulling the tablecloth from under wine glasses. Frank laughed as he rolled into the leaves. "What's the hurry?"

"It's five o'clock. Mum will be expecting me home to help with the dinner, and you don't want her or my father coming here to look for me, do you?"

The very thought sent all the ardour from his mind and body. "No, you run along. I'll be gone in a few minutes as well".

"You can stay as long as you want, but please put the fire out before you go. You will find a small shovel under one of the logs around the fire. I'm going to keep these as a souvenir", she said holding up his boxer shorts. I'll see you tomorrow same time".

He began to say that he wasn't sure...

"If you don't say now that you will be here, I might ask a boy from school... Most of them are very keen to get to know me..."

He was horrified. He found that he could no more countenance the thought of his Boo with another boy than he could Joy with another man.

"I will be here..."

"You are jealous! You cannot bear the thought of me sucking another boy, can you?"

He tried to give a dishonest answer, but he had to admit that he could not.

"Good, I will see you tomorrow. Bye-bye, sweetheart!"

She ran through the bushes at the opposite end of the copse where she had entered it and he heard a motorcycle engine firing up and driving off. He listened until the noise had vanished. He sank deeper and deeper into his own despair, and then started to dress himself commando style, sans underwear.

When he reached the outer circle road, he had an idea. He knew that Joy's sense of smell was terrific, and she had told him that all Thais shared the same ability. He personally couldn't smell anything on himself, but he knew that Boo had rubbed her pussy all over him, so he sat by the fetid irrigation channel that ran between the outer circle road and the rice fields and lowered himself into it. He ducked his head under with some trepidation, and remembered to hope that no-one had witnessed his charade. Then he walked a hundred yards or so back towards the glade and walked back to the road. It was five thirty, but the sun and his body heat were enough to dry his two items of clothing to just 'damp'.

Satisfied that he had masked 'his girl's' body smell, he walked to Elle's. When she saw him, she tried to ask him why he smelled so bad and was damp, but she didn't get anywhere.

He wanted to fire as many beers into himself as he could within an hour or so to provide an excuse for falling into the ditch. When it was obvious to him that that tactic wasn't going to work, he ordered a half bottle of Johnny Walker and took a shot after every swig of beer.

That worked a treat. He stood up when Elle brought his three beers to go home and the bill, and fumbled in his pocket for his wallet. It was under his handkerchief, but he could not extract it. He had drunk too much, so he pulled everything out together and put it on the table.

He was looking at Elle's face in apology for his clumsiness, when he saw a smirk spread over her countenance. He followed her gaze and was horrified to see his wallet enveloped in a pair of small pink knickers with a white lace bow and trim. He snatched them up quickly, but he realised all too late that that seemed to accentuate his guilt.

He smirked, pretended to be embarrassed, not that that was difficult, and said, "Da, my wife, washing machine…" while imitating the drum revolving and the clothes becoming entangled. As a finale, he put the wet knickers back in his pocket.

He never found out whether, Elle either just didn't understand his explanation or didn't believe it, but he sensed that the knickers were another nail in the coffin of his fate.

When he got home, Bew definitely noticed the smell coming from him, saying, "Min!" One word which has many meanings, but in this case, 'What a horrible smell'. The opposite was 'hom'. He knew those words because of his socks and the aftershave lotion that Joy had bought for him at Christmas.

"I fell in the irrigation ditch", he said, wafting a hand before his nose.

"Da is upstairs".

"Thank you, Bew", he replied, noting that it was the most they had spoken to each other in three or four days. He hoped that the ice between them was starting to thaw, that his punishment was over.

He ran upstairs, making such a row that Joy was turned to face him when he arrived at the top. He held up a hand in greeting and walked over to her.

"Hello, what happened to you? You look as if you have been dragged through a hedge backwards and then thrown in a lake".

"I was walking through the rice fields", he started, sitting down and opening a beer, "when I saw an irrigation channel. I was looking down into it for fish, but I thought I saw a snake, so I tried to get a closer look. I slipped and the next thing I knew, I was in the smelly water with whatever I had seen, but I don't know what it was because I didn't see it again".

"I see. You should take more care. It could have been a cobra or any of the other dozen types of poisonous snakes around here. You can't sit here drinking beer smelling like that… you look like a farm labourer. Go shower and change".

"Yes, darling, right away". Under the shower, he thought about flushing Boo's panties down the toilet to get rid of the last piece of evidence, but he didn't want to part with them, and if they blocked up the awful plumbing, he would have some explaining to do. He decided to burn them on the fire after Boo left the next day.

The next day! 'What was he going to do about her smell tomorrow?' he wondered. He couldn't fall in a ditch again. He transferred the panties to his new trousers and rejoined Boo.

"What a life!" he murmured regaining his seat and beer.

"Did you say something, dear?" asked Joy.

"Just 'what a bloody life?'".

"Am I becoming a burden? I'm sorry... I'm sure I must be... and this house and this village..."

"No, Joy, no! I didn't mean you. Definitely not! I was referring to falling in that smelly water... You will never become a burden to me. I love you very much. I do miss the old Joy though... but I know that she will come back to me one day... I just hope and pray that it is soon".

Joy held out her hand. He took it and began to cry. "I am still with you, Frank... it's just that I get dragged or blown away sometimes... You are my mooring and when the rope tying me to you breaks and I drift away from you, I struggle and struggle to get back to you to tie up again, because I know that you will always be there waiting for me... You will, won't you, Frank, always be there waiting for me to come alongside and moor up again?"

"Of course, I will, Joy! Always. Never doubt that. For forty years, I thought I was the big, strong loner who didn't need anyone. You taught me the joy of loving someone, of having somebody special... I have always thought that you were so aptly named. You are my joy and my wife". He felt so guilty, but meant every word that he had said. He squeezed her hand tightly, still weeping, and Joy squeezed it back, holding onto the one and only rock left in her world.

∞

After lunch the following day, at which Joy seemed abnormally lucid, he asked her to take him for a walk to look for snakes. She declined the offer, saying that she wanted a nap, so he left on his own as always. As he passed through the gap in the bushes at the end of the trail, he could see Boo's head above the log that had shielded them from casual view the day before. He guessed that she was lying on their blanket with her head propped up on her hand and he was right, but she was also stark naked. As he stepped over the log, the first thing that he noticed was that the sparse hairs on her pussy had been shaved off. Her vulva was pouting as if she had been playing with herself while waiting for him. He put a hand down and stroked it.

"Do you like?"

"Yes, that style suits you, madam", he replied trying to be witty.

"I am not a madam", she said rather coldly. "Now come here and let me undress you". She cupped his balls and wanked his cock until he could take it no longer and she directed the spray over her torso. "You always come so quickly the first time, so I thought it was a good idea to get it over with. Are you happy with my decision?"

He was still too out of breath to reply in words, but he nodded, smiled and lay down beside her.

"Did I upset you by calling you 'madam'? If I did, I didn't mean to".

"No, you didn't upset me. I was only playing with you. Before, a long time ago, but even now sometimes, when rich falang ladies used to come here and look down on us, they often insisted that we call them 'madam'. We hated them, but didn't mind using the word, because in Thai it is two words: 'ma' meaning dog, and 'dam' meaning black. Since the dog is just about the lowliest of mammal creatures, we thought it apt and funny".

"Nice, but where do you get all these sayings from... like prick sauce?" She moved her hand down from tweaking his nipples to checking the readiness of his undercarriage. As she pulled his foreskin back to his scrotum, he missed a breath.

"Oh, that's nice. Don't stop doing that..."

"My cousin tells me them. Remember? I told you about her... she works in Bangkok. She meets lots of falang in the bars. She says that they are very kind, and very generous..." He felt the hint, but was silenced by the feel of her hand.

"Here is another one for you. Why are many men who make love in the dark gay?"

"I, er don't... er, know", he said coming again. She drew every last drop out of him, licked her hand clean provocatively inches from his face, and dried it on his hairy chest, before taking him in hand again. "Easy! Because 'dark' means bumhole in Thai. Get it?"

"Yes... that's very good". He put a hand down to her and she put her foot the other side of him to allow him easy access.

"I was wondering when you would remember my pussy, after I shaved her especially for you this morning. Yes... that's lovely..." She spoke Thai in loud groans for a few seconds and then came, hugging his neck to her with one hand and working his member with the other. They had both given up watching for intruders long ago.

It took a lot of coaxing and a lot of trying on both parts for him to come inside her, but that was the way she seemed to like it... long and slow. After forty-odd minutes, the magic happened and they lay back panting. Ten minutes after that, she sprang up and announced that she had to go. He watched her get dressed and pull her knickers on.

"I can't give you these, as much as I'd like too. Mum asked me where yesterday's were this morning. 'I don't know', I said, 'I put them in the machine with everything else; they must be where all the missing socks go'. I think I got away with it, but I'll have to be careful now. See you tomorrow, lover!"

She bent down, kissed his cock and was gone. He lay there for quite a while with a huge smile on his face, until he noticed the light starting to become dimmer. He got off the leafy bed and sat on the log, then took the large bottle of mineral water that Bew had given him and washed himself. He didn't bother drying, but got dressed wet. Then he unwrapped the sandwiches she had made for him also, took one to eat on the way and scattered the others in the glade for wild animals. The thought that the wildest animal he had ever seen there was Boo brought a smile to his face. He looked around him and liked what he saw. Boo was lucky to have a place like this, he thought and he was lucky that she had shared it and herself with him. He decided to keep her panties a little longer and so started off to Elle's with these happy thoughts in his head.

After a couple of bottles, he went home. Everything was the same, nothing had changed. Joy was on the verandah with the left-over food after she had eaten enough to earn her tablets.

"Did you find any snakes, dear?"

"Only this one", he said showing her a selfie of his one-eyed trouser snake.

"I haven't seen that one for ages", she said taking his phone and touching the picture. "At least you didn't fall in the klong this time... er, the irrigation channel".

19. UPS AND DOWNS

Joy's old personality was almost recognisable on Monday. Nobody knew the reason for it, but Frank hoped that it might be the result of his reassurances and his joke about his snake the previous day. Everybody else hoped that it was due to the daily visits to the Wat and the new medication that she had been taking, but Frank didn't know that the family had taken her to another doctor behind his back.

However, whatever the reason for her sudden recovery, it was all for nothing on Tuesday morning when the letter arrived from the government confirming that she had to make an appointment at the Phitsanuwed Hospital in Phitsanulok.

"I am finished", she muttered. "Now, I will lose my job, lose my visa and lose my husband. Please, Frank, do not let that happen to me... I want you to kill me first... Please, allow me the dignity of dying as your wife, not your divorcee".

He held her close, reassuring her that none of what she feared would happen and shouted for Bew - the first time that he had openly admitted that he couldn't cope. She noticed that as well and came running. As Joy wept into his chest, he handed Bew the letter. She read it, spoke to Joy in Thai and nodded at what she eventually said.

"I will make an appointment for this afternoon or tomorrow... It is best to be as helpful as possible" Frank nodded to Bew in agreement, touched her forearm in gratitude, then felt awkward about having done that and said it verbally. She nodded, gave a brief smile and went downstairs for her phone.

That night, Joy cried, Bew cried and so did Frank, all night under Joy and Frank's mosquito net; they were all fully clothed but slept together on either side of Joy when she got off, but this time, neither of them worried about their arms touching.

∞

The three of them were a bundle of nerves in the morning, but none more than Joy. She was convinced that her life was over and that the old lady in her head had been right, and nobody could convince her otherwise. It seemed to Frank that his wife was sowing the seeds of her own dismissal, even though that was the last thing that she wanted to happen. Which doctor could find her fit for work, even with all the goodwill in the world? He knew that not even he would employ her in her present state of mind.

The son of one of the old fogies drove Mae, Joy, Frank and Bew to Phitsanulok the following morning. They started off at ten for the eleven thirty appointment. Nobody but Bew was allowed to accompany Joy through the tests and interview and that was only because Joy was obviously so fragile that she needed someone with her.

Frank had not even been considered for the role.

The complete examination took over four hours, but they weren't asked to contribute towards it financially and they were not given any of the findings. Perhaps, Joy would be allowed to ask for them one day, but they certainly were not being offered freely.

The car, full of people, was an exceedingly sombre place to be during the ninety-minute drive home. Everyone knew that Joy had made a hash of it, just as she had known she would. No-one wanted to speak, lest they say what was on everyone's minds - that she had blown it and would be sacked.

The three of them slept together again, when Joy wasn't crying.

Frank was glad that Bew was getting used to sharing their bed, because he was soon going to have to broach the subject of his visa, and he wanted someone to sleep with Joy in his place. It was strange, he thought, in Bangkok he had found Bew so attractive that he couldn't take his eyes off her, but now he considered her a sister-in-arms, albeit a pretty one. His respect for her had transcended the physical despite her tender years.

Remembering Boo, suddenly, he was amazed at how quickly Thai females grew up. Maybe they weren't any different from girls all over the world, he thought, but he didn't know. He had only ever tried to get to know girls for one reason all his life. Even his wife, but she had opened his mind to another dimension of womanhood.

It was his problem, not theirs that he found it difficult to see them only as sex objects. Pretty or not pretty, young or old, available or not... that was how he had always judged a woman. He had to talk to all his female colleagues, but socially, he only spent time on the ones whom he fancied and who might succumb to his patter.

He was beginning to think for the first time in his life that that might be wrong. After all, he had never wanted to sleep with a man, but he still talked to them. It was all so confusing. He raised his head above his wife's and looked at Bew's beautiful young face. Her eyes were closed but he could not be sure that she was asleep and the last thing that he wanted was to be caught staring at her... not after winning her respect back, or so he saw it, because she was now talking to him. He ducked behind Joy's head again quickly and tried to sleep.

∞

He was awoken by Bew coaxing Joy to go for a shower and breakfast. The room was beginning to light up naturally, so it was dawn. He decided to keep out of it and pretend that he was still asleep. Joy resisted a little, but soon went with her young nurse. However, it surprised him that they did not return for several hours. When he arose at what had become his normal time - about ten - they were both on the veranda. As usual, Bew stood aside when he approached.

"It's all right, Bew, this concerns you as well. Please stay where you are. Joy, I know I said I would never leave you, but my visa will expire soon, so, from what I have read, I will either have to go to Laos or Nan. Is that correct? I need your help on this".

She looked at him for a few seconds. Her face told him that she could not comprehend how any anybody could possibly value her opinion.

"Come on, girl, I need your advice. This was your job and your husband needs your help. I need your help... What should I do?"

She stared at him, and he stared back, challenging her.

"Er, if, er, you want a visa extension", she said slowly as if racking her brains for distant memories, "of, er sixty days to do something specific... You must go to Nan... but if you, er, have a non-specific reason like tourism, you must obtain the visa from outside the country".

"Thank you, darling. What is classified as a specific reason?"

"Er, voluntary work, to become a monk, to study, to visit your family, to play football..."

"Wait there... to visit family, eh?" She nodded. "Well, you are family, aren't you? So, I can apply for a visa on those grounds, or not?"

"A visa extension, yes... thirty or sixty days..."

"OK, I'll take the sixty days... I will wait for you no matter how long it takes, my dear, and after that one has expired, I'll get ten more, if I have to..."

"No, you cannot... You would be better getting a married extension of twelve months..."

"Then I'll do that, girl. I will wait for you to get better no matter what!"

"Thank you, my dear, but what about your job?"

"They can stuff their job... if it's a choice between you and them, you win every time".

She turned her attention from the bamboo to look at him, tears in her eyes. "You mean that, really?"

"Of course, I do! I have been saying it for weeks... you just don't remember, do you?" She looked at him with the inscrutable face that Orientals are famous for, but admitted nothing. "OK, Joy, how do I get one of those?"

∞

Frank's life was sad and lonely and had been for almost a month. Joy's life was notable for its bad days and less bad days over the time from when she had fallen ill to the present, but there was no distinct pattern. Boo continued to demand Frank's attention and he gave it guiltily, but he felt that she was the only friend he had while his wife's mind was elsewhere. He was extremely grateful to her, but also sometimes resented her demands on his time, which he knew was selfish, but it softened the guilty pain of being unfaithful to his beloved Joy. His life was a mess of contradictions, but then, everybody else was struggling too. The only difference was that, without Boo, as young as she was, he was completely alone eleven thousand kilometres from his friends and family, whereas the others had them on their doorstep.

He was not proud of his affair with Boo, but despite her age, she was the only person on the vast continent of Asia, who took away his fears, even if it was only temporarily, and even if she frightened him half to death for other reasons, and he loved her for that... not as a sixteen-year-old, but as a person who was capable of keeping him sane, while his whole world was disintegrating around him. He knew, without a shadow of a doubt, that if it wasn't for Boo, he would be on the verge of a nervous breakdown himself, and would have to go back to Britain and abandon his wife, who needed him more at that moment than she probably ever would again.

If they were both lucky, and Boo was the glue that kept him sane enough to help Joy.

He knew that it sounded like a hollow justification for his affair with a horny, ambitious teenager, but no matter how much he thought about it, it still rang true.

If he gave up Boo, he would eventually give up Joy and go home.

That was the bottom line as he saw it.

∞

One morning, after Joy and the family had returned from the Wat, he re-raised the subject of his visa.

"Joy, you said that if I go to Nan for a visa extension of sixty days, you would have to go with me. Well, I have been looking at the map, and that's about three hundred kilometres away... Are you up to that? Otherwise, I have to go to Laos, and that will take three days".

Joy looked confused. "You want me to go with you to Nan?"

"Er, yes, if you are up to it, but do I need you there?"

"I'm not sure now. I don't know any more..."

They could see that see was becoming distressed because she couldn't remember.

"I will find out for you, Aunty Da. Perhaps the rules have changed". She pushed a few buttons on her phone and was soon talking to Nan Immigration. She confirmed that Joy would have to be there too for that visa. Frank and Bew exchanged glances; they both knew that it was dubious whether she could make such a journey.

"I could go to Laos alone", he offered, but Joy shook her head. "Ladies, there are two options! Either I go to Laos alone, or I go to Nan with my wife! There is no third choice! I will do either, but I must do one and within a couple of days. I don't want to leave it until the last minute.

"Look, I'll tell you what, I'll go to Elle's for an hour and you can tell me what I am going to do when I get back. OK?" Bew just gave him a non-comital stare, but Joy was unhappy. "I'm sorry, kids, but we only have two choices and since I am obviously only a foot soldier here, I will go to the pub and await your highness' decision". It did not go down well, but what he had said was accurate, and he knew it. He walked off with the air of the righteous.

He really didn't mind which option they chose, except that if he had to go to Laos he might be able to get out of the crazy situation he was in for a day longer. He loved his wife, and he loved Boo, but not in the same way, and he had a lot of respect for Bew, but the three of them and all the old fogies were doing his head in. He didn't know how much longer he could take it. Getting away for two or three days sounded wonderful. An hour later, he went back to receive their decision.

He found them where he had left them. "OK, what are we going to be doing, ladies?" he asked sitting down.

"Aunty Da wants to go to Nan with you".

"Right, OK, but she gets very travel sick and she cannot take pills for that with the prescription medicine, so how are we going to get around that?"

"We thought that we would try to keep Aunty Da awake a little longer each night and only give her half a sleeping tablet. Then, when we drive up to Nan, she will be tired and we can give her a whole tablet. She should sleep all the way there and back, with luck. It might mean carrying her into the immigration police office to give her signature though".

"All right, if that's the way you want to do it, that's OK by me. It will still be hard on her though".

"Yes", agreed Bew, "but Aunty Da wants to make sure that nothing happens to you".

"I am touched. Thank you, Joy. I understand what a sacrifice that will be for you". She only looked at him and shook her head for a reply.

"When will we go?" was his only other question.

"We think that we will need three days to prepare, so we can leave on the fourth", replied Bew.

"That's fine by me", he answered.

∞

The following afternoon, he went down to Deo's shop to see Boo and tell her that he would be away for a couple of days getting a sixty-day visa extension, so that she wouldn't think that he was avoiding her and do something stupid, by which he meant go off him or ask his mother-in-law where he was.

"Where are you going?" she inquired.

"Nan for two days. They seem to think that we will be coming back the same day, but I think that Joy will need a night or two in a hotel up there before she will be in a fit state to travel".

"How are you getting there?"

"Bew said that one of the family will take us by car".

"I went there once on a school trip. It's beautiful all the way, but it's high up in the mountains and the roads are rough. It might be less than three hundred kilometres from here, but it is a four or five hour drive each way at least. It's great fun, if you're well, but I wouldn't want to do it if I were sick like Aunty Da... Why don't you fly up there?"

"I didn't know that that was an option... Where from and where to?"

"Er?"

"Airports... where are the airports?"

"Oh, I see. At this end, there is one at Phitsanulok and one at Sukhothai. You will need to check if they fly to Nan Airport, but I should think so... I think it's about two thousand Baht per person each way and takes twenty or thirty minutes".

"Boo, you are a darling. Thank you so much". He looked around to see if anyone was watching and kissed her on the forehead.

"My pleasure", she said, "I'm glad to be of service, but 'darling' is one of those words like 'madam'. It means monkey shit".

"Oh, sorry about that, my, er, my dear". She smiled and nodded at the revised endearment.

When he arrived home at seven, his wife and Bew were already in bed. He waved at Bew as he passed their mosquito net and held up his Kindle. He saw her nod in the shadows as he walked on through to the balcony. He opened one of his carry-outs and sat down. The moon was almost full and all the light that he needed. He went online, and typed 'flights from phitsanulok to nan' into a search engine. He didn't like to tout a new alternative until he was certain that it existed. His reputation with the family and Joy's health would not bear a false hope.

He was glad that he had taken the cautious approach, because it was not possible to fly from Sukhothai or Phitsanulok directly to Nan, but it was possible to fly from either airport to Bangkok or Chiang Mai and then fly to Nan. It added an extra four thousand Baht per person, but that was not an issue. It cut the actual travelling time to about two and a half hours. It would still take about five hours each way, but Joy would be sitting in an airport for half that time, not a car. By the time he had worked everything out, including the itinerary and flight plans, it was gone ten, so he showered and went to bed. He drifted off to sleep, pleased that he had good news for Joy in the morning.

He was awoken abruptly by a kick in the shin. It took him a few seconds to realize what had happened. He had always been slow to regain consciousness, but he was also a little hungover.

Bew was comforting Joy, but Joy was lashing out with her arms and her legs saying things in Thai. It looked for all the world to him as if she was having an epileptic fit. Bew was doing her best to restrain her, but without using excessive force. Joy was mumbling about something, which he correctly guessed to be her medication. Joy held her head and shouted 'Shut up!' The only two words he understood, but he assumed that she was talking to the old lady in her head, not Bew and him. Nevertheless, he was shocked and horrified to witness his wife behaving in such a manner. It was outside his experience, way outside and he didn't know how to handle it. He wanted to roll over and let Bew take care of her, but Joy was his wife and his responsibility, as he had rightly asserted in Bangkok. He was beginning to wish that he had thought before opening his big mouth. He had often thought about the expression 'Be careful what you wish for'. This was his own real life lesson, and he was not enjoying it.

Bew helped Joy out from under the net, and led her to the table, but

Frank could hear everything, even if he had to guess what they were talking about. He wished that he were deaf, because the anguish in both women's voices was too painful for him. Joy wanted the tablets that stopped the voices, but Bew insisted that she take them with food, as the doctor had recommended. Joy argued that she was not hungry, and couldn't possibly think about eating until the voices had been silenced.

Bew capitulated, but demanded that she eat some of the food that had been prepared beforehand. He was later to discover that the scene that he had witnessed that morning was a repeat of similar such fiascos before. It was difficult for him to realize, as a fairly high-ranking officer in his bank, that he didn't know how to handle this situation… that he didn't know how to take care of his own wife.

After Joy had taken her tablets and was making a show of fulfilling her end of the bargain by eating miniscule amounts of food, Frank joined them. He realised that this was the point in the day when he normally first saw Joy, after the tantrum and when the tablets were having their calming effect on her troubled mind.

"I have some good news, ladies", he said leaning on the veranda rail in front of Joy. "We can save half the travelling time by flying to Nan".

"There is no flight from here to Nan", said Bew, "I checked".

"That is correct, but it still takes less time to fly to Chiang Mai and then fly on to Nan than it does to drive there from here. We could even have a night or two in each city on the way back, if you like. What do you say, Joy?"

"It's up to you".

"Is that all you've got to say? I thought you'd be pleased. No, I thought that you would be more than pleased, I thought you'd be ecstatic".

"Yes, I am, darling, of course I am. It's a good idea", but she still said it with all the enthusiasm of a condemned man who has the choice of being shot or hung.

"Have you ever been to Chiang Mai before, Joy?"

"Yes, it is very beautiful. I have never been to Nan through".

"How about you, Bew?"

She shook her head. "I've never been to either of them".

"Nor have I. It will make a lovely break for the three of us, won't it?"

"It's up to Aunty Da".

"Yes, all right… What do you say, Da, er, I mean Joy?"

"Er, yes, OK".

"Great! Can you book us three flights to Nan via Chiang Mai, Bew? The sooner the better for me, but in any case, no later than Monday the eleventh and not on the weekend, because the visa office isn't open then. Here's my credit card. Joy knows any details about me you may need. Have a chat and see which day suits you best".

While Frank went for his shower and Bew went to prepare his breakfast, Joy was left on her own. Through the almost constant fog that was her current existence, she knew that it would do them all good to get out of the claustrophobic, and for Frank, even depressing atmosphere of her mother's house, but it took a lot of effort to maintain that thought. All she could really imagine was the effort it would take to get up out of the chair, go down to the taxi, wait for the plane et cetera, et cetera. It was wearing her out just to think about it.

She was dreading the journey already. All she really wanted to do was sleep... or die. She had asked Frank to kill her several times, she remembered that... She didn't think she had asked Bew, that would be too awful, but she might have. She hoped she hadn't put the child through that though... although she still wouldn't mind being dead... the confusion in her mind when the effect of the tablets was waning was too much to bear. She felt as if all her life, she been admiring the view from the edge of a cliff when a sudden fog had come down. She wanted to go back to safety, but was frightened to take a step lest she fall over the edge.

The fog was cold and damp and she wanted to be warm again, but where was that place? She was too frightened to move from where she was, although it was horrible to be there. The tablets took all that worry away. They didn't lift the mist, they made her not care about the clammy chill of the fog and the pain in her legs from being rooted to the spot. She saw Frank return, sit down and hold out his hand to her. She grasped the lifeline and began to weep. She was safe again for a moment at least.

"Frank?"

"Yes, darling?"

"I love you... you won't leave me, will you?"

"No, of course not. Whatever gave you that idea?"

"Chiang Mai..."

20. THE VISA RUN

Bew informed him that Joy would like to leave on the Monday and handed him back his credit card. "I only booked the one way", she said. He nodded wondering why Joy couldn't have told him herself, but he didn't ask. He would be counting the days down to be able to get away even if it was only for a few days.

What he didn't know was that Joy had consulted a monk that morning on which of the days left to them was the most propitious one to fly on.

The flight was from Phitsanulok at nine ten in the morning, so they had to be there for eight. They would be in Chiang Mai within thirty minutes, have to wait thirty-five for a connecting flight and be in Nan by ten fifteen. The immigration office was seven kilometres down a dual carriageway from the airport and the city centre another five from there. He and Bew were looking forward to the trip. They were new cities for both of them and Bew had never flown before. Joy was the only wet blanket, but then she was still unwell and had flown hundreds of thousands of miles on business.

Joy and Bew did the packing the night before and went to the Wat to pray for a safe journey and a good result at six. Joy's cousin picked Frank up from the house just before six thirty and then met the ladies at the Temple and they were off. Joy was sick less than thirty minutes into the ninety-minute journey to the airport, but he had seen her worse. She didn't want to take sleeping tablets until just before the first flight.

When they were eventually sitting in the aircraft on the runway, Bew was a little frightened by the roar of the engines in the small plane, but she put on a brave face and held Joy's hand. The half a sleeping tablet that she had taken was being to take effect, but she managed to comfort Bew before she fell asleep. Their strategy with the medication worked quite well, but Joy and Bew still made straight for the ladies on touch down. Frank sat in the bar over a coffee and waited for them, but they didn't appear until the call to board for Nan was made twenty minutes later.

"You were both an awfully long time in there, were you that sick?" They both glared at him, but neither offered an explanation, so he just followed them to the jet and waited to see what would happen next. Again, Joy and Bew held hands for the take off and then they both appeared to go to sleep. The food was unusual for him. He was offered a curry or a box of chocolates on both fights. He knew from his association with Joy that his stomach would not put up with curry before seven pm, so he opted for the chocolates, which were hand-made and delicious. When they touched down in Nan Airport, they had to hire a taxi to take them to the immigration office, since Frank had not taken his driving license on holiday with him, Bew didn't have one and Joy was incapable of driving.

They filled out the visa extension form, stuck Frank's photo on the front and awaited their turn with an immigration officer. It was not long in coming.

"Two copies of your house book, please", said the female officer at desk number two.

"I don't have a house in Thailand", replied Joy, "we are staying with my mother. I work at the Thai Embassy in London. We are on honeymoon, but I have fallen ill".

"I see, but I cannot process this form without the correct paperwork, you should know that".

"Yes, I am sorry, but I am not well".

"What's going on?" asked Frank since all the talking had been in Thai. They all ignored him. "Excuse me, but this is my visa application and I demand to know what is going on".

"One moment, sir" said the officer and Joy put her head in her hands. The white strings around her left wrist and neck became obvious to the officer. Frank saw her looking at them. People received a string bracelet every time they went to the Wat, usually once a week, but sick people often went once or twice a day. Joy had a dozen or more on her wrist and three amulets on string around her neck.

"Did your mother inform the police that she had a foreigner staying with her?"

"I shouldn't think so. She's in her sixties. She wouldn't know that she had to do that".

"It is an offence not to inform the local police within seventy-two hours".

"Look, I'm fed up with this! My wife should not even be here! The doctor said she was too sick to travel! This is my visa, leave her alone!"

"Please, Frank, the officer is correct; she is only doing her duty"

"Perhaps so, but if I had known that I was going to get all this bullshit here, I would have gone to Laos..."

"Frank, please, leave this to us. You may think that it is your visa because it is going in your passport, but you are here because of me, and I have to vouch for you".

"OK, but I want to know the problem". Joy explained and Frank muttered something under his breath, but let them proceed.

After a lot of debate to which the station commander was called. The first officer addressed Frank.

"Two colour copies of your passport; two recent copies of the house book where you are in residence and two copies of your wife's Thai ID card".

Her accent was poor and Frank unwisely responded, "I didn't understand much of that, will you say it in Thai to the ladies, please". Joy was pacing the floor waaing something or someone invisible. Bew was walking with an arm around her shoulder. The officer addressed Joy, but Frank intervened.

"I think that you will get further talking to my niece". She did so. "Do you know what we need, Bew?"

"Yes, photocopies", she replied.

Frank looked around the room. "There's a photocopier over there. Why can't we use that one?"

"Please to go outside and bring me the correct paperwork", the officer said directly to Frank. "If you cannot find a copy machine outside, perhaps I will help you".

"Outside? Outside where? In the bloody garden?"

"Please, Frank, let's go". They led him back to the taxi, but he was tamping mad. "You don't understand, Frank. Didn't you notice the sign on the door? Immigration Police. They are not just immigration officials as in the UK. They are armed police officers and, although we have all been requested to be nice to the public, we don't have to tolerate abusive language or behaviour. Please remember that when we come back. You should apologise to the lady".

"Yes, you are right, my love. I was out of order. Come on then, what now?" Bew phoned her grandmother and asked her to get a lift into Phichai immediately and have a copy of her house book made at the Civic Offices. Then she was to have it scanned and emailed to her phone. Her grandmother didn't understand, but the man who had given them a lift that morning did, and he offered to help get things sorted out within the hour. Bew pointed out that it would be lunchtime at noon, and that would mean that they would lose an hour. Meanwhile, their taxi driver took them to a print shop where they could get photocopies made.

They arrived back in the police station with fifteen minutes to spare before lunch, but both of the immigration officers were free and they had Joy sign the copies and put the stamp in Frank's passport within that time.

"Thank you very much for all your help, madam", he said with a smile remembering Boo's words. "I apologise for my rudeness earlier, but I am very concerned about my wife's state of health. I am sure that you understand".

She nodded curtly, said, "It is my duty and my privilege", and walked away, presumably for her lunch.

"Thank you, darling", said Joy, "I am proud of you".

"OK, now that that is over, let's go and have a look around Nan, shall we?" Joy was obviously reluctant, and Bew followed her lead.

"I'm not really up to it... Do you mind?"

"Well, we have come a long way and we do have the taxi until six. We could get a couple of rooms?"

"No, let's ask the driver to show us a few sights and then take us to a good restaurant and then we'll just go home, eh?"

"You don't want to stop in Chiang Mai either?"

"No, not this time. We'll come back next year for a better look around... when I'm well again".

"All right. Whatever you say, my dear".

Nan proved to be an exceptionally beautiful city, and the food at The Isaan Garden was wonderful. He had heard that Isaan food was some of the hottest in Thailand, but the Nan version was just to his taste.

They booked the return flights from the outdoor restaurant and caught the two thirty flight back to Chiang Mai. Again, the ladies surprised him by going straight to the toilet and not coming out until boarding time. They were back in the village by five thirty. Frank went to Elle's a rather disappointed man, despite the fact that the main reason for going had been achieved. He could now stay with Joy until she was well enough to return to London.

Boo had seen the taxi pass through the village and followed it on her bicycle. She sat opposite him in Elle's.

"You're back soon. I thought you'd be away at least a couple of days. Did you get your visa?"

"Yes, all that went well enough, but Joy didn't want to stay in Nan long, and she spent all of both of the stop-overs in Chiang Mai locked in the toilet".

Boo began to laugh.

"It's not that funny!"

"Oh, yes, it is, but you don't get it again. One of Thailand's biggest and most famous mental institutions is in Chiang Mai! She must have thought that there was a chance you were going to take her there... Oh, I shouldn't laugh really... It must have been awful for the poor woman. Yes, excuse me. Anyway, it's nice to have you back. I had better be going home for my dinner. See you".

"Yes, see you, Boo". It was no wonder that Joy had wanted to get back to the safety of her mother's house as soon as possible, he thought. She must have been going through all sorts of mental torture for days, wondering whether she could trust her new husband not to have her locked up in an asylum.

After his three beers, he trudged home, wondering how he would put his foot in it next time, and whether he should broach the subject with her, but that would involve telling her who had explained about Chiang Mai to him, and admitting that he had told a girl about her odd behaviour. He was torn: he wanted to comfort his wife and tell her that he understood her anxiety, but did not want to make her think that he had been discussing her with a young girl. He decided to say nothing for the time being.

Joy was in a good mood, when he arrived. She was on the balcony, but she took the dishes from Bew as she brought them up and placed them before her husband herself - the first time she had done that for weeks.

He knew that she had noticed that he was aware of the fact and smiled at him broadly. "This is far better than Chiang Mai, isn't it? Aren't you happy now that we didn't stay there?"

"Yes, my darling, this is much better, but I would never have left you in Chiang Mai on your own... We were only ever going to be there for a visit".

"Yes", she said, not letting on whether she knew that he had divined her fear, "but we can always go back another time, when I'm a hundred percent better".

21. THE FOG BEGINS TO LIFT

It seemed that the realisation that Frank hadn't been plotting to have her locked away, had a beneficial effect. She began to take more interest in her appearance and was more thoughtful of others. She still wanted her mind-numbing tablets on time, but she stopped throwing tantrums for them like a spoiled child wanting sweets in a supermarket check-out queue, and stopped promising to eat after having been given the tablets and then breaking that promise. In short, she became better behaved.

However, this new behaviour did not mask the fact that she still relied heavily on her medication to stop the voices, which she insisted came from outside her head. When the effectiveness of the drugs was on the wane, she could tell you where a voice was coming from. Sometimes, she would beckon you to help her surprise someone who was annoying her from a hideout nearby - behind a door or under the stairs, and the fact that there was never anyone there did not deter her from wanting to try again the next time. She was like a puppy dashing around trying to catch its own tail, but instead of being amusing, it was heartbreaking.

Frank would often try to talk to her about the voices, and he guessed that Bew did too. He had been horrified to witness her mother screaming at her one day, so had recorded it on his iPhone for Boo to translate. She repeated several times, "Bai loei, khun ba", which Boo had told him meant, 'Go away, you're crazy!'

It sounded terribly harsh coming from a mother, so Frank looked for alternatives. He was not a linguist by any means, but he didn't know how good Boo's command of English idiom was. Of all the options he could think of including the very rude alternative to 'go forth and multiply', he hoped that she had been saying 'Get away with you, you're crazy!'

However, no matter how much he could mitigate the meaning of the first half of the phrase, he could not soften the second half. 'You are mad/crazy/bonkers/as nutty as a fruitcake', all sounded like the wrong things to say to someone who was nuts, even if only temporarily. It seemed overly harsh, taking telling the truth too far. Her mother seemed to be lacking in compassion. It seemed to say more about her than it did about Joy. Had she always been so heartless, or did her age make the stigma of Joy's mental illness too much to bear. He had been on a course at the bank on Asians and

Face, since more and more of his bank's customers were from that continent and many of them were wealthy, some exceedingly so.

Despite that, he didn't know whether there were regional variations or differences between how seriously individuals took a loss of Face.

However, whichever way he tried to justify his mother-in-law's words he found that he could not. It also made him realize that he had never once seen her put her arm around Joy, or pat her shoulder or hand, kiss her or simply speak to her in a manner that sounded even remotely tender. She and Joy hadn't even touched each other when he and Joy had walked in through the gate and he knew for a fact that they hadn't seen each other in at least a year.

There was no escaping the fact that they seemed to have a cold mother-daughter relationship by Western standards. Joy seemed closer to Bew than she did to her mother.

He had no way of knowing anything at all about the other people who sat on the garden table most of the day and sometimes stayed the night under mosquito nets in the same room as them. Neither Bew nor Joy were offering any information about them, although Joy had implied once that they were local members of the family. They seemed a cold, heartless bunch to him as well after the way they had kept on to Joy about going to the doctor until she was crying. He wasn't particularly close to his own family by any standards, but they would never have done that to him, never in a million years.

Bew neither offered an opinion nor asked for his. He could see that she loved her aunt, but she was a sealed unit as far as he was concerned. She seemed to speak to him only when she had to, and never about the elephant in the room - Joy's mental health. However, he and Joy needed her help more than any other single person's. In many ways, she was more useful than a doctor, whom you visit once a fortnight, because she was the nurse who took the aggravation from the patient night and day, twenty-fours hours relentlessly. There was no relief shift for Bew; she was truly on her own no matter how much he tried to help. Perhaps that was why she kept her feelings locked up, under guard, he thought. Perhaps it was the only way she knew of dealing with the pressure.

Joy talked to Bew often, he had heard them, but he didn't know what they talked about. They never volunteered the information and he never asked, not liking to intrude.

His own conversations with Joy were hit and miss, in that sometimes she revealed snippets about what was bothering her and sometimes she didn't. More often than not, she revealed nothing in fact. It annoyed him intensely that he found himself becoming angry with her if he thought that she was not trying to help people to help her. He could feel himself losing patience with her and he didn't like himself for that. He thought that he would have boundless patience for his wife, but it seemed that he did not. It dismayed him as much as her illness did. It displayed a flaw in his character that he thought he didn't have.

It made him ashamed of himself more than his liaison with Boo did. She was often his rock. He admitted to himself that he enjoyed the sex, and he admitted that he was flattered by her attention, but often there was no-one else for him to turn to, despite her youth. He was also aware that Joy had told him that many girls were desperate to escape village life. In his less egotistical moments, he knew that that was the real reason for her interest in him. He usually quickly forgot it again, but the seed was well rooted in his mind. He had been a fool to take up with her, despite the comfort she had been. He should have tried to keep her as a friend, not as a lover, in spite of what had happened at their first encounter. She was another unknown, a loose cannon, as the saying went, and as such could prove to be more trouble than she was worth. He knew that he would have to decouple himself from her very gently. Very gently indeed.

After several days of this improved behaviour, he and Joy were sitting on the balcony one night talking about the stars, when she suddenly changed the topic.

"What do you think about going back to Bangkok? Moving back in with my sister?"

"Sure, if you want to, but I thought that you have more friends and family here, more support?" He checked his mind for any selfish motivation for not wanting to go because of Boo, but there was none.

"Yes, that's true, but I don't like everyone thinking I'm crazy here and Bew should go home". He had forgotten that this was not her home. Of course, she had her own disrupted life elsewhere... a life that she had to try to piece together again one day. She was sure to be missing the support of her girlfriends and maybe there was a special boy there as well.

"Who thinks you're crazy?" he asked innocently.

"Everybody".

"Who, for instance? I don't".

"I hear people talking at the Wat and people who come to visit here... Even my mother thinks I'm mad and that means that at least half the people at the table do too. Thank you for saying that you don't think I'm barmy".

"I don't think it... I think that you are having some kind of nervous breakdown - causes unknown, but exacerbated by those people who did those horrible things to us in Fuengirola for whatever reason they had for doing that. This is just a temporary phase; I'm convinced of that. You are not bonkers".

"Thanks. Will you call Bew, please?" He went to the top of the stairs and called her name, although he could just as easily have learned over the balcony and done it. She followed Frank to the balcony and leaned against it in front of Joy. "Yes, aunty?"

"Frank and I have been discussing what to do. You need to go back to Bangkok, don't you?" she asked in English.

"Yes, soon", she replied in Thai.

"Let's keep it in English, so that Frank can take part, shall we? So, soon, eh? How soon?"

"That is up to you".

"No, not really. We need to be where you need to be".

"OK, thank you. It would be nice to be there by next weekend".

"Fine, then we will try to leave on Friday. Shall we fly again? You like flying, don't you?"

"Yes, it's a bit scary taking off and landing, but scary can be fun too".

"Great! Well, get Frank's credit card off him tomorrow and book three singles. Oh, I suppose we had better ask your Mum first".

"She won't mind. She'll be glad to have us back... in spite of Frank's snoring".

"It's not that bad!" he interjected.

"Oh, yes, it is", replied Joy, "especially if you're a bit tiddly and lying on your back". The both women giggled behind their fingers and Frank was so happy to see his wife smile again. It was the only time he could remember Bew laughing too, which he found sad for such a pretty young girl. She had had everything going for her, and then she had been lumbered with their problems. It was a shame, but she had stood the test well and would be all the stronger for it. This whole nightmare would pass, indeed, was already passing.

That night as the four of them lay inside their mosquito nets, Joy suddenly sat bolt upright put her hands together high before her face and began to chant something in Thai, probably a prayer, Frank conjectured. The light was switched on and her mother shouted something at her. Bew slipped under their net like a fish being released back into the water by an angler. Mum stood outside the net still shouting. Frank discerned the words 'ha more' again.

"Go and see the doctor! I told you to go and see the doctor, didn't I, but you never listen to me, do you?" she said in Thai.

"I did go to the doctor! Can't you remember? You're the one who needs to see a doctor. I did go in Bangkok and here a few days ago. It's these new bloody tablets, they don't work".

"Well, go to another doctor and get some new ones!"

"I can't keep running from doctor to doctor hoping for the best. That really is stupid!" and then in English, "Frank, can you hear a woman, the old woman, outside? She is saying that I am going to die now". Bew translated for her grandmother.

"No, I'm sorry love, I can't". Joy waaied and started chanting again.

"Stop praying to dogs! You crazy girl". Joy jumped up, slipped under the net, held the curtain back an inch and peered out. Her mother ran to a cupboard. "Perhaps the old woman is in here? Come out, old woman and say your piece! Oh, she's not in there either. Maybe on the balcony? No, or on the stairs? No, again! Why? Because she is in your head, you stupid girl! I keep telling you, go to see a doctor!"

"It's midnight in the middle of nowhere! How can I go to see a doctor now?" she screamed. All this was lost on Frank, but he could feel the emotions, especially the anger and anxiety, and he could see Bew and Joy crying. His mother-in-law's face was very stern, and it made him feel like joining the younger women in shedding tears. He felt so useless. He put a hand on Joy's knee and squeezed it.

"I will die here, Frank, or they will put me in a home and I will die there. You will have to go back to London alone and find a good, new wife. I am so sorry that I let you down, my love".

That did it. He burst into tears. "You are not going to die any time soon, and I am not going back without you... I love the wife I've got, I love you, I don't want a new one... I just want the old one back".

Mae went back to bed grumbling to herself, and eventually Bew went to, leaving them both staring into a non-existent distance with tears rolling down their faces.

"Lie down, darling... try to get some sleep".

"I cannot sleep", she whispered tapping a temple.

"Try, please. Do it for me. You look worn out". She nodded, dried her eyes on the inside of her nightdress, and put her head on the pillow. He held her hand and she snuggled her backside into his stomach. Minutes later, he heard her breathing change. She was at peace, but he didn't get a wink of sleep himself, until he felt her get up at six. She was calling Bew for her early morning fix of mind-numbers.

He dreamed that he was on a battle field fighting a real war. Bullets were whizzing by and shells exploding all around him. Soldiers were falling down, but when he looked more closely, they were all made of plastic, cast in fixed stances. He was the only real person there.

He got up at sevenish and went to join Bew and Joy on the balcony. Joy looked the same as most mornings, but a little less helpful than she had been of late. He thought that she might be embarrassed.

When Bew went for his breakfast, he said, "So, what are we going to do?"

"Do about what?"

"He looked at her incredulously. "About you, about last night! It was pretty horrible... We can't go on like that, can we?"

She shook her head. "No, you will have to go home alone... Leave me here. I will walk around the village all day with the other crazy lady until a drunken car-driver puts us out of our misery one day".

"Oh, please, Joy... No wonder, people think you're crazy, if you talk like that. That is crazy talk. No more, eh? Concentrate on how you're going to get well, not how you're going to die".

"I will try, my dear, but that is how I am thinking. I feel that I have led a charmed life. I went to university, met some great people, got a wonderful job and moved to one of the most exciting cities in the world. There I met my dream lover and married him. For my honeymoon, he took me the place I had always wanted to go. I came from here", she emphasized by spreading her arms around her, "but I have led the life of a princess, but now it is my time to pay for it all. It is my Karma and no-one can escape one of the immutable laws of nature. Not even a princess". Tears welled up in her eyes. "I fear, no I do not fear anything with Buddha beside me, I think that my time has come. I just don't want you to go back to your old lonely ways. I want you to be happy, and I like to believe that I made you happy some times..."

"You have always made me feel like a king... I have never been happier. You are the best thing that has ever happened to me, Joy. Please don't talk about leaving me, I couldn't bear it. I need you more than you will ever know".

When he recovered from his despair, Joy was holding his hand tightly. He hadn't remembered holding it out to her, and he hadn't noticed Bew deliver his food either, but there it was on the table: coffee, toasted bacon sandwiches made with Boo's titty-bread and banana cakes. It was a meal fit for a king and he offered half of it to his princess, but she would only accept a banana cake the size of a large modern coin. Bew had obviously seen the emotional outburst and slunk away to give them some privacy.

One of the few things that he had learned about Thais was that they abhorred public displays of emotion, especially love and anger.

Joy drifted in and out of sleep and Frank read his book over the next few hours until it was time for lunch and Joy's second batch of tablets for the day. There was a noticeable difference in the hour before she took her tablets and the hour after. It was as if she had taken a highly-charged vitamin drink. She was full of life and ready to talk. Frank could only assume that the accumulation of tablets for weeks on end was helping, but that there needed to be a minimum amount of medication in her body to achieve a positive effect. After his lunch and shower, at about three, he asked Joy if she would like to go to Elle's with him. To his utter surprise, she accepted and even called Bew herself over the balcony to help her get ready. It was indeed a red-letter day.

Joy insisted that Bew accompany them, but Frank did not object to that. It seemed that the only place she didn't accompany her to was the bathroom anyway.

When the time came, they set off. Joy on his arm and Bew half a pace behind on the other side holding a parasol over them, ready to catch her if she should fall. The parasol only covered the two women. They looked like high society rich people out for a stroll accompanied by the lady's handmaid. In Europe, Frank would have found the scene embarrassing, but in the 'old worldliness' of Thailand, it did not seem out of place. Elle rushed out when she saw the group coming and wiped the table and benches. Joy and Frank sat on the inside of the table looking out over the street and Bew sat opposite them.

Frank had his customary beer, Bew wanted an ice cream and Joy wanted mineral water. They sat there like an estranged couple sharing a day with their child. No-one had a word to say except Elle, who found numerous petty excuses to visit them and ask questions. It all went over his head, but he was becoming bored with the constant interruptions, and he could see that the incessant questions were wearing his wife out too. After about twenty minutes, she pressed down on his thigh and looked into his eyes. She closed hers and shook her head almost imperceptibly. She had had enough and wanted to go home, but he was proud of her.

He walked her home then returned to finish his beer. He had one more and took three home. Elle had tried to question him further in her unique variety of English, but he wasn't playing ball. In fact, for the first time in weeks, he was glad to get back.

That night, Joy lay awake for almost an hour gripping Frank's hand in bed. There was a look of fear on her face as she stared at the ceiling through the mosquito net, but he didn't believe for one moment that that was what she saw. He could only imagine the terrors before her eyes by watching the grimaces on her face and the fear in her eyes. However, she did not cry out and they both eventually found sleep.

∞

The following morning, Joy actually woke him up when she returned from the Wat at eight thirty, which was a first.

"I have some wonderful news for you… for us", she announced. "Come out onto the balcony, Bew will be bringing you your breakfast soon". He was excited by the excitement and enthusiasm in her voice. He slipped out under the net that Joy held up for him and then offered her his hand up.

"What is it, darling?"

"Outside", she replied and dragged him along. She was like a child who wanted to show someone her new bicycle. "Sit down. We are going to get married tomorrow!", she exclaimed clapping her hands, bouncing at the knees, eyes wide. He didn't know what to think. "Aren't you excited?" she asked, noting his lack of enthusiasm.

"Er, yes, but I thought that we were already married".

"Yes, we got married in the UK, I'm not completely crazy, but we said that we would hold a Buddhist Wedding Ceremony as well. Don't you remember?"

"Yes, of course! Sorry, how stupid of me… but that doesn't give us much time to practice, does it, or organise everything?"

"Don't you worry about a thing. The family and I will do all that".

"But, don't I have a rôle to play as well?"

"Of course! You're the groom! You're the leading man! What has got into you? Shock, I suppose, eh? Nerves? Well, you just leave everything to us. You just spend the day as if nothing is going on. Read your book, go for a walk, go to Elle's, do whatever you normally do, because Bew and I are going to be busy all day.

"Bew! Oh, there you are". Bew put the tray down for Frank and allowed Joy to lead her away talking excitedly in Thai.

"So, I'm getting married tomorrow in Thai in the Buddhist style and I am not to worry about it. How the bloody Hell am I going to manage not worrying about it?" he said to himself aloud.

He showered after breakfast and returned to the balcony to read his book, but he could not concentrate. He could hear constant activity below, so he shifted the angle of his chair so that he could observe the front yard. People came and went by foot and by car, but no-one came to see him, and then at about midday, Mae, Bew and Joy got into a car and left without saying goodbye, so he left the house and started a full pub crawl of the four shops.

He would have his stag party on his own.

When he returned home some time after dark, he was very much the worse for wear. There were a couple of dozen women of all ages in the front yard. Some were sitting on the table and some were scurrying about, but the atmosphere was fantastic. They were all laughing and talking, cooking and drinking and there wasn't a man in sight. He spotted Joy on the table with a glass of wine in front of her. Her mother had one too and there was a third glass, which he presumed was Bew's.

Joy ignored him, but most of the other women waaied or smiled at him. Suddenly, Bew was at his side.

"This is the ladies' party. Aunty Joy said you must go upstairs and shower. You can watch from the balcony. I will bring you food and a beer in ten minutes".

He did as instructed, and watched the ladies enjoying themselves for a while, but woke up at two o'clock and went to bed. Everyone else was already fast asleep.

The Ghouls of Calle Goya

22. GETTING MARRIED AGAIN, AND AGAIN

He was awoken at five o'clock by the loudest music he had ever heard coming from a house, and it was the house he was staying at. Joy had already left, so he took her pillow and his own and clenched them to his ears, but the sound was reverberating through the wooden floorboards into his body. There was no escape.

Bew was waiting for him outside the bathroom. "Ah, good, you are awake. Aunty Joy sent me to wake you up"

"You are kidding me, aren't you? Every living thing for blocks around is awake. What could sleep through that?"

"It is an alarm call for all the women in the village who want to come and help Joy prepare to get married. Go up onto the verandah, I will be with you in a few minutes".

He took his usual seat and waited. He, or he presumed someone else had put the cap back on his unfinished beer. It was a third full, so he flipped the cap off and took a swig. A hair of the dog that bit him, he thought, but it was foul – as warm as tea. It was at least thirty degrees Celsius above nice.

Bew returned with a tray and placed it before him as she took Joy's usual perch. "Aunty Joy sent me up with this for you. Pork, chicken, buttered bread, cakes, sweets and a bottle of beer. She said to eat as much as you can, then shower and put on long trousers and a white shirt. The shirt has been washed and ironed and your shoes are being cleaned, or you can wear your sandals if you like. They have been washed too. You are to remain here until someone comes for you and you are allowed one more beer before the ceremony".

"When is that?"

"At ten fifteen. Do not come downstairs until someone comes for you". She got up to go.

"Wait a minute. Is that all you're going to tell me before we go to the church, or the Wat?"

"We are not going to the Wat; the monks will come here. People get married at home in Thailand. I'll see you later".

He took some comfort from knowing that the ceremony was to be held 'at home', but not a lot. He shuffled his chair around to get a better view of the yard and started on the four-inch mound of roughly cut hot pork before him. at five thirty, the music was turned down to just loud. An hour later, Bew returned with another beer for him and two paracetamol tablets. "I forgot to give you these before, sorry", she said and left again.

Below, a couple of dozen women were cooking and cleaning and about a dozen men were setting up trestle tables and a canopy to provide some shelter from the sun or rain, if it should fall. Inside the house, two men were preparing the living room for the ceremony. Joy and her mother were overseeing the whole shebang and Bew was doing whatever they asked her to. Everyone, except Joy and Bew were having nips of Thai whisky called lao from time to time.

It was soon light. Time was passing quickly for everyone; for Frank because he was nervous and for the others because there was so much to do. After all, it wasn't every day that the village monks were invited into one's home, and hopefully, one's only daughter only got married once. Everything had to be perfect.

Frank had no timeline to work to, but at seven thirty, he took his shower and sat on the veranda in shorts awaiting further instructions. At eight, the three leading ladies, Joy, Mae and Bew peeled off for their showers and to get changed. Then their stylists arrived to give them a makeover. At nine, a new shift of guests arrived to relieve the workers so that they could go home to change.

At nine thirty, two old men, dressed as he had been instructed to by Bew came to sit with him. They brought him a third beer but couldn't speak English. However, he understood that it was time to dress, when they started to take his short trousers off him. They smiled warmly when he returned dressed still drinking his beer, then they took him by the forearms and led him downstairs still clutching his bottle.

There were about forty people in the yard waiting, all drinking and all smiling at him as he made his appearance. Many wanted to waai him or shake his hand. He was more concerned with finding Joy, but she was not there. Nor was Mae and nor was Bew. At ten to ten, someone relieved him of his half bottle, gave him a full one and led him out of the gate. About half the guests followed him and Bew appeared at his side. She took his arm and led him up the street followed by 'his people'. The music was turned up again and Frank spotted its source: a low-loader parked outside in the street with a bank of Marshall speakers that would have graced any Rolling Stones outdoor rock concert.

Bew led him and the followers in a strange dance that was basically three prancing steps forward, one step back, turn in a circle and start again. In this manner, it took them over thirty minutes to walk around the small block, the streets of which were lined with people drinking, many of whom wanted to give the groom and his escort a sip. He had never seen Bew accept a drink before but she was doing so that day. When they got back to the house the gate was barred and a dozen women were defending it, shouting at him and his entourage. Bew confronted them and shouted back. After five minutes of mock arguing, they admitted Frank, Bew and his crowd.

The yard was packed, but they parted for him and Bew, who still had his arm. Someone took his empty bottle from him and Bew led him inside. All the walls were draped with orange sheets – the glow was calm and relaxing. Joy was kneeling before a stool at the mouth of an arc of nine seated monks, who were also dressed in orange robes. Every square yard of floor space had someone sitting on it. Bew led him to Joy, encouraged him to kneel beside her and withdrew. He had never seen Joy look so beautiful, so serene, so radiant. She was wearing a sarong, a traditional Thai blouse, had her hair up and wore talc on her face.

The monks chanted and the leader sprinkled them with water. Then, those who wanted to, bound Frank's left wrist to Joy's right with white string. It was done about thirty times. The monks filed out and were driven back to the Wat. They were not allowed to eat after noon, so had to get back for their main and last meal of the day.

The couple was asked to kiss and cameras captured the moment. Some said that they hadn't been ready and asked them to kiss again. After five or six kisses, Frank realised that it was a joke. An old man led them upstairs to a bed and Joy pulled him onto it. As the old man left closing the door behind him, he winked at Frank. They lay there quietly, but Joy's lips were moving. Frank thought she was praying, so he tried to think of something appropriate as well. He later found out that she was counting, because the old man burst back in with a big grin on his face.

Mae was sitting next to a bowl with a lot of one-thousand Baht notes in it and a pile of gold jewellery. She looked around herself furtively, picked it and ran out of the house. Frank was encouraged to go after her to retrieve the loot, but he could not because he was tied to his wife who would not budge. People laughed and so did he.

When all the guests were in the garden, Joy cut the bonds between them and took Frank outside. "That's it, my love. We are married Thai style. That wasn't so bad, was it?"

"It was nerve-racking before it started, but everyone was so helpful and friendly that I thoroughly enjoyed it. Bew was a great help. What was the money for?"

"That was supposed to be my dowry".

"What, your mother was supposed to give me all that money and gold?"

"No, silly, you were supposed to give it to me! A bride like me could cost you half a million Baht and ten baht in gold".

"Ten Baht in gold? Twenty pence? That's not worth having, is it?"

"Not ten Baht! Ten baht, with a small 'b'. A baht is fifteen point two grammes, so that's more than five ounces".

"In Britain, the bride's parents used to give the dowry…"

"Not here, matey. Come on, let's join the party".

Between five and six o' clock, most people went home to sleep, shower and get changed. Joy changed into less formal clothes too, but about seventy people returned in the evening to dance and finish off the food and drink.

By midnight, everyone was worn out, but Frank got the feeling that that was about the traditional time to close such parties anyway. He was very proud of the way Joy had managed to behave and dared to think that organising and going through the wedding had 'straightened her out'.

∞

Despite the way Joy had behaved on their wedding day, the pattern of irregular responses to everyday events and auditory hallucinations continued to favour the unfavourable after the event, but gradually the balance shifted back in their favour.

They left for Bangkok two days later when Gail had to return to go to work. The parting from Joy's family and Boo was amicable, but both Frank and Joy were glad to leave. Boo did not make a fuss, which sort of surprised him and Joy's mother did not say goodbye to him, which did not surprise him at all

Being back in Bangkok helped Joy, but not Frank. He missed Boo, and he thought that she felt the same way, judging by their daily phone calls, but as they diminished into several times a week, he realized that he had been replaced in her affections. That was how it should be, he thought, but could not help experiencing a few twinges of jealousy. Deep down, he suspected that he missed her more than she missed him. She certainly never made the trouble for him that he had feared, and that gave him all the reason he needed to dispose of her knickers. He kissed them goodbye, put them in a paper bag and threw them into a skip while out walking one afternoon.

The end of an era.

∞

They had not been able to make the flights on the fourteenth, so they had put them back to the twenty-eighth, a Thursday, which would give them the weekend to recover before going back to work. That was the grand plan, anyway, but neither of them honestly considered it achievable. They reckoned that they would need at least a week in London before they could go back to work, which would make it the first of June. They both thought that June 1st sounded an auspicious date to put this ghastly episode in their lives behind them and start their lives again as a happily married couple.

Frank came to be fascinated by Thailand and the ways of its people, even if he couldn't find much respect for his wife's family with the exception of Bew. In his opinion, Boo was worth more than all the rest of them put together, although he was aware that Gail had done her best for her sister.

Gail, Bew and Frank began a co-ordinated campaign to reintroduce Joy into society. Bew took her to meet her friends for coffee, Gail took her to meet her colleagues for lunch, and Frank took them all out for evening meals. In this manner, they slowly rebuilt Joy's self-confidence, in the hope that she would be able to slide effortlessly back into her job and community in London.

Frank was willing to go along with this belief, so that he could get his wife back to the UK, but he was sure that it would take longer. As an employer in the bank, he knew that he would blackball her for a job, if she came before his interview panel. There was just no way that she was ready to work again, although he did think that she was fit enough to travel, if she was given compatible travel sickness tablets, and that had to be possible. Joy seemed to perk up when Frank told her that a date had been set to fly back to London. It was as if she no longer had to worry about being left behind in Thailand by a husband who no longer cared about her.

As a final effort to bring Joy back into the fold, the four of them organised a civil, or registry office wedding for them. They invited all the people they had introduced Joy to in Bangkok and Joy invited a few of her old friends from university and the Foreign Office too. About thirty people witnessed the signing of the documents. Frank paid for everyone who could make it to lunch immediately after the short ceremony to a good Thai restaurant, which Bew had hired exclusively for their party in his name for two hours. It was great fun with lots of laughter and good food.

The night before they were to leave, they took Bew and Gail out for a meal at the most expensive restaurant they knew of and bought new clothes for all of them. Joy gave Bew twenty thousand Baht for taking care of her. Frank gave her another twenty thousand, not realizing that forty thousand was more than the average teenager could hope to earn in a year, although even if he had known it, he would not have begrudged her the money.

∞

When they waved each other goodbye at the airport the next day, there were many tears, but they had all hugged and kissed each other and the air between them was clear, although he was less enthusiastic about the family in Baan Lek.

23. LONDON

Joy was heavily sedated for the flights back to London. They had to change at Istanbul as before, but then fly on to London instead of Malaga. In hindsight, he wished that he had changed both flights for a direct trip from Bangkok to their final destination. Joy was nervous that her thin mask of normality would slip and reveal her to be the crazy lady from Baan Lek. Between them they pulled it off though by Frank doing most of the talking and Joy being asleep for a lot of the time. He found an old record by Jimmy Cliff of the in-flight entertainment channel and played it for Joy. It was one of his all-time favourites and became one of hers too. It was *'I Can See Clearly Now* (the rain has gone. I can see all the obstacles in my way. Gone are the dark clouds, they've passed me by, it's going to be a bright, bright, sun shiny day). The bright lyrics and reggae beat uplifted her and replaced 'Ghost Riders' as her favourite song, although she still liked to sing that too.

They arrived at Frank's apartment on Friday afternoon. Joy was still groggy from the travel sicknesses pills, so all she wanted to do was doze in front of the television, but Frank felt that he ought to speak to Mike again.

"Hello, Mike, we're back in London... thank you. We just got back to my flat... not twenty minutes ago. I thought that I'd bring you up to speed, since you don't work the weekend".

"Hey! Some lucky people don't have to work for months!"

"It was hard work, Mike. Really hard... the most difficult job I've ever had to accomplish". Tears slowly filled his eyes.

"I believe you, don't worry. I've had a bit of it too, don't forget. Jocasta is, well, let's just say that she is not always the easiest of women to live with. So, how is Joy?"

"She's here asleep on the couch. She's much better than before. The doctor deemed her fit enough to fly, but she had to be drugged up to the eyeballs because she suffers so badly from travel sickness. Still she's here now".

"So, will you both be in work on Monday?"

"I probably could be. The problem is that Joy still worries about everything... and I mean everything... every tiny detail. First, she worried that I wouldn't get a visa to Thailand, then she worried that it wasn't valid; then that I wouldn't get a visa extension. When we had accomplished all that, I thought she would calm down, but no, then she worried that we would lose our jobs, that she would lose her visa to the UK, that we would be separated, get divorced… Oh, and lots more in between".

"Yes, I get the picture. Was she always the worrying kind, do you think? I mean, she didn't appear to be to me, but deep down?"

"It's difficult to say, isn't it? She had, I mean, has a great job, and everyone worries about losing a good job, don't they? But on the whole, no, I don't think that she was a born worrier. Thais seem pretty laid back on the whole. They believe in Karma, fate, predermination and all that… it takes a lot of the stress and worry out of life. I would say that what she has now is very unThai, to be honest".

"So, what are your plans?"

"I thought that we would just laze around the flat for the rest of the day, perhaps look for a new doctor for her tomorrow and phone the Embassy. I can come in on Monday, if you like and try to take Joy to the doctor's on Monday evening".

"That sounds like a good idea. It is best to show your face as soon as you can, not that you have anything to worry about jobwise… er, I mean besides getting Joy well. Er, I could let you have the name of the doctor that Jocasta sees, if you want. She's very good".

"Yes, that would be a big help, Mike, thanks. I'll be behind my desk on Monday, then, Inch Allah - God willing!"

"See you on Monday, old chap. Chin up… give Joy our love. Make sure that you keep me informed of every development, won't you? I mean first and foremost as your friend but also as your manager, OK? Bye for now".

Mike was good to him, he thought. The best friend he had, more of an older brother than a friend. He carefully removed the pillow from under Joy's head and slipped his lap underneath it, then he settled back to see what she had been watching. Tennis! He wasn't a sporty person, and only played squash and badminton because it was de rigeur at the bank. Likewise, with circuit training. He flicked through the channels until he found a film and watched that instead.

∞

With the problem of finding a doctor already taken care of, they didn't have a lot to do on the weekend. They took Frank's old Jaguar E Type out for a spin on Saturday afternoon on the pretext of having lunch in a country pub and doing some shopping. However, Joy even needed travel sicknesses tablets to be able to do that, which reduced the amount of fun or even conversation they could have, so they were back home by four. Joy cooked a mild Peneng with Jasmine rice, Frank's favourite Thai dish. They washed it down with iced water flavoured with chopped fresh lemon, because Joy was still on medication, although drinking alcohol at both of their recent weddings hadn't seemed to do her any harm – and perhaps the opposite. Then they watched films and went to bed.

They didn't go anywhere on Sunday, but telephoned friends and family to report that they were safely back. Both Frank and Joy spoke to Somchai. He advised not going in to the Embassy on Monday if Frank was unable to accompany her for reasons of safety. Instead, he recommended writing a detailed report for the personnel manager and faxing it in. This suited her too. It gave her a project, something to do.

However, as Frank demonstrated his ability to cook a Sunday roast of chicken, roasted and boiled potatoes, carrots peas and French beans with real gravy, Joy helped him, always eager to learn more British traditions. He followed it up, most would say let it down, by serving microwaved Roly-Poly pudding and tinned custard, but nobody was complaining. In good old British tradition, they slept lunch off on the couch in front of a film.

There had been no nightly terrors for Joy for ten days and so it continued, although he instinctively kept a close watch on her during the time between getting into bed and falling asleep. It was her danger zone. On Monday morning, they breakfasted together and Frank went reluctantly to the bank. It was the first time that she had been left alone since she had become ill, and he didn't like doing it.

"Don't worry about me", she urged him. "I'll put a few things away, have a shower and write my report. I'll be all right, honest. Anyway, I know where you are. I'll ring you at lunchtime. Go on now or you will miss your train".

He kissed her goodbye and left, still not happy about having to do so.

Joy was apprehensive too, although she hadn't wanted Frank to know because she knew that he would worry about her. She took a sheet out of the airing cupboard, wrapped it around herself and curled up to watch TV.

Frank went straight in to see Mike upon arrival greeting his colleagues as he passed them. He felt their eyes on his back and heard the rustle of whispers. He knew that everyone was talking about him and his crazy Thai wife. He was glad to get into Mike's office and close the door behind him.

As he leaned back on the closed door, he closed his eyes and it occurred to him that that must have been similar to how Joy had felt. She could hear whispering voices, and 'knew', at least in her own mind, that people were there 'watching' her. Taking the medication was her way of closing the door on it all. He opened his eyes, although he hadn't remembered closing them.

Mike was staring at him from across the room with a look of utmost consternation on his face.

"Are you all right, old son? You look terrible... as if you've seen a ghost or something. Come on, sit down before you fall down".

He did as he was told. "I think I did, in a way. It was just the worry of leaving Joy, and then people whispering about me out there... I think I felt like Joy has been feeling these last couple of months. It was awful... but it only lasted a minute or two for me, for her it was constant. It must have been Hell for the poor woman..."

"Yes, yes... here drink this. I know that it's early and we're not supposed to, but I'm your boss and I'm going to have one with you". He handed Frank a double vodka. Downed his and then refilled both glasses adding half a small bottle of slimline tonic to each. "Phew, your face scared me then!" He was secretly wondering whether he had ever looked like that and hoped that only strangers had seen him if he had.

"Look, old son... you have shown willing, so why don't I send you home to take care of your wife? I can see that you are not going to be much use to us in this state. No, you will be far more useful at home. Make an appointment to see Mary, our doctor. Here's the number I promised you. It was lovely to see you again, but my advice is that you call in sick when you get home. I'll vouch for you.

"Go on, get off home with you... I'd be gone like a rat up a drainpipe if anyone said that to me".

Frank stood up, held out his hand and walked to the door. As he went through it and then turned to close it, Mike was pouring himself an even larger drink. He closed the door quickly and quietly so as not to embarrass his friend. He hurried through the outer office ignoring everyone, then walked swiftly to the nearest pub. He ordered a pint of bitter and a double brandy, then phoned his usual taxi, with which the bank had an account.

When he put the key in the latch, Joy hid under the sheet. Frank found her shivering from fear seconds later. "What is it, Joy? Have you been like this since I left?"

"Er, yes, er, no... I don't remember... I was watching TV in this sheet, then I heard something in the hall and hid".

"I'm sorry... it was stupid of me not to call ahead. Mike has given me sick leave. I think I caught a tiny glimpse of what you have been going through today. It was awful. Can I get in there with you and I'll tell you about it?" They huddled together completely wrapped in the sheet and he told his story.

"Oh, my poor dear!" she said with a slightly mocking tone. Would Daddy like some of Mummy's crazy tablets?"

"You're taking the Micky, aren't you?"

"No, of course not. I'm sure that it was a very harrowing experience for you". She was already holding his hand, but she kissed him and chuckled. "I'm sorry. Not very nice is it when you feel completely alone and that everyone is talking about you?"

"No, it's not... I did say that I only caught a tiny glimpse of what you were going through".

"Yes, you did. Sorry for mocking you".

"I'm not... You have my permission to take the Mick out of me whenever you want, if it makes you smile". He put his free arm around her. "It's cosy in here, isn't it? Shall we just stay in our own cosy little bubble and let the world get on with it?"

"Wouldn't that be nice?" she replied dreamily, "But we can't, can we? You make lunch and I'll finish unpacking".

Later that afternoon, they kept an appointment with Dr. Mary, as they came to refer to her. She was a very pleasant psychiatrist in her sixties. She must have enjoyed her job or didn't want to leave her patients in the lurch, because she could probably have retired years before. She was slightly plump, had short hair and horn-rimmed spectacles. Her surgery was an addition to her lovely country cottage. She could easily have passed for the family's cook. However, her husband had retired from practice ten years before, and their three children worked all over the world. When talking to Dr. Mary, they felt more as if they were discussing a minor family problem with a wise old aunt. At a given point, Frank suspected that she had pushed a button, because there was a tap at the door and her husband, Ronald, brought in a trolley of tea and cake and then left again with only a smile to his wife and the 'friends' she was having to tea.

Dr. Mary changed Joy's prescription before they left saying that she thought that Joy had made so much progress that the medication that she was on from Thailand was too strong for her now. Whether that was the truth or not they would never know. They obtained the tablets on the way home and she started taking them that night. When they visited Dr. Mary four days later, Joy could not swear to feeling any better, but she certainly didn't feel any worse, was glad to be on weaker medication and liked her new doctor to the point of friendship.

Frank had similar feelings, but was not a patient. Dr. Mary heard about Spain and Thailand and her fears for her job. She sympathized about the real, problems that they had encountered, but suggested that the ghouls, ghosts and devils that she had seen were either fictions of her imagination or real people playing nasty practical jokes on them. This concurred with Frank's own point of view, but Joy was yet to be convinced. Dr. Mary did not push her point of view forcefully having studied the beliefs of several different cultures during her career. She described Joy's problems to them as 'random and sometimes inexplicable anxiety attacks of varying severity'.

They had shown her the MRI CD from Bangkok, and she agreed that there was no inherent physical reason for the attacks. Joy was not physically ill, although the attacks did sometimes cause leaps in her heart rate and blood pressure, which could of themselves be distressing.

She was given two sets of tablets. One to be taken every morning and every night before retiring; and one to be taken as and when needed, if she experienced a sudden attack. Dr. Mary also recommended a book on pranayama or yoga breathing exercises, which she would be able use to control an attack in the future.

They were both highly impressed.

∞

Joy was called in at the beginning of the following week for an interview concerning her report. Under the circumstances, Frank was allowed to accompany his wife, but no provision could be made for an interpreter for him and he was not allowed to bring one. He was there for moral support for Joy only.

Frank had met all three members of the panel before. There was her immediate superior, Somchai, the head of personnel and the ambassador. Frank learned later from Joy, that Somchai had argued her case strongly and it was only because of his high opinion of her and her work record that prevented them from returning her to Bangkok for 'lighter duties'. However, given the severity of her mental problems as described in the report from the Phitsanuwed Hospital in Phitsanulok, she could not be allowed to continue in her present function, because it involved a great deal of contact with the public. The risk of her damaging the Embassy's and therefore Thailand's image was too great. Therefore, she would henceforth be assigned to a less senior role within the Embassy.

Joy's face was like stone throughout the thirty-minute interview. When asked whether she had anything to say, she simply said in English, "No, thank you. We will be collecting the rest of my personal possessions tomorrow", she looked at Frank for confirmation, and he nodded. On that note, the meeting was closed and they left. They went to the pub where they had met for lunch. Joy excused herself to go to the Ladies immediately and was in there some time. Frank rightly suspected that she was crying her heart out and taking a tablet.

When she returned, she told him the gist of what had been said. He sighed heavily, but had to admit to himself that he would have come to the same conclusion having read only the Phitsanuwed Hospital report.

"We could submit a new report from Dr. Mary?" he suggested.

"Maybe, but my heart has left the Embassy... I worked very hard for them and this is how they reward me. If I lose, or give up my job, will I lose my visa?"

"I don't see how, you are married to me and I earn more than double the twenty-one kay a spouse has to earn per month to bring in a non-EU national. No, I am sure that you are as safe as houses..."

"I will keep my job for a while, but stay on the sick as long as possible, then tell them what they can do with their filing clerk's job".

"Whatever you say, my feisty little firecracker, I'm right behind you, whatever you want to do".

"OK, get us a bottle of cava and I'll join you in a drink".

"Are you sure? Let's ring Dr. Mary and ask if you can have a drink". Dr Mary told Joy that the occasional glass or two would not do any harm, so they carried on. They had had two bottles before they called a taxi, and Joy had had four glasses. She was as drunk as a lord, but then she hadn't had a drink since they had gotten married for the third time nearly two weeks before.

∞

That evening, Frank had to phone Somchai to ask for the name of a removal company that the embassy would allow on their premises. He also let him knew know that Joy had told him how he had stuck up for her and thanked him on their behalf. Then he hired a minivan for the following afternoon. The van driver picked them up at noon and they were finished by five thanks to the two helpers who rode in the back. Frank tipped them well and said goodbye. That night, his London bachelor pad of twenty-odd years was transformed into a beautiful home with both Western and Oriental features. Joy had collected some stunning Thai pieces in several media.

"I had never seen how drab my flat was until tonight", he admitted when they were in bed.

"I was frightened of dominating the place. You don't think that it's too much. do you?"

"Never!", he replied hugging her. "You dominate all you like".

∞

On Friday, he phoned Mike for what had become his weekly update. When Mike had finished appraising Frank of the latest events in the bank, Frank told him about Joy's interview at the embassy.

"I'm terribly sorry to here that... the bastards. You wouldn't be able to do that over here, but I suppose that our laws don't apply on embassy territory. Hard luck, she really loved that job, didn't she?"

"You know what they say about Orientals... We have a stiff upper lip, but their whole face is inscrutable. I think that it has hit her very hard though. Her whole career is down the pan, as far as she is concerned".

"Did it come as a big surprise?"

"Not to me, Mike... to be perfectly honest, she was practically catatonic when the doctor made the report that the embassy is going by... it's not fair though, because that was then and now she is much closer to her old self".

"Yes... believe me, I don't know what to say".

"Thanks, Mike, you've been great and so has Dr. Mary. We are both so impressed with her. She reminds me of Miss Marples... you know, the original one played by, er..."

"Dame Margaret Rutherford?".

"Yes, that's the one... They are both lovely old ladies".

"I think you will find that Margaret Rutherford is dead".

"Well, you know what I mean".

"Yes, I do and I agree. Look, Frank there's something I have to do before the end of the day. Can we chat again?"

"Yes, of course. I've been a man of leisure for so long that I've forgotten what it's like in the Power House".

"Yes, well, dodderiness comes to us all one day - only joking. See you soon".

They hung up and Frank went back to what he had been doing, putting up an extra Ikea shelf in the kitchen to accommodate all the herbs and spices that she insisted she needed in order to prepare authentic Thai cuisine.

Mike buzzed his secretary to hold all calls and appointments for fifteen minutes. He doubted that he would need more than that. He took out his phone, unlocked a secret folder and dialled one of the numbers in it. His call was answered on the second ring by a man speaking a language he had become accustomed to hearing, but which he still could not understand. He waited politely until the man had said his set piece and then whispered four words, "Is Francisco there, please?" He could hear his phone being reconnected.

"Francisco speaking", came the calm, cool voice at the other end, "how may I help you Brother Painter?"

"Worshipful Grand Master Artist, I bid you well, my name is Brother Master Artist Michael Stockton of the Surrey Atelier 1503. I bring you fraternal greetings but bad news also".

"And I bring you the fraternal greetings of the Inner Circle too, Brother Artist. We have known each other for many years, what is the current situation Michael?"

"I am afraid that we have all but destroyed the lives of two decent people. We have caused them extreme anxiety, which has resulted in the woman suffering a major nervous breakdown and the loss of the job that she cherished. In my opinion, it is not an exaggeration to say that we have ruined the young woman's promising diplomatic career".

"I see. Can you be here tomorrow to bear witness?"

"Yes, Brother Artist".

"Very well, Brother. Try to make it for three o'clock. You are welcome to stay the night, if you wish".

"Thank you, Brother Francisco, you are always most generous. Until tomorrow".

Mike waited for the other man to hang up first and then did likewise. He then closed the secret folder, and called his secretary.

"Ok, Maureen, open the floodgates, we're ready for business again!"

The Ghouls of Calle Goya

24. THE GOYA SOCIETY FOR TRUTH AND BEAUTY

The Baron ordered the meeting to be convened at three o'clock at the Inner Circle's Round Table in his castle in simple ceremonial dress. This meant that all the Brothers and Sisters who were called to attend would look similar except for the dabs of paint on their artists' smocks, which denoted their Atelier of origin and rank within it. However, not everyone was able to read these signs as they were designed to be indecipherable to outsiders. At precisely three o'clock Central European time, the Baroness, the Worshipful Master Artist of the Inner Circle Atelier Number 1 banged her gavel and all twelve other members looked at the clock and stood up. "Brother and Sister Artists, I now ask you to assist me to open this Atelier, The Inner Circle number 1. To what do we owe our allegiance?"

"To search for and always uphold the Divine Principles of Truth and Beauty", they all said as one.

"Thank you, Brothers and Sisters. Would you now assist me to sing 'All Things Bright and Beautiful'? After the hymn was over, she banged her gavel again. "Please be seated. As some of you may be aware there has been a possible breach of conduct, and at this stage, I may only say 'possible' because this is a trial into the behaviour of four of the future leading lights of our organisation. The four artists in question have been indirectly accused of gross misconduct and so it is our grave duty today to hear the evidence, assess the defendants' innocence or guilt and determine a sentence if necessary.

"I do not need to remind you that a task such as faces us this day, is almost without precedent. No-one here present today has ever been asked to adjudicate at such a hearing - so rare are they within our Society.

"With those thoughts in mind, Brothers and Sisters, I will hand this meeting over to The Worshipful Grand Master Artist, Worshipful Brother Francisco, who has spent the last week researching the procedures for handling such complaints". She passed the gavel and block down the left-hand side of the table and sat down.

"Thank you, my Grand Lady Artist", he said using the short form of address. "This is indeed a grave complaint against four fellow Artists. We could be here for some time, so I suggest that we get started immediately. I call the first witness, an Englishman who is well known to every Artist at this table. I have known him personally for thirty years, so if you think that that might prejudice my findings, please bear it in mind when deliberating. Call Worshipful Brother Master Artist Michael Stockton of the Surrey Atelier 1503. The Baroness pushed a button under the lip of the tabletop and Maximillian outside admitted Mike.

The third member to the president's left stood up and showed him to the witness box slightly behind and to the left of the president. "Please state your name, rank, and accusation". Mike did so.

"Brothers and Sisters, you have heard the accusation. I will now ask Brother Artist Michael to elaborate and then you may ask him questions".

He told about the fake hauntings, the video and the going-away sign. He told how the couple's honeymoon had been ruined, how the woman in question had been demoted and her career blighted because of the extreme nature of the nervous breakdown she had suffered as a direct result of harassment from four members of their Society. People gasped in disbelief and drank copious amounts of water. Such things were totally unheard of, as the Worshipful Master Artist of the Atelier had said.

"Brothers and Sisters, you have heard the complaints in detail, does anyone have ought to ask of this witness?"

He was asked whether he knew the defendants, and he replied that he had met them at their Initiation Ball' on March the 30th, but otherwise did not.

He was asked how he knew the couple and told them honestly.

He was asked how he knew that the complaints were true, and produced the photo of their going-away card, all the documents and receipts that Frank had submitted to the bank, he showed them photos that Consuela had taken of the onion and garlic hanging in his apartment and finally held up his phone and offered to run the video of them making love in his place in Calle Goya.

The Baron banged the gavel. "We don't want to see the video, but I do want to remind the Brothers and Sisters that our organization owns the apartments above and to the right of the one that Brother Artist Michael owns. It is how we met... thirty-odd years ago, and why he joined our organization. I offered him our ideals, long before I became President, but I believed in them then and I still do now. I found a kindred spirit in Brother Artist Mike and we have been friends ever since.

"Any further questions of this worthy Brother? No? In that case, I would ask him to wait outside while we question the accused. Since having multiple defendants at one hearing is unprecedented in the four-hundred-year-old history of our organization, I put it to the Inner Circle, should we hear them singly or severally?"

The vote was unanimous to hear them together so that they could not hide behind one another if they were guilty.

The two boys and two girls were shown in and into the dock. They identified themselves as Painters Robert, Sven, Millicent and Suzanne of various Ateliers and their sponsors were allowed to sit and watch. Michael's verbal evidence had been filmed so that it could be replayed if necessary, but his accusations were played back without video so as to hide his identity temporarily.

"How do you plead, Brother and Sister Artists?" They looked horrified at the extreme nature of the suffering that their antics had caused.

"It was only a joke!" said Millicent. "I didn't think that any of this would come of it... really! And I don't believe that any of the others did either". They were all looking down and shaking their heads.

"Does anyone have any questions for our Brothers and Sisters?" asked the Baron.

"Why did you choose this poor, innocent couple for your inane pranks?" asked a Sister.

"Er, their names... Frank and Joy... it seemed as if they were mocking our leaders..." ventured Suzanne.

Sven spoke out in their defence. "When we arrived there was a letter addressed to them. We read their names and felt insulted. How were we supposed to know that a Worshipful Grand Master Artist owned the apartment and that they were his friends?"

"Whether you knew that or not, it is no excuse for terrorising innocent people. That is a ludicrous statement to make in your defence! How could you possibly think that our illustrious Society could ever, ever condone such actions?"

"We thought that we were upholding the honour of our institution..." said Millicent.

"Well, that was a serious error of judgment, Sister Painter! Very serious", said a Worshipful Master Artist from Finland. "We are about helping mankind, not terrorising innocent individuals on their honeymoon just because of their names! It is preposterous..."

His use of the word 'Painter' instead of 'Artist' was meant as a veiled insult. Both words could be used interchangeably, but 'Painter' was generally used to describe the lowest-ranking members of the Society.

"We didn't mean anything, honest", said Robert.

"Again, that is utter nonsense! You intrude on a couple's bed chamber, film them in flagrante delecto, play it in front of them in a local bar and put it on the Internet, and you say that you didn't mean anything?

"Do you take us for morons such as yourselves? I have not been so insulted for decades".

"Does anyone have any more to say? Either in defence or in question?" The defendants and their sponsors just studied their hands or their feet. The Baron looked around the table, but people were shaking their heads, some in disbelief of what they had just heard, others because they had no questions.

"Very well, how do the defendants plead?" He called out their names one by one and waited for the responses. They all pleaded guilty. "In that case, I will ask the defendants and their sponsors, if they are not within the Inner Circle, to please step outside".

When they had left the room, there was silence and a lot of shaking of heads. "Just what are we coming to?" asked one elderly member not of anyone in particular, and perhaps only of himself.

The Baron gave the Inner Circle a few minutes to collect their thoughts and then called them to order. "The ballot, please". The third person on the President's right left the table, gave a white and a black ball to each member and waited.

"Brothers and Sisters, we are voting on the guilt or innocence of the four Painters. Black signifies guilt and white innocence".

The ballot box was handed to the Baroness as Master of the Atelier. She tipped the contents out into a bowl and then passed the bowl around for all to see. There were twelve black balls.

"We, the Inner Circle, have spoken", she announced. "We find guilty, unanimously. We now need to proceed to the unenviable task of passing sentence".

There followed a debate that lasted seventy-five minutes and it ranged from the expulsion of the guilty to the expulsion of the guilty and their sponsors for such poor judgment as to recommend people like that into their Inner Circle. After allowing the members to have their say and come to a natural quiet, Francisco gathered the reins of the committee and continued. "I have listened to the opinion of every member here. Permanent exclusion has never been inflicted on members before, so it would be unprecedented, as is the infringement we have heard spoken of this afternoon. Furthermore, ostracising these young Painters will not help the victims, the perpetrators or the organization. Therefore, I have a proposal to put before you for your consideration. Please feel free to offer alterations, as you see fit".

He handed the sheet of paper that he had been writing on to the person to his left. The man took it to a booth in the shadows of the room and returned with thirteen copies of it. He gave each member a copy and the President a copy and his original to vouch for its authenticity.

"I vouch that my photocopy is a true copy of my script and I prove it to you thus". He held up his copy and the original for the others to compare their copies with his. The Barron's recommendations were passed with only a few minor adjustments. The Baroness scooped up the minutes and her husband's original proposed sentence along with the amendments, which she had annotated on her copy. The matter was deemed to be of such importance, that the minutes of the meeting were typed up that evening and approved by the members of the Inner Circle. The sentences were passed that evening and the four miscreants dismissed from the castle in the dark without transport. Their sponsors were left to arrange a taxi for their disgraced fledglings.

A barbecue was organized in the garden for those who had been invited to stay, but the Baron spent the time in his office composing a letter - the most difficult and perhaps the most important letter he had ever had to write in his life.

And it had to be ready by the morning, even if that was only for his own satisfaction and the honour of the Society that was his life - and that of so many others.

25. THE LETTER

The Baron worked until the early hours of the morning to draft and then write out the letter which would go out to every Atelier in the world, all 2,909 of them and eight individuals in particular. When he was confident that he had accurately conveyed the verdict of the Inner Circle, he wrote it out in longhand. Then he started on the second and last letter that he had to write that night, but it was the more difficult of the two.

When he was finished, it was past three and he didn't have the strength to shower before collapsing onto his bed.

Only the Inner Circle and Michael had been invited to stay the night; the perpetrators had been dismissed in a display of disgust. That morning, only Maximillian was allowed to serve them at breakfast, because their business was still not concluded, not by a long chalk. The atmosphere in the dining room was sombre.

"Ladies and Gentlemen", for they were outside the Atelier Room, "I have written out the verdict that the Mother Atelier came to last night. You will find your personal photocopies in front of you in the envelope with 'Verdict and Sentence' written upon it. Please read it over breakfast and we will ratify it in fifteen minutes. Then we will discuss the second letter".

The diners used spoon handles and knives to open the dark-green envelopes and continued to eat. There were no disagreements, only nods and grunts of approval. When the time came to vote on that latter's contents, there were no objections.

"Thank you. Copies of that letter will be sent to every Atelier in our organization through the usual channels tomorrow. We expect and need every Atelier to comply immediately. That means within two days of receiving the communication. Please impress that on the Ateliers where you have influence.

"Now, we come to the second letter, the most difficult and perhaps most important one that I have ever had to write in my current capacity within our organization. Please open the second letter now. We will return to it in twenty minutes".

Again, it was passed without hesitation, and he thanked the members once again.

"Michael, I know that you have to leave early, so my car and chauffeur are awaiting you outside, whenever you are ready. When the car returns, it will be at the disposal of my other friends".

Michael finished his tea, and then went to his room to check that he had left nothing behind. A youth carried his case down for him and placed it in the boot of the Baron's Rolls Royce. Everybody saw him off as the car pulled away; slowly at first on the long gravel drive, but it accelerated once on the tarmac road.

Michael phoned Frank from the departure lounge of Oslo's Gardermoen Airport.

"Hello Frank, look, I'm sorry to have to disturb you on a Sunday and all that, but I have some news that is probably to your advantage. Can you meet me for lunch at the Highwayman at say, er, twelve thirty? Bring Joy if she's up to it, but if she can't manage it that is all right as well"

"Sure, we can be there, but what is this all about?"

"I'm sorry, my friend, but I cannot tell you that until I see you. Look, if you are late, I will wait, but please do your best to get there. You know what Jocasta is like".

"Yes, of course we'll be there! I'm intrigued, and Joy will be as well. See you then".

"OK, until then".

When he explained the mysterious phone call to Joy, she wasn't sure whether to be nervous, trepidatious, or happy to see Mike again. Her emotions were flowing in all directions.

She needed a tablet.

They met in the pub, as directed. Frank and Joy arrived first by almost thirty minutes, which only served to increase her anxiety. However, when Mike arrived, he was so charming that he soon had her giggling like a schoolgirl. The three of them had always got on and Joy trusted Mike. If the truth be told there was some chemistry there, but Frank trusted both of them too.

"Are you allowed a glass of wine, Joy?"

"Yes, I can have two, and I have had four, but don't tell Dr. Mary!"

"I wouldn't dream of it. Chateau Neuf all right for everyone?" They both nodded.

"What's this all about, Mike?"

"Oh, no... I'm famished, let's order first". When they arrived at the cheese and biscuits, as was his Atelier's custom, he raised the reason for their meeting.

"Now, I imagine that you are anxious to know why I have asked you to meet me here."

"Yes, most definitely", replied Joy for them both.

"All right. First of all, I have to tell you that I cannot promise you anything. However, I have had that apartmento in Fuengirola for thirty-odd years, and so I have met a lot of people there, as you can imagine. Landlords come and go, and their tenants even more quickly, but as it happens, I have stayed friends with the man who owns the two apartments, the tenants of which you say gave you problems. Don't get me wrong on this one, I believe you and I am on your side.

"Anyway, I have spoken to the man who owns those flats, and he is most concerned about what has happened to you as a result of the behaviour of his tenants. However, he has to hold his own inquiry and he is not from this country, so, it could take a while. I trust this man though, although he is a little eccentric. A really nice guy, but a little, er, old fashioned, shall we say, but he will be in touch, I know that for certain".

"How, by carrier pigeon?" Nobody laughed.

"It has been known!" joked Mike, "But usually by letter. Hand-written letter on dark-green vellum in a double-sized, dark-green envelope sealed with sealing wax and or ribbon. Have you received anything like that?"

"No, not yet..." said Joy.

"It sounds more like a parcel", added Frank.

"Yes, well, you should receive it soon... When you do, if you have any questions about it, phone me and I'll see what I can do"

"All right, Mike, thanks a lot, my friend... You have been good to Joy and me these last two months".

"Think nothing of it... We are friends. I'm just sorry that all this happened in my flat. If I hadn't offered it to you, you would have had a wonderful honeymoon in a hotel..."

"No, Mike", said Joy, "we cannot allow you to think like that. You were trying to help us. What happened to us does not reflect on you in any way".

"Thanks, Joy, I appreciate your saying that. I was feeling guilty". The truth was that he had hoped to recruit the couple into the Goya Society, if everything had gone well.

"Well, look, kiddos, I have enjoyed our lunch, we must do it more often, but I have to get back to see how Jocasta is... I'm really surprised that she hasn't phoned yet". She had, but he had switched his phone off. "I'll see you both soon. Bye for now". They kissed and shook hands, and Mike left. On the way, he phoned a motorbike delivery service that he had used before and asked them to meet him in a pub in the village next to his. He handed Francisco's letter over to the rider and instructed him to deliver it at seven am through the letterbox of the address that he gave him.

"There is no need to ring the bell, or wait for a receipt", he said. "I know that's unusual, but, I am paying in advance and I will know if it doesn't arrive. I know the recipient and I know your boss". The implied threat was unnecessary, but the letter was vitally important, so he didn't feel as if he could afford to miss a trick.

∞

When Frank went down to check the post the following morning, the first thing that he noticed was a huge, dark-green envelope. There was no stamp on the fifteen by six-inch envelope or any sign of where it had come from.

He presented it to Joy. "This must be the letter that Mike was talking about. Do you want to open it?"

"No, er, no, you do it..." Frank wanted to keep the unusual seal intact, so he cut around it with a sharp knife, then he unfolded it carefully.

Their address was below a header of an artist at his easel, and above that was the name of the organization: The Goya Society for Truth and Beauty. There was no return address, phone number or email address. He held it up for Joy to see before he read it. The watermark was also of an artist standing at an easel.

"Impressive, or what?" he asked his wife. She nodded.

"OK, here we go, are you ready?"

"Yes, I can hardly wait... I'm nearly wetting myself! Get on with it!"

"OK. Here we go.

"Dear Mr. and Mrs. Jones,

"I am sorry for what has befallen you through no fault of your own. My name is Francisco, Frank, if you like, and I hope that you will not mind me using your first names throughout the rest of this letter.

"My dear Frank and Joy, and I do not say that lightly, please be assured of that. I represent the owners of the apartments from where your problems originated. The fact that the people occupying our premises were the cause of your misery is not in dispute.

"The fact is, that I represent a large organisation, the aim of which is to spread Truth and Beauty among the population of the world, so what has befallen you is completely abhorrent to us. That it was perpetrated by four of our members makes the crime far worse. The only point that I will make in their defence is that they are young, although even I cannot accept it as an excuse. They thought that you were part of a test, so they tell me. You see,

184

the names Frank (Francisco) and Joy (Joielle) have a historic significance to us. We are sometimes referred to as the Goya Society, referring to Francisco de Goya, the Spanish painter. He and an ancestor of mine, Joielle, had a liaison while they were in Italy. She posed for him on many occasions, but they could not marry because of the strict distinctions of class in those days. She was of noble birth, but he was only middle class, and by the time he was famous, she was already married with children. It was sad, very sad for both of them, but their problem was not uncommon.

"Anyway, when the four youths from our organization saw a letter addressed to Frank and Joy, they thought that you were part of their initiation test.

"I cannot pretend to understand why they chose to denigrate you. My reaction would have been so revere you. Such is the difference sometimes between the young and the old.

"We, the executive committee, if you like, have levied a severe punishment on the four youths, their sponsors into our organization, each branch of that organization, and upon me as its president. I will detail the amounts of those fines for you just so that you may better judge the severity, with which we have taken this gross, hitherto unknown, infringement of our very core principles.

"Each of the four youths in the two apartments in Calle Goya is being fined twenty-five thousand Euros. The four senior members who sponsored them are being fined fifty thousand Euros each; each Atelier in our organization will contribute towards another five hundred thousand Euros and I will top the fund up to one million Euros.

"Not an inconsiderable amount, I am sure you will agree. We normally donate all the money that we raise to worthy causes around the globe, but in this case, that sum will be made available to you.

"You also have the organisation's and my most heartfelt regret that this dreadful event befell you.

"It goes without saying that you may do with the one million Euros whatsoever you will. There is no caveat on the, er, let's say, prize money, since prize money is tax-free in your country. We will set up a prize draw and have you win it.

"The rules of the competition are simple. By entering the prize draw, you agree unconditionally, not to discuss with anyone except your doctor, the events that took place in Calle Goya. You further promise never to discuss the contents of this letter with anyone who may use it to their own or your advantage. In order to enter the prize draw, and win it, just send an email from your most-used account to free-email-prize-draw@free-lottery.ng Entry into the competition means that you have accepted the terms and conditions above. Please enter within forty-eight hours. If you need advice, talk only with your most trusted male confident.

"I wish you well,

"Frank,

The Goya Society for Truth and Beauty, President.

"Well, well, well... What do you make of that?"

"I don't know, but who is our most trusted male confident? If he had said female, I would have said Dr. Mary".

"Oh, that has to be Mike. Mike lent us the apartment; Mike knows this guy, Frank; Mike told us to be on the lookout for a large green envelope; and Mike is my most trusted male confident. You are my most trusted female confidente".

"Aw, thank you, my darling... Well, what are you waiting for? The clock is ticking and there is a million Euros at stake. Phone our dear old trusted confident, Mike!"

"Certainly, madam, anything you say, madam".

"And less of the cheek, dah ling".

"Touché", he grinned, speed-dialling Mike. "Good morning, Mike! And how is my most trusted confident today? Fit and healthy, I hope".

"You sound very chipper today. Get your oats, did you?" he replied remembering the phrase from the letter.

"Oh, I'm just feeling on top of the world. We received a large green envelope this morning..."

"Oh, good. Did it contain anything interesting?"

"Yes, it did, as a matter of fact, and we would like to discuss it with you. Can we meet you for lunch?"

"Certainly, you know me, I love business lunches. Shall we say The Highwayman at twelve?"

"Perfect".

"I'll book a table in the name of the bank, seeing as it's bank business".

"See you there, bye".

∞

"Do you mind if I have a look at the letter?" asked Mike maintaining his ignorance, although he had already read it in Norway. He read it quickly, but stopped now and then to make appropriate noises. "Well, I never... a million Euros, eh? I hope that you will be depositing that in our bank... or will you be moving to Couts now?"

"What? The NatWest? The Royal Bank of Scotland? That mob, never!" he replied with a grin and some pride in the company that had employed him for thirty-four years.

"You are in good company with us... With that sort of dosh, you will be moved to our Preferred Clients list, along with all the other big nobs".

"You've been peeping in the showers, haven't you, Mike? You'll have to watch him at the sports club, Frank!" said Joy giggling behind her hand. "No, what am I saying? If you watch him, you'll both be Peeping Toms!" She laughed out loud, and Frank and Mike exchanged knowing glances. She was getting back to normal.

"Yes, well, enough of that kind of slanderous innuendo", said Frank in mock seriousness. "What do you think about the letter, Mike?"

"I love everything about it! Beautiful colour, the best vellum I have ever seen, and the most skilled penmanship too. You don't see hand-written Gothic script like that very often... in pen and ink too. It is a work of art, truly a thing of Beauty!" Frank noticed the special emphasis he had placed on the last word, and met his friend's gaze when he looked up.

"You know more about this than you are letting on, don't you, my most trusted male confident?" They were playing word games and both of them knew it.

"Yes, all right", he said after a pause. "I can tell you more, but I must beg of you both never to reveal a single word of what I am about to tell you. But, it is a long story, so let's order the pud first and another bottle of wine, courtesy of the bank for one of its most highly respected representatives, myself, and two of its most important soon-to-be Preferred Listed clients, to wit you two. Are you sitting comfortably, then I shall begin...."?

Mike paused while the waiter brought their order.

"This is better than Story Time on Watch with Mother!" squeaked Joy. Frank put an arm around her and they cŵtched together for a few seconds until the waiter had left.

"Right, now where was I?" said Mike toying with them.

"At the beginning!" exclaimed Joy with a mock serious expression on her face. "Get on with it or I'll kick start you under the table!"

"Your wife is being rude again, Frank, she's making me blush".

"Well, get on with it then or I'll kick start you under the table as well, and I've got bigger feet than Joy has".

"All right, all right... Are you ready?" Joy tapped the underside of the table near Mike with her foot.

"Drat! I can't reach him", she said.

"If there is one thing that I have learned after being in banking for nearly forty years, it is to sit far enough away from clients so that they can neither strike nor kick me".

"We could throw things at you though" retorted Frank. Joy picked up a spoonful of apple tart and custard and aimed it at him.

"OK, I give in, here we go...

"Francisco de Goya was a famous painter in the late Eighteenth and early Nineteenth Century... Please stop me if I am telling you things that you already know". Joy took aim with her sweet again. "Point taken. Anyway, before he became famous, he travelled a lot to develop his skills in the ateliers – the studios - of Master Artists in various parts of southern Europe. While on one particular journey, he met a beautiful, young Norwegian aristocrat by the name of Joielle, who was doing the Grand Tour of the cultural capitals of Europe as part of finishing her education. She met the young Goya in Italy and they spent hours together, suitably chaperoned, of course, discussing Truth and Beauty, which were fashionable topics in those days. They fell in love, as was inevitable. She posed for him in several paintings, which he gave to her as gifts. Anyway, Joielle's parents had already chosen a suitable, rich, Scandinavian aristocrat for her and refused to allow her to marry an impoverished, unknown painter. As a dutiful young lady, she did as her parents wished, but closely followed the career of dear friend. It was she who founded the Goya Society for Truth and Beauty, of which Frank, or Francisco, the writer of this letter is the president and I am a member. He is also a direct descendant of Joielle".

"How romantic, but how sad too", murmured Joy. "She set up a shrine to her lover and never forgot him".

"That is true, Joy. Very true. The paintings and sketches that he gave her are still in the family's private collection. They have never been catalogued by any art historian and are completely unknown to anyone outside our Society.

"Anyway, to continue... Oh, by the way, just a small, but interesting detail, I think, since this secret Society was founded by a woman for herself, originally, and then her offspring, it is open to both men and women, which is unique we believe for a society as old as ours. Our lodges, we call them Ateliers, are mixed - men and women have equal rights with us. We sit side by side at our meetings, and in fact, the leader of our premier Atelier is a woman.

"But, to continue my tale… I've forgotten where I was…"

"Goya's paintings in your secret society", prompted Joy.

"Ah, yes, thank you, my dear. It is a secret Society, which is why I beg you never to divulge what I am telling you. The Society started as a woman's dedication to her lover; then she let her children in on the secret, and they their children and so forth. In time, friends of the family were invited to join, and as people moved to live around Norway and even abroad, the Society expanded. It is now four hundred years old, and there are ateliers in many countries, although it still retains a lot of its original Norwegian flavour. We have kept it a secret Society for fear of retribution from non-members. For example, if I were to promote another member of our Society at the bank, everyone would be screaming 'favouritism', wouldn't they? Which is ironic, since one of our Guiding Principles is Truth, which would preclude us from taking any action, which is not true. Such is the ignorance of folk.

"And, I might add, not only non-members, which brings me to the four youths who terrorised you - and we, the organisation, do not consider 'terrorised' too strong a word. We held an Initiation Ceremony on Goya's birthday, your wedding day, which was why I had to leave immediately after the ceremony and couldn't go to the reception, and those two boys and two girls were the initiates. I cannot reveal any of the secrets of that Initiation Ceremony, naturally, but parts of it do represent some of the characters to be seen in some of Goya's work. At this special initiation, it was our one-hundredth, these four people were awarded a fortnight's holiday at two of our apartments in streets named after Goya... we sort of collect accommodation in streets named after Goya - you could call them investments, and they have done very well, I might add - but we see them as holiday homes for our members, who have done something special to deserve them. You can imagine the kick it gives us to stay in a street named after our hero.

"So, those four arrived in Calle Goya, Fuengirola, on the day before you did, I believe. Anyway, one day, they saw the names on the letter I sent you, put two and two together, made five and thought that you were a part of their test. None of us can understand, why they thought that, or, if they did, why they decided to treat you exceptionally badly, instead of exceptionally well. It is completely beyond us, but there you go. It still happened...

"Francisco and I bought our apartments in Calle Goya at about the same time, shortly after the block had been built. In fact, I must have bought mine just before him, otherwise he would have bought mine as well and my life would not have been changed, and nor would yours. Anyway, we were inspecting our new properties at the same time and we got on. Two young men... we went on the town together and got to know each other very well. He told me about the Goya Society and eventually I joined up. To be honest, I thought he was taking the piss, er sorry, Joy, at first. I mean, it does sound a bit bizarre, doesn't it? I have been a member, an Artist, as we say, ever since...

Or I should say that I started as an Apprentice Painter, then became a Painter, and finally an Artist.

"I offered you the flat out of pure friendship, but in the back of my mind, if I am honest, which I must be, I was hoping that you would join me in our Society one day. Fat chance of that happening now, I should imagine".

"What a story!" said Joy under her breath, "So, the million dollars thing might be true?"

"There is no 'might be' about it, Joy. If Francisco says something, he means it. Except that it is jot a million dollars, it is..." he flicked open his phone and touched a button, "it is currently one point two three six million dollars and rising, so let's have another bottle, or shall we move on to the coffee and Cognac?"

"How much more of the story is there?" asked Joy.

"Oh, enough for wine and Cognac".

"What about getting back to work, won't you be late?" asked Joy.

"What do you mean 'getting back to work'? I'll have you know that I haven't stopped working since the moment I got up, young lady. This is bank business now. Frank and Francisco are clients of ours, so an extended lunch on expenses is perfectly justifiable. Truth, remember, is crucial to us".

"My apologies", she said with mock humility.

"Accepted, Gracious Lady", he replied. "So, to continue, you need to enter that competition now. Go on, I want to see you do it right now. No more story until I've seen you do it". Mike passed Frank the letter, as he took out his phone.

"Ok, done".

"In that case, you will have a million Euros before the end of business today. Congratulations!" He held up his glass and clinked it with each of them. "What do you think of the Nigerian thing?"

"It's a nice touch... You hide amongst the scammers", said Frank.

"Oh! You wound me! Truth, dear friend, Truth! I invented this method of transferring legitimate assets from us to worthy causes, in order to avoid paying taxes and fees. All our funds come from donations from our members. They have earned that money and already paid tax on their salaries. It is post-tax cash. However, some countries want another slice of our money, so I came up with this work-around... Oh, some fifteen years ago, or more. It is because it works so well that scammers have copied me, or us, I should say. Having said that, I will not argue that the scammers have created an excellent camouflage for our financial activities. The Nigerian Connection was a stroke of pure genius, even if I do say so myself".

"So, why Nigeria then?" asked Frank

"That was just a pure accident. I happened to be 'on holiday' there, helping to set up a new Atelier. I often wonder at how strange it is the way things work out. A whole new industry was born because I was on holiday and you are Euro-millionaires because I bought a small flat in Spain before a Norwegian got his hands on it. How much stranger can life be than that?

"Now, is there anything I can tell you that I have missed out?"

"We don't know what we don't know, and we don't know what you are allowed to tell us, do we, Mike?" replied Joy to Mike's rhetorical question.

"Of course not, it was a silly thing to say, dear lady", he replied generously.

"I have a question, but I don't know whether you can answer it... You are a member of this society, right?" Mike nodded. "So, does that mean that you have to go to Norway to attend your lodge, I mean atelier?"

Mike nodded and smiled. "When I first joined, I used to have to go to mainland Europe, if I wanted to attend an Atelier. It was great! I used to pop over to France, Spain, Belgium, The Netherlands, Norway and other Scandinavian countries to attend Ateliers there, but there is now one in Surrey, so I don't hop about as often as I used to. I do miss it though... although as you get older travelling alone is not so much fun as it is when one is younger".

"If we were to join, you wouldn't have to travel alone. What do you think, Joy?"

"Truth and Beauty sound great principles to me. I'd join if they would have me".

"Any Atelier, my Atelier, would be proud and honoured to have you as members... not only because you are worthy people, but I don't think that any Atelier in the world has a Frank and Joy married couple in it, except Number One, and you are famous throughout our network..." Mike noticed a flash of dread on Joy's face. "They don't know what you look like, but the membership had to know your first names because it was vital to the evidence". Joy relaxed and nodded.

"Yes, I can see that... It's just, er, that video". She looked at her husband. "Does he know about the video?"

"Yes", admitted Frank. The three of them studied their empty glasses. "Let's have some coffee and Armagnac to cheer us up again".

"Armagnac! What a good idea!" agreed Mike. Joy was glad of the change of subject, but Mike hadn't finished with it yet. "As for that footage, some of our legal guys have had it banned, de-listed, I think they call it, from all the search engines on the Internet, and, they assure me, if that happens, no-one can find it, and so no-one can watch it. It's called a DMCA, and any company that still has the title in its catalogue risks having all its stock de-listed, which would effectively kill the company. Therefore, it no longer exists. No company would risk extinction for one film when they have thousands of others to sell. Consider the matter dealt with".

"Thank you, Mike", said Frank.

"Don't thank me, that was Francisco's work. He is a very clever and resourceful man, and what he doesn't know, his wife probably does. You will most likely meet them one day, if you join up".

When they were done, they shared a taxi home not wanting to end the party yet, but Jocasta had phoned. Mike left his car in the bank's underground car park and bought a bottle of champagne and three glasses to travel with. They didn't live in the same village, but they were close enough.

In the back of the limousine, Mike flicked on his phone. "Guess what! You have just won a million Euros in a Nigerian email lottery, and furthermore..." he added clicking a few more buttons, I can confirm that the funds have already left the prize draw company's account, so they must be in yours, but I cannot check that for you". He popped the cork and filled their champagne flutes. "Congratulations!" he said again clinking glasses.

26. EPILOGUE

When Frank and Joy arrived home late that afternoon, they checked their six-month-old joint account, into which they had both been paying since the New Year, and there was slightly more than a million pounds in it. They walked down to the nearest decent restaurant and continued their celebrations alone. They also decided to quit work. Joy finished first on the grounds of ill health, which Dr. Mary supported with written and verbal evidence at the tribunal. Joy was awarded a reduced pension commensurate with her number of years of service. Then Frank applied for early retirement on the grounds that he needed to take care of his wife. He also was awarded a lump sum and a reduced pension.

Then they put Frank's fashionable apartment on the market for just short of half a million pounds. It went almost immediately, but the paperwork took six weeks to complete, which was enough time for them to buy a small holding in the West Country overlooking the Severn Estuary and Wales. It comprised a fairly large, completely modernised cottage and several acres of land. Joy had always had a passion for sheep, so they decided to specialize in rare breeds and their first were Welsh Llanwenog, because they were tough and bred prolifically with few problems due to the small size of the lambs, although they grew quickly. They had been advised that they were ideal for novices wanting to promote rare breeds. Joy was impressed.

They both joined the Surrey Atelier number 1503 of the Goya Society for Truth and Beauty and met dozens of new friends from all over the country. Their Initiation Ceremony was the biggest ever held in the UK, and the biggest that most people had ever seen. All of the Inner Circle were there as were the Worshipful Grand Master Artists of many European Ateliers. After the ceremony, when the lights went on and people removed their masks, they were surprised to see that Mike was the Worshipful Grand Master Artist of the Surrey Atelier and that Dr. Mary also held an office. They were overwhelmed at meeting Francisco and Ingrid, whose nickname was Joielle, who stayed the night with them at Mike and Jocasta's large country house.

They would drive down the M4 to go to Atelier meetings every month and kept their promise to accompany Mike on jaunts to other Ateliers across the English Channel. They went back to Mike's apartment in Calle Goya many times with no fears that the demons or ghouls that had haunted them would ever make a re-appearance. They also stayed at several of The Society's other properties in other Calle Goya's and Goya Streets around the world. The Society opened up a whole new world to them and they had the money to enjoy it.

Mike stayed on at the bank until his retirement age of sixty, which was only a year or so later on, then he groomed Frank and Joy full-time to start a new Atelier in Bristol or Cardiff, with the help of other members who lived in the vicinity.

They continued to fund Bew's education until she had gone as high as she wanted to and paid for annual trips to Europe. They also sent Boo a million Baht, so that she could attend university to study English, but Frank never suggested that they invite her over. Neither did Joy, and that made Frank wonder whether she knew or suspected that there had been anything between them, but the subject was never raised.

They both went to Thailand every year, but Frank would not go back to the village. When Joy went to visit her mother for a few days, he would wait for her in a hotel nearby. He could not bring himself to pretend that he wanted to see her again, especially after taking the vow to always be in search of Truth and Beauty at his initiation. Joy understood that and respected him for it.

The Sedolfsens became special friends and Frank and Joy underwent the ceremony of initiation that one day might lead to their election to the Inner Circle. They also met the perpetrators of the injustices against them and forgave them. The four youths, and Frank and Joy, wept as they hugged and accepted their apologies. It was a soulful experience for all who witnessed it at the Grand Atelier that night in the Baron's castle.

Joy was the first Worshipful Master Artist of their new Atelier several years later and the most memorable Worshipful Master Artist for many of the attending Painters and Artists who attended the opening night of The Society's newest Atelier, number 3003, the first one in Wales.

The End

Bonus chapter of a new book:

THE DISALLOWED

The Humorous Story of a Contemporary Vampire Family

by

Owen Jones

1 MR. LEE'S PREDICAMENT

Mr. Lee, or Old Man Lee as he was known locally had been feeling strange for weeks and, because the local community was so small and isolated, everybody else in the vicinity knew about it too. He had been to seek the advice of a local doctor, one of the old kind, not a modern medical doctor and she had told him that his body's temperature was out of balance, because something was affecting his blood.

The woman, the local Shaman, Mr. Lee's aunty in fact, was still not quite sure of the cause, but she had promised that she would know in about twenty-four hours, if he left a couple of samples for her to study and came back when she sent for him. The Shaman handed Mr. Lee a clump of moss and a stone.

He knew what to do, because he had done it before, so he urinated on the moss and spat on the stone after hawking deeply. He handed them solemnly back to her, and being very careful not to touch them with her bare hands, she wrapped them separately in pieces of banana leaf to preserve their moisture for as long as possible.

"Give them a day to rot down and dry out, then I'll have a good look and see what's the matter with you."

"Thank you, Aunty Da, I mean, Shaman Da. I will await your summons and return immediately when you call me."

"You wait there, my lad, I'm not finished with you yet."

Da reached around behind herself and took an earthenware jar from the shelf. She uncorked it, took two mouthfuls and then spat the last one all over Old Man Lee. As Da was incanting a prayer to her gods, Mr. Lee was thinking that she had forgotten about the 'cleansing' – he hated being spat on by anyone, but especially old ladies with rotten teeth.

"That alcohol spray and the prayer will tide you over until we can sort you out properly," she assured him.

Shaman Da stood up from her full-lotus position on the earthen floor of her medical sanctuary, put her arm around her nephew's shoulder and walked with him outside, rolling a cigarette as they went.

Once outside, she lit it up, took a deep draw and felt the smoke fill her lungs. "How's that wife of yours and your lovely children?"

"Oh, they are well, Aunty Da, but a little concerned about my health. I've been feeling a bit dicky for a while now and I've never been sick in my whole life, as you know."

"No, we Lees are a strong lot. Your father, my dear brother, would still be fit now, if he hadn't died of the flu. Strong as a buffalo he was. You take after him, but he never got shot. I think that's what has caught up with you, that Yankee bullet."

Mr. Lee had been through this several hundred times before, but he couldn't win the argument so he just nodded, handed his aunt a fifty Baht note and set off home to his farm, which was just a few hundred yards outside the village.

He was feeling better already, so he put on a jaunty pace to try to prove it to everyone.

Old Man Lee trusted his ancient aunty Da completely, as did everyone else in their community, which consisted of a small village of about five hundred houses and a few dozen out-lying farms. His aunty Da had taken over as village Shaman when he was a boy, and there weren't more than a dozen or so who could remember the one before her. They had never had a university-qualified medical doctor of their own.

That was not to say that the villagers did not have access to a physician, but they were few and far between – the nearest permanent doctor was 'in town', seventy-five kilometres away and there were no buses, taxis or trains in the mountains where they lived in the very top north-eastern corner of Thailand. Besides that, doctors were expensive and prescribed expensive drugs, from which everyone assumed they earned high commissions. There was also a clinic a few villages away, but it was staffed by a full-time nurse and a part-time circular doctor who worked there one day a fortnight.

Villagers like Mr. Lee thought that they were probably all right for rich city-dwellers, but not much use to the likes of them. How could a farmer take a whole day off work and hire someone else with a car to do the same to go to visit a city doctor? If you could find someone with a car that was, although there were a few old tractors about within ten kilometres.

No, he thought, his old aunty was good enough for everyone else and she was good enough for him and besides, she hadn't let anyone die whose time wasn't up and she certainly hadn't killed anyone, everyone would swear to that.

Everyone.

Mr. Lee was very proud of his aunty, and anyway, there was no alternative for miles around and certainly no-one with all her experience – all…? Well, no-one knew how old she was really, not even she herself, but probably ninety if a day.

Mr. Lee reached his front yard with these thoughts in mind. He wanted to discuss the matter with his wife, because although he appeared to the outside world to be the boss in his family, the same with every other family, that was only show, because in reality, every decision was made by the family as a whole, or at least all the adults.

This was going to be a momentous day, because the Lees had never had a 'crisis' before and their two children, who were no longer children either, would have to be allowed to have their say as well. History was about to be made and Mr. Lee was well aware of it.

"Mud!" he called out, his affectionate name for his wife since their first-born had not been able to say 'mother'. "Mud, are you there?"

"Yes, I'm out the back."

Lee waited a few moments for her to come in, but it was hot and stuffy indoors, so he went out to the front yard and sat on their large family table with its grass roof where the whole family ate and was wont to sit if they had any free time.

Mrs. Lee's real name was Wan, although her husband affectionately called her Mud, since their eldest child had called her that because he hadn't been able to say 'mother' yet. The name had stuck with Mr. Lee but not with either of the children. She came from the village, Baan Noi, as did Lee himself, but her family knew nowhere else, whereas Mr. Lee's family had come from China two generations before, although that home town was not far away either.

She was fairly typical of the women of the area. In her day, she had been a very pretty girl, but girls were not given much opportunity back then and nor were they encouraged to be ambitious, not that things had changed much for her daughter even twenty years later. Mrs. Lee had been content to look for a husband on leaving school, so when Heng Lee had asked for her hand and shown her parents the compensation money he had in the bank, she had thought that he was as good a catch as any other local boy she was likely to get. Neither did she have any desires to wander away from her friends and relations to a big city to increase her scope.

She had even come to love Heng Lee in her own way, although the fire had long gone out in her short love life and she was more of a business partner now than a wife in the family firm dedicated to their mutual survival.

Wan had never sought a lover, although she had been propositioned both before and after her marriage. At the time, she had been outraged, but now she looked back on those moments with a degree of tenderness. Lee was her first and only, and now would surely be her last, but she had no regrets about that.

Her only dream was to see and take care of the grandchildren that her kids would surely want in the fullness of time, although she did not want them, especially her daughter, to rush into marriage like she had. She knew that her children would have children as sure as eggs were eggs, if they were able, because it was the only way to provide some financial security for themselves in their old age and have a chance of developing the family's status.

Mrs. Lee cared about family, status and honour, but she did not want any more material things than she already had. She had learned to do without for so long that it didn't matter to her any more.

She already had a mobile phone and a television, but the signals were poor to say the least and there was nothing she could do about that but wait for the government to get around to upgrading the local transmitters, which would surely happen one day, if not any time soon. She didn't want a car because she didn't want to go anywhere and besides the roads weren't very good anyway.

However, it was not only that, people of her age and station had thought a car so out of reach for so long that they had ceased to desire them decades ago. In other words, she was content with the bicycle and old motorcycle that formed the family fleet of transport.

Neither did Mrs. Lee hanker after gold or fancy clothes anymore, as the realities of raising two kids on a farmer's wage had knocked that out of her many years before too. Despite all that, Mrs. Lee was a happy woman who loved her family and was resigned to staying as she was and where she was, until Buddha called her to go home again one day.

Mr. Lee watched his wife walking towards him, she was adjusting something under her sarong, but from the outside – something wasn't sitting right, he supposed, but would never ask. She sat on the edge of the table and swung her legs up to sit like a mermaid on a Danish rock.

"OK, what did that old crone have to say?"

"Oh, come on, Mud, she's not that bad! OK, you and she have never hit it off, but that's just the way it goes sometimes, isn't it? She never speaks a bad word about you, why, just thirty minutes ago she was asking after your health… and the kids'."

"You can be such a fool sometimes too, Heng. She speaks nicely to me and about me when people are around to hear, but whenever we are alone, she treats me like dirt and always has done. She hates me, but she's too devious to let you see that, because she knows that you would take my side and not hers. You men think you are worldly-wise but you can't see what's going on under your own noses.

"She has accused me of all sorts of things over the years and many times too… like not keeping a clean home, not washing the children and once she even said that my food smelled like I'd used goat droppings for flavouring!

"Bah, you don't know the half of it, but you don't believe me either, do you, your own wife? Yes, you can smile, but it has not been very funny for me these last thirty years, let me tell you. Anyway, what did she have to say?"

"Nothing, really, that was just a check-up, so it was the same old routine. You know, pee on some moss, spit on a stone and then let her spray you with alcohol from that toothy old mouth. It makes me shudder to think of it. She said she'd get word to me tomorrow, when she could let me know the outcome.

"Where are the children? Shouldn't they be here to take part in this family discussion?"

"I don't think so, not really. After all, we don't know anything yet, do we? Or have you got any ideas?"

"No, not really. I thought I might have a massage off that Chinese girl… that might help, if I ask her to go easy on me. She learned her skill in northern Thailand and she can be a bit rough, can't she… so they say. You know, especially with my insides being like they are. Perhaps, they'll benefit from a gentle rubbing though… what do you think, my dear?"

"Yes, I know what you mean by gentle rubbing. If that's the case, why don't you ask your uncle to do it? Why choose a young woman?"

"You know why, I don't like having men's hands on me, I've explained that before, but all right, if it upsets you, I won't have a massage."

"Look, I am not saying that you can't go! Heavens, I couldn't stop you if you wanted to go anyway! However, as you say, they say she is a bit rough, and she may do more harm than good. I think that it would be wiser not to, until we've heard fro your aunty, that's all."

"Yes, OK, you're probably right. You never said where the kids are."

"I'm not really sure, I thought they'd be back by now… They went off together to see about some birthday party or other on the weekend."

The Lees had two children, one of each, and they counted themselves lucky for them, because they had been trying to have children for ten years before their boy was conceived. They were twenty and sixteen now, so Mr. and Mrs. Lee had long given up hoping for any more.

They had stopped trying long ago too.

However, they were good, respectful and obedient children and they made their parents proud, or at least, what their parents knew about them made them proud, because they were just like any decent kids: 90% good, but could get up to mischief too and had secret thoughts that they knew their parents would not approve of.

Master Lee, the son, Den, or Young Lee, had just turned twenty and was nearly two years out of school. He, like his sister, had a happy childhood, but the fact was beginning to dawn on him that his father had a very hard life planned for him, not that he hadn't worked all his life both before and after school anyway. However, there had been time for football and table tennis and the girls at the school dances back then.

That had all finished now and so had his prospects of a sex life, not that there had ever been much to boast about – just the rare kiss and even rarer fumble, but now he had had nothing for nearly two years. Den would have left for a city at the drop of a hat, if he had any sort of clue what to do when he got there, but he had no ambition either, except to have sex often.

His hormones were playing havoc with him to such an extent that some of the goats were looking very attractive to him, which worried him no end.

Not very deep down, he realised that he would have to get married, if he wanted to have a regular relationship with a woman.

Marriage, even if it came at the cost of having to have children, was starting to look decidedly attractive.

Miss Lee, better known as Din, was a very pretty girl of sixteen, who had left school in the summer, having studied two years fewer than her brother, which was quite normal in their area. Not because she was less bright, but because both parents and the girls themselves assumed that the earlier they started their families, the better it was. It was also easier to get a husband when a girl was younger than twenty even a few years older. Din accepted this traditional 'wisdom' without question, despite her mother's misgivings.

She had also worked before and after school all her life and probably harder than her brother, although he would never have been able to see that, as girls were virtually slave labour everywhere roundabouts.

However, Din did have fantasies. She dreamed of romantic entanglements, in which her lover would whisk her away to Bangkok, where he would become a doctor and she would spend all day shopping with her girlfriends. Her hormones were also troubling her, but their local culture forbade her from admitting to them, even to herself. Her father, brother and even mother too, probably, would give her a hiding, if they caught her even smiling at a boy from outside the family.

She knew that and accepted it without question too.

It was her plan to start looking for a husband straight away, a task that her mother had already offered to help in, because both the ladies Lee knew that it was best accomplished as soon as possible, in order to prevent any risk of shame befalling the family.

All in all, the Lees were a typical family for the locality and they were happy to be so. They got on with their lives within the constraints of local mores and thought that right and proper, even if the two children did harbour dreams of escaping to the big city. The problem there was that the lack of ambition that had been bred into the hill folk for centuries held them back, which was a good thing for the government otherwise all the young people would long ago have disappeared from the countryside into Bangkok and from there to foreign countries like Taiwan and Oman where the wages were better and the freedom from rigid peer pressure was alluring.

Many young girls had taken the trip to Bangkok though. Some of them had found decent jobs, but many had ended up working in the sex industries of the larger cities and from there, a few travelled even further abroad and even outside Asia. There were many horror stories about to dissuade young girls from taking that route and they had worked on Din and her mother alike.

Mr. Lee liked his life and loved his family, although it was not the done thing to admit that outside the confines of the home and he didn't want to lose them to some sickness that might have started building up in him when he was still only a lad.

Mr. Lee or Old Mr. Lee, as he was better known (although he knew that some of the less respectful youngsters in the village called him Old Goat Lee) had been an idealist in his youth and had signed up to fight for North Vietnam as soon as he had left school. They lived right on the border with

Laos, so North Vietnam was not far away, and he knew of the bombs that the Americans had dropped there and on Laos and he wanted to do his bit to have it stopped.

He had joined the communist cause and gone to Vietnam for combat training as soon as they would have him. Many of the people he was training with were just like him, part Chinese, but fed up with foreign powers meddling in his countrymen's future. He could not understand why Americans living thousands of miles away cared who was in power in his little part of the world. He had never worried which president they had elected.

However, as fate would have it, he never had the chance to fire a shot in anger because he was hit by shrapnel from an American bomb as he was being transported from the training camp to the field of battle on his very first day out of boot camp. His wounds had been very painful, but not life-threatening, although they were sufficient to get him invalided out of the army, after he was fit enough to leave hospital. He had been hit in the upper left leg by the biggest piece, but a few smaller bits had peppered his abdomen, which he now thought may be the source of his discomfort. That had also been the source of the rumour that he had been shot.

He had returned home with a bad limp and enough compensation to buy a small farm, but since his leg was bad, he had bought a farm and a flock of goats and bred and sold them instead. Within a year of his return, his leg was as good as it would ever get and he was married to a pretty local girl that he had known and fancied all his life. She was also from a farming background, and they settled down to a happy, but meagre existence.

Every day of the week ever since, except Sunday, Mr. Lee had taken his flock up into the uplands to graze and in the summer, he would often stay overnight in one of the bivouacs he had here and there which he had learned to make in the army. He looked back on that time with nostalgia, as happy days, although he would not have called them that at the time.

There were no predators in the mountains any longer, except men, because all the tigers had been killed long ago for use in the Chinese medicine industry. Mr. Lee had mixed feelings about that. On the one hand, he knew that it was a shame, but on the other he had no desire to have to defend his goats from marauding tigers every night. When the illness had struck him only a week or so ago, he had been a goatherd for almost forty years, so he knew the mountains as well as most people knew their local park.

He knew which areas to avoid because of landmines and strychnine packets dropped by the Americans in the Seventies and he knew which areas had been cleared, although the sappers had missed one or two as one of his goats had discovered only a month previously. It had been a shame about her, although her dead body had not gone to waste and the end had come quickly when a dislodged stone had triggered a mine and been blown skyward, taking her head clean off with it.

It had been too far to carry her carcass home, so Mr. Lee had spent a few days in the mountains gorging himself while his family were worried sick about him back on the farm.

Mr. Lee was a contented man. He enjoyed his work and the outdoor life, and he was long reconciled to the fact that he would never be rich or go abroad again. For this reason, he and his wife were now happy to have only had two children. He loved them both equally and wanted the best for them, but he was also glad that they had left school so they could work full time on the farm, where his wife grew herbs and vegetables and kept three pigs and a few dozen chickens.

Mr. Lee was thinking of how much he could expand his farm with the extra help. Maybe they could manage another dozen chickens, a few extra pigs and a field of sweet corn perhaps.

He awoke from his reverie, "What if it's serious, Mud? I haven't mentioned this before, but I fainted twice this week and came near to it two or three times more."

"Why didn't you tell me this before?"

"Well, you know, I didn't want you to worry and you couldn't have done anything about it, could you?"

"No, not personally, but I would have got you to your aunty earlier and maybe tried to get you to see a medical doctor."

"Ach, you know me, Mud. I'd have said, 'Let's wait to see what aunty has to say before spending all that money'. I must admit to feeling mighty queer sometimes though and I am a bit scared of what aunty will say tomorrow."

"Yes, so am I. Do you really feel that bad?"

"Sometimes, but I just don't have any energy at all. I used to be able to run and jump with the goats, but now I get tired just watching them!

"Something's up, I'm sure of it."

"Look, Paw," which was her unimaginative pet name for him since it meant 'Dad', "the children are at the gate. Do you want to bring them in on this now?"

"No, you are right, why worry them now, but I think that aunty will send for me late tomorrow afternoon, so tell them we are having a family meeting at teatime and they have to be there.

"I think I'll go to bed now; I feel tired again. Aunty's spittle livened me up for a while, but it has worn off. Tell them I'm all right, but ask Den to take the goats out for me tomorrow, will you? He doesn't have to take them far, just down by the stream so they can eat some river weed and get a drink… It won't hurt them for one or two days.

"When you get ten minutes, could you make me some of your special tea, please? The one with ginger, anise and the rest… that should buck me up a little… Oh, and a few melon or sunflower seeds… perhaps you could ask Din to crack them for me?"

"How about a mug of soup? It's your favourite…"

"Yes, OK, but if I'm asleep, just put it on the table and I'll have it cold later.

"Hello, children, I'm going to bed early tonight, but I don't want you to worry, I'm all right. Your mother can fill you in with the details. I've just got some sort of infection, I think. Good night all."

"Good night, Paw," they all replied. Din looked especially concerned as they looked anxiously first at Mr. Lee's retreating back and then at one another.

As Mr. Lee lay there in the quiet darkness, he felt his sides throbbing even more, just as a decayed tooth always seems to be more troublesome in bed at night, but he was so worn out that he was fast asleep before his tea, soup and seeds were brought in to him.

Outside, on the big table in the half-light, the rest of the small family discussed Mr. Lee's predicament in hushed voices, despite the fact that no-one would have been able to hear them if they had spoken out loud.

"Is Paw going to die, Mum?" asked Din almost in tears.

"No, dear, of course not," she replied, "at least I don't think so."

About the Author

Owen Jones was born in Barry, South Wales, where he lived until going to Portsmouth to study Russian at 18. After finishing his degree, he moved to s'Hertogenbosch in the Netherlands where he lived for ten years.

At 32, Owen moved back to Barry to work with in his family's construction company, first as a painter and then as a director, or, as the bank once corrected him, a painter and decorator. He was also office manager for ten years.

At the age of 50 Owen moved to Thailand to live with a Thai girl that he had met while there on holiday. He married the woman and now lives in her village of birth in remote northern Thailand.

As Owen puts it:

<u>**'Born in the Land of Song,**</u>
<u>**Living in the Land of Smiles'.**</u>

The Ghouls of Calle Goya

Review Request

Would you, please, leave a review of this book wherever you bought it right now before you forget

It will help the author and the readers who come after you - it really will. Your opinion counts more than you may think it does.

Thank you,

Owen

PS: Please be my friend and keep in touch on social media.

Contact Details

BlueSky: owen-author.bsky.social
Facebook: AngunJones
Instagram: owen_author
LinkedIn: owencerijones
Pinterest: owen_author
TikTok: @owen_author
X: @owen_author
Blog: Megan Publishing Services

Owen Jones

Books by the Same Author

Alien House
A Story of Love, Hope and Alien Intervention
-

Andropov's Cuckoo
A Story of Love Intrigue and The KGB
-

Annwn – Heaven - *series*
A Night in Annwn
The Strange Story of Old Willy Jones's NDE
Life in Annwn
The Story of Willy Jones's Life in Heaven
Leaving Annwn
Returning to Earth on a Mission!
-

Asian Shorts
An Anthology of Short Stories Involving Asians or Asia
-

Behind The Smile - *series*
The Story of Lek, a Bar Girl in Pattaya
Volume I: **Daddy's Hobby**
Volume II: **An Exciting Future**
Volume III: **Maya – Illusion**
Volume IV: **The Lady in the Tree**
Volume V: **Stepping Stones**
Volume VI: **The Dream**
Volume VII: **The Beginning**
-

Daisy's Chain
A Story of Love, Intrigue and the Underworld on the Costa del Sol
-

Dead Centre - *series*
Dead Centre
Not All Suicide Bombers Are Religious!
Dead Centre II
Even The Wrong Can Be Right Sometimes!
-

The Bull at the Gate
The Day the Sky Fell !
-

The Disallowed
The Story of a Contemporary Vampire Family
-

Fate Twister
The Strange Story of Wayne Gamm
-

The Ghouls of Calle Goya
When Malice Results From Good Intentions!
-

The Psychic Megan Series
A Spirit Guide, A Ghost Tiger, and One Scary Mother!
The Misconception
Megan's Thirteenth
Megan's School Trip
Megan's School Exams
Megan's Followers
Megan and the Lost Cat
Megan and the Mayoress
Megan Faces Derision
Megan's Grandparents' Visit
Megan's Father Falls Ill
Megan Goes on Holiday
Megan and the Burglar

Owen Jones

Megan and the Cyclist
Megan and the Old Lady
Megan's Garden
Megan Goes to the Zoo
Megan Goes Hiking
Megan and the W. I. Cooking Competition
Megan Goes Riding
Megan and the Radio One Beach Party
Megan Goes Yachting
Megan at Carnival
Megan's Christmas
Megan Catches Covid-19

-

Tiger Lily of Bangkok – *Series*
Volume I: **Tiger Lily of Bangkok**
When the Seeds of Revenge Blossom!
Volume II: **Tiger Lily of Bangkok in London**
The Tiger Re-awakens!

-

Non-Fiction

How to Give Your Dog a Real Dog's Life
(and make him love you for it)

-

The Eternal Plan
– Revealed
(written by Colin Jones, compiled by Owen Jones)

-

Authorship
Publishing Your Book On You Own

Plus 195 other self-help manuals.